CONNECTIONS

by

Vera Berry Burrows

Connections

"Ah, well, I guess that partly answers your first question. You find me infuriating…Yes?" Richard said with more than a little confidence. "And I would agree with you that some women would have given up before now and indeed have done so many times previously, so that's a point in your favour in trying to stick it out."

"I guess so, but why are you putting me to the test? That in itself is infuriating and I'm beginning to feel I simply ought to tell you to get lost!" Jane could not fathom this man at all, but instead of bidding him a hasty goodnight, she took a swig of her wine and prepared to go into battle with this intriguing character that had somehow got under her skin. "Now, please explain this impenetrable wall you have built around yourself."

Richard appeared to shift uncomfortably in his seat. "That's only for me to know," he said bluntly. "We only met yesterday and there is no way I would bare my soul to a stranger. Like it or lump it, Jane. I intend to maintain my mystery in the same way you are maintaining yours."

"There is no mystery about me, Richard, or whoever you are. I'm Jane O'Connell, former teacher, taking a break to find myself in my new found freedom."

"Ah, but it isn't that simple, is it?" Richard observed.

"What do you mean?" she asked, her heart thumping in her chest at the thought that he had detected the insecurity which she had not yet found the courage to openly acknowledge and accept herself. She lowered her eyes and twirled her wine glass between her fingers to hide her uneasiness.

"You know what I mean, Jane." He emptied his glass with a flourish and stood to leave. Walking round to her, he took her hand and pulled her up until they were standing only inches apart. Taking her into his arms, he kissed her full on the lips, tenderly and with affection. "Maybe that will help you decide," he said. "Goodnight."

Not another word was spoken and he walked away without looking back.

CONNECTIONS

Vera Berry Burrows

A Wings ePress, Inc.
Mainstream Novel

Wings ePress, Inc.

Edited by: Jeanne Smith
Copy Edited by: Leslie Hodges
Senior Editor: Jeanne Smith
Executive Editor: Marilyn Kapp
Cover Artist: Trisha FitzGerald

All rights reserved

Wings ePress Books
http://www.wings-press.com

Published In the United States Of America

Wings ePress Inc.
3000 N. Rock Road
Newton, KS 67114

Dedication

Andrew, this one's for you with love.

One

1988

He was already in the kitchen making their morning cups of tea when Jane appeared. "You haven't done that for a while," she commented.

"Done what?" he asked, making a bold effort not to react to her sarcastic observation.

"Made tea for us both," she told him.

"Well, the situation hasn't lent itself to amicable breakfasts just recently," he stated. His thoughts were clear. *I must make this as easy as possible for both of us. Jane does tend to get the wrong end of the stick sometimes. I need her to know exactly where we stand if our lives are to be happy and meaningful again.* "Shall we sit on the deck?"

Jane smiled and nodded. *Good start anyway,* she thought as she opened the sliding doors for him.

Mick placed the cups on the table—on opposite sides. Jane was confused. *He's sending mixed messages. First he makes the tea and then makes sure we aren't sitting side by side.* She sat facing outward, looking towards the garden as Mick walked round to face her, his position significantly looking away from what had thus far been his retreat, his sanctuary.

Holding his mug in both hands on the table, he stared at it for a while before he looked directly at Jane. "I don't want this to turn into an argument, Jane," he said gently.

She looked at him and said. "Okay. I understand." *I can see that vulnerability in his eyes again. He feels the same as I do. He wants to start again—to put the past few months behind us.* She took a deep breath and waited expectantly for his plea.

"I want a divorce."

For Jane time stood still. With her shocked eyes telling him exactly how she was feeling, the only word she was able to gasp was, "What?"

~ * ~

Ten months earlier:

Jane looked at the clock by the side of the bed. *Oh blast! I'm going to be late,* she thought in a panic. "Mick, wake up! It's eight o'clock," she cried as she jumped out from under the doona and began running round the room to find her clothes. *Why didn't I put them out last night as I always do?* she thought amidst her panic.

Suddenly she stopped and tutted loudly as Mick stirred. "I don't have to go to work," she said out loud. "You're an idiot!"

"Who's an idiot? Me? What did I do?" Mick asked sleepily.

"No, I don't mean you, darl. Sorry. I got up to go to work."

"Oh well, yes you are an idiot. Come back to bed and we can celebrate." He grinned cheekily, because he knew exactly what Jane's reaction would be, what her attitude to sex had been for a while.

"I'm up now, so I'll make a cup of tea and some toast," she told her husband of twenty-seven years. "Stop being lecherous and come and sit on the deck with me."

She placed the breakfast tray on the table and looked pointedly at her husband. "Time and tide wait for no man," she said reflectively as they sat in the early morning sunshine that bathed their beautiful garden in a wonderful healthy glow. She was unnecessarily forceful. "I gave that old adage much thought when I decided to end my career. I'm beginning to question the wisdom of anybody who goes into teaching these days. I intend to start living after too many years of the relentless demands of education. My time has never been my own until now..." She paused deliberately, "...and I'm strangely overwhelmed by a very unfamiliar feeling."

"All that sounds very philosophical for so early in the morning, even though it is a bit clichéd," Mick observed as he sipped his tea thoughtfully. "Who are you trying to convince, Jane? Me or yourself?" His expression clearly conveyed his bemusement.

"I have looked forward to this day for so long," she told him. "I can't believe my subconscious woke me to go to work this morning. I genuinely believed momentarily that it was a normal Monday morning and by eight o'clock I ought to have been in school."

Mick looked over his cup at his wife, her hair still tousled and her robe open to reveal a creased cotton nightie that had been ironed and crisp the night before. He smiled affectionately. "You've been at it for too long, Jane, running around for other people's children. Now you can run around for your own."

She wasn't sure she liked what she was hearing. "I never thought of my job as running around for other people's children as you put it," she said, unreasonably irritated by Mick's observation. "You are intimating that my life's work was simply a child-minding service."

Mick eyed his wife, a completely mystified expression on his face. "Why are you so bothered about it? You should be on top of the world. No more working for others, your own boss, pleasing yourself in what you do and don't do. What could be better than that?" he stated, still not quite certain how he should be reacting.

"It's a weird feeling. I'm not sure how I feel. It isn't anything like being on holiday and I thought it would be," she informed him. "School holidays were always welcome, what we looked forward to at the end of every term. They were what kept us going... waiting for the next break, but enjoying the hard work in between. Does that sound silly?"

"Yes it does. You're contradicting yourself," Mick told her bluntly. "How can you enjoy what you're doing if you're looking forward to it all being over? It doesn't make sense to me."

Jane sighed. "You wouldn't understand, because you've never been a teacher," she said, still incongruously and ridiculously prickly about her situation.

Mick stood and stretched noisily, breathing in air filled with the perfume of the Chinese jasmine growing by the side of the deck. "Hmmm," he sighed, "That's beautiful, just beautiful. My plants are calling. I can't waste my day off. I'll have a shower when I've finished my jobs in the garden. I'll be outside for a while until the sun gets too hot. See you later, darl." He bent to kiss her cheek. "You need a hobby,' he said with feeling. "Look at me—gardening, sailing and fishing—and still managing to earn a living in between," he continued pointedly and then he was gone.

Jane leaned back in her chair and put her slippered feet up on the one that had previously been occupied by her husband. She closed her eyes and felt the warm sun on her face. *I ought to feel happy and relaxed,* she thought, *but I'm tense and restless. Suddenly I have the feeling that I'm not in control and I don't like it. Perhaps I do need a hobby. I never had time for hobbies.* She stood abruptly and marched purposefully inside to take a shower. She dried her hair quickly, put on shorts and sun-top, opting to wear runners instead of sandals. Calling to Mick as she left to inform him that she was going for a walk, she climbed into her car and drove the short distance to the coast where the cliffs were high and the scenic pathway offered time for quiet reflection. "You need a hobby," she said out loud, her sarcastic tone revealing it still irked that Mick had picked up on the fact that she was at a loose end. Her mind was full of confused thoughts, most of which were completely irrational since this was ostensibly the first day of her retirement, the past weekend excluded of course. *This is ridiculous,* she silently brooded. She was suddenly and inexplicably irritated with herself and could find no reasonable explanation for her inability to see where her future lay. *Get a grip, Jane!*

When she arrived at the gate of the nature walk, she read the notice she had seen many times before—*Easy route*—the arrow pointed straight on—*difficult to the right.* She stood for a moment mentally tossing a coin. *Easy?* That was the road she and Linda, her friend of many years, had often taken. It was a bit twisty, but mostly level with awesome views over the rocks and across the bay. She smiled at the analogy. *That just about sums up my friendship with Linda,* she thought. *Usually on a level playing field, but with the occasional twists and turns. Should I give myself a challenge and take the difficult route? Oh what the hell,* she considered significantly. *Difficult it shall be.* She smiled to herself again and wondered if, at forty-nine, she would be able to climb the steep pathways without feeling that her lungs were bursting. *I need to prove to myself that taking early retirement was worthwhile. This will tell me one way or the other whether or not I am physically fit enough to take on the challenges of life after work.*

She breathed in deeply, duly regarding the twenty-something steps up to the track. "Ah well, here I go." Being there in the morning, especially on a Monday meant that the place was very quiet, just how Jane liked it. Surrounded by ghostly trees and forbidding thick undergrowth, she found there was still something very peaceful and relaxing about it. The sun was struggling to break through the leaf-laden branches of the

Moreton Bay fig trees. Where the foliage was less dense, the golden rays pierced the air with laser-like beams that gave the pathway an almost magical aura.

The going was slow, but not arduous and the leisurely pace allowed her time to ponder on what lay ahead. "I am forty-nine years old," she reminded herself again. "I took early retirement so I might enjoy my own time before I grow too old and infirm to do all those things I never had time to do before. Why then do I feel so lost and dejected? And talking to yourself, Jane, suggests dementia!" She grimaced, shrugged and sighed deeply. *Have I made a mistake? Should I have carried on working for a while longer and what are those things I never got around to doing? I can't remember now what I intended to do with my time,* but the mere thought of going into school again to face the ever increasing number of disruptive pupils filled her with horror. *It never used to be like that,* she thought sadly. *It takes just one unruly pupil to ruin a lesson. When there are several in one class...* "Kids!" She spat out the word loudly and continued her walk, mentally trying to justify her decision now that reality had kicked in. *At this point in time, I feel an odd realisation that I am a victim of circumstance and admittedly, circumstances of my own making.* "You have to sort this out soon, Jane O'Connell," she said adamantly, "or you'll lose all sense of self-worth. What's done is done and nothing ventured, nothing gained." She smiled at the thought that she seemed to be overdoing the clichés that morning. By the time she reached the bench strategically placed for unfit people to take a necessary rest, she uneasily accepted that her decision to retire had been the right one for her. *Money isn't a problem. Mick and I have earned well and saved well. Mick is still working, the house is mortgage free and now my super is providing me with a regular income.* "And anyway," she told the gum tree to her right, "as long as there is a roof over our heads and food on the table, that's all that matters." She was beginning to unwind and she smiled again at the supposedly physically unfit person sitting on the bench deliberately put there for her and she presumed other out-of-condition recently retired women, she felt the sun shining not only on her face, but also on her future.

Intermittently, when the sun went behind the trees, she again began to question her wisdom in giving up a satisfying and well paid career. *I prefer to call it a career rather than a job. Jobs could be done by any Tom, Dick, or Harry. Careers are vocations, life's work. Teaching is exactly that.* "Are you sure you have done the right thing, Jane?" she asked herself for the umpteenth time in the past hour. Yet when she took in the view across the bay, when she saw the sun shining on the sparkling, blue ocean and the sea birds calling to their young on the cliffs, she tried to rid herself of the doubt and accept that this was indeed what she needed to do at this point in her life.

"It *is* what I need," she affirmed out loud, "but more to the point..." She paused as the doubt irritatingly crept in again. "Oh heck, is it really what I want?"

Two

Jane Peterson and Mick O'Connell met at university in Queensland in the late fifties. She was the free-spirited girl whose personality attracted a host of admirers. She was everybody's friend—sporty, academic and committed to her studies, but she always found time to enjoy life to the full.

"What's a nice girl from Dubbo doing in Brisbane?" he asked her when they met. A group of students were congregating in the local bar after a long day in lectures and Jane's dazzling smile and vibrancy had attracted Mick from the start.

"I guess I'm doing what you're doing," she said light-heartedly, "studying."

"Not at the moment, you're not," he observed. "I'd say you were partying and studying doesn't come into it."

She gave him a look of undisguised disdain. "Don't be facetious," she advised him and haughtily turned to talk to her friend, Linda, who had also travelled from Dubbo to study sociology and philosophy. Linda and Jane had been friends for as long as she could remember and although they were close, they each knew when the other needed space. *The perfect friendship,* Jane mused.

Undeterred by the apparent brush-off, Mick tapped her gently on the shoulder. "Will my heart-felt apology be accepted?" he asked sheepishly.

"Only if you buy us a drink." She grinned cheekily, her eyes sparkling when she actually took in the boyishly handsome features of ... "Who are you?" she asked.

"Michael James O'Connell," he announced, "of true Irish stock, only son of Seamus and Molly O'Connell, ten pound Micks and proud of it."

Both Jane and Linda laughed. "I've heard of ten pound Poms, but never Micks," Jane told him. "Are there really such people?"

Mick put an arm around each girl and pulled them close so he might whisper in their ears. He looked around furtively as if to make sure nobody was listening. "Actually," he confided quietly, "I made it up, but we're originally from Northern Ireland, so that makes us British ...well, Mum and Dad anyway. I was born in Western Australia and so were my sisters, so we're Aussies."

"So you're really ten pound Poms after all, with an Irish slant..."

"To be sure, to be sure," Mick joked.

Jane was warming to this very personable young man. "I like your style," she told him, "but your chat-up line is so dorky..."

"Dorky? What do you mean?" he asked, amused by her forthrightness.

"You sounded like a throw back from the thirties or something," she told him. "You might as well have said *do you come here often?* What a dork!"

"That's personal, young lady. I'll have you know I'm a straight A student," he bragged, "Straight and a student ...get it?" It was a very flippant remark and Mick was about to give up. He could see he had no chance with this girl. "Sorry," he said almost shyly, "that was a bit near the knuckle. Sorry." He squirmed at his own audacity.

"Quit while you're ahead," she told him, "and what happened to those drinks?"

Mick was a year ahead of Jane and so nearer to qualifying than she was. He was studying for a Bachelor of Pharmacy degree. "I'm very impressed," she told him. Contrary to what he had intimated to her, he was extremely studious and so when they started seeing each other on a regular basis, they often studied together in the library, or on the beach. When he qualified, he chose to do his pre-registration year with the local pharmacy so he could remain close to Jane.

"What if I get sent out to the bush when I qualify?" she asked him plaintively as her final exams approached.

"We'll deal with it if and when," Mick reassured her. "Don't stress about it. I'm here for you, Jane and always will be."

"Is that a proposal?" she asked.

"Hey, hold on a bit," he told her. "I didn't say anything about marriage, but now you mention it…" He stood up from the lounge where they had been ensconced for the past couple of hours and walked towards the window.

Jane realised she'd said the wrong thing. "Just joking," she said to relieve the tension. She looked longingly at the strong back of the boy she had fallen in love with. He was staring out of the window and she struggled to find the words that would convince him that she was happy with things as they were. "It was just a flippant question, Mick. It didn't mean anything…"

He turned slowly, his hands pushed deep into the pockets of his boardies. His expression was steely and Jane shivered. *I've really done it this time,* she thought nervously. *You stupid idiot, Jane. Why couldn't you keep your big mouth shut?*

Mick walked slowly towards her. "I knew this subject would come up eventually and I've no intention of avoiding it if that's what you're thinking," he informed her seriously.

Tears welled up in her eyes. "I'm so sorry, Mick. You have to believe me. Please don't run..."

"Sh-sh-sh," he said gently and bent to take her hand in his. Kneeling at her feet, he hugged her closely and whispered in her ear. "I love you."

"And I love you too and it doesn't matter that we're not getting married..."

Mick released his hold on her and stood again reaching into his pocket, supposedly to find his handkerchief to dry Jane's tears, but in reality it was to retrieve what had been hidden there for the past week. He knelt again and took her hand. "Will you marry me, Jane?" he asked smiling. He opened a tiny leather-bound box to reveal a most beautiful antique diamond ring that had belonged to his Irish grandmother.

"You bast...!" she halted abruptly. *I've already put my foot in it today and I don't want to ruin the moment by further stupidity.*

"You were saying?" Mick urged, his eyes shining with happiness.

"Yes," she replied, "Oh yes, please." With the ring on her finger, they kissed passionately, urgently and cemented their relationship right there in the wonderful heat of the moment.

~ * ~

Twenty seven years and one daughter later, she sat on top of the cliff, her favourite place, still pondering her decision to retire amidst the fond memories of Mick's proposal. "Have I really done the right thing?" she tediously asked herself again. "This is the first day of the rest of my life," she said loudly and smiled again at the cliché. "Is it possible that my life will be one big cliché from now on? Oh my goodness, I hope not." But there was something else making her tense and restless, something she was unable to fathom, an itch she was unable to scratch.

Three

Jane felt her life had stopped. "That's what it's like," she told her husband. "I'm not living; I'm just existing. What's the matter with me, Mick?"

Mick eyed Jane questioningly. "What do you want me to say, Jane? You made the decision to retire without my input. What's so different now?"

"What do you mean? You told me it had to be my decision and you refused to discuss it at the time," Jane reminded him.

"It was already a *fait accompli* when you first mentioned it to me. Your exact words were *'I've decided to retire. Don't try to stop me. I've made up my mind.'*"

Jane remembered the conversation and was surprised by his precise recall. "Yes, I did say that, but you walked away without saying a word either for or against, even when I asked you point blank what you thought."

Mick sighed deeply. "Jane, you told me not to stop you, so I didn't. To be perfectly honest, I assumed you would sleep on it and then change your mind, but in true Jane style, you dug in your heels and did your own thing, regardless of what I thought or felt. Why are you suddenly asking for my advice so long after the event?"

"Oh, just forget I spoke, Mick," she said, feeling unreasonably irritated again. "I'm just your wife after all, so you don't have to be interested in what I do. You don't half get on my nerves at times."

Mick sighed. *Menopause or just female unpredictability?* he mused. "I'm going to work," he said. "Hopefully you'll be a bit more accommodating when I come home." He kissed her on the cheek and left her to ponder on her predicament, deeming that in his opinion, concentrated thought was what was needed.

Apathy had never been one of Jane's characteristics and she wondered why she had allowed it to take over her life in the past few weeks. *I have to weigh up the pros and cons of my present life,* she silently decided and took out a notebook to write down her thoughts. "Setting it out in black and white will help, I'm sure. Right... *Pros,*" she wrote as she talked to the photograph of her daughter, Sally, with her husband, Bill and their beautiful children, Jacob and Holly. She smiled. "Sally is just like me, wilful and impetuous. Bill will have to be strong to cope with her... but back to my list. *Pros: My time is my own; I can stay in bed late if I so wish; I can have friends in for morning tea...* She paused. *But most, if not all of my friends still go out to work. And Linda hasn't much time for me these days as she thinks her most important role in life is to fetch and carry after her husband and grown up sons. She hasn't exactly put herself out to make time to see me recently.* She inwardly chastised herself for being judgmental. *If Linda wants to live her life that way, that's her business.* She crossed out the last item. *...I can spend time doing the things I never had time for before I retired... I hate that word 'retired.' It makes me sound old and doddery. Only old people retire. I'm not old, so why have I put myself in the retired* *category? Should that go down as a pro?* She sighed deeply and forcefully closed the notebook as she threw the pencil across the table in frustration.

She wandered outside onto the deck that overlooked the immaculate garden—Mick's obsession, Mick's hobby. She bristled at the intensity of her feelings. She suddenly had this weird, inner urge to find fault with Mick's pride and joy. "If I were a rose, or a frangipani, I'd get more consideration from my husband." She knew she was being dramatic, but she said it anyway. "What *are* all those things I intended to when I had the time?" she asked herself again. She returned to retrieve her notebook and searched for the pencil that had skittered across the kitchen table and found its way to the farthest corner of the room. Remarkably, it had not broken and Jane shrugged as she inspected the point. "Maybe that's a sign," she commented. "Pick yourself up, dust yourself down and start all over again."

"Right. *Painting, writing, quilting, scrapbooking, cake decorating, flower arranging, computing and the Internet...*" She paused momentarily as the idea clicked in her brain. "That's it! It's about time we kept up with the times and bought a computer and I can enrol on a course to learn all the basic skills. Alleluia! Thank you, thank you," she said as she looked up to the heavens. "Wait till I tell Mick..."

~ * ~

"...and I'll enrol at TAFE to learn how to use a PC..."

Mick stared at Jane uncomprehendingly. "Why on earth would you want a computer, Jane? Computers are for young people, not for us. Isn't there enough for you to do in this beautiful land of ours without sitting in front of a computer screen all day? That's why we moved to Queensland, why we were so excited about living on the Gold Coast."

"We have to move with the times, Mick. Computers will take over the world in the next few years."

"Don't be ridiculous, Jane. We've only just got used to everybody having a television and a telephone in the house."

Jane looked at her husband with disdain. "I give up with you," she told him. "The one time I feel I'm doing something positive with my new found freedom and you pour cold water on the idea." She walked away before she said something she might regret and she realised she'd said enough already.

They ate dinner in silence, each consumed by their own thoughts. When eventually Mick spoke, his words were not what Jane wanted to hear. "Whatever you decide, Jane, you're on your own. Don't expect me to get involved in your hare-brained ideas. It'll be a waste of time, not to mention a waste of money and then you'll have an obsolete piece of electronic equipment nobody will want."

"That's rubbish..."

"Exactly—that's what I said. Think about it, Jane. What will you do with a computer?" Mick's tone was nothing short of scathing.

Jane took a deep breath, determined not to lose her temper. "I intend to explore its uses and it might benefit you to do the same," she said with measured control, "and I think I'll write a novel. I'll learn how to do word processing. It's much better than a typewriter; even you should appreciate that and I'll thank you not to say another word. The least you could do is to give me some encouragement, but that would be like agreeing with me and just recently, you have been in your own little world of your work and your garden and your boat..." She paused deliberately. "What will happen when your precious yacht becomes old and rusty, Mick? I don't like spending time sailing aimlessly around the Broadwater, but I don't stop you playing with your big boy's toy, so your view of my plan smacks of selfishness as far as I can judge." She wanted to speak her mind. She'd been dwelling on the problem for days, but perhaps this wasn't the right time. "It's about time you listened to me without that look of contempt on your face."

Mick stared at his wife with total bewilderment. "Where is all this coming from?" he asked.

Jane sighed. "You don't listen to me anymore, Mick. Since I stopped work, you haven't been interested in me at all, not that you ever took that much interest in my work before, but now..." She stopped mid-sentence. She needed to clear her mind of all negativity before she might discuss the issues that really concerned her. "I'm going to bed," she said.

"Shall I come too?" Mick asked weakly.

"No, Mick. Just leave me alone for a while."

She lay in the semi-darkness staring into space. She sighed deeply. Her mind was so full of confused thoughts and she was unable to answer Mick's question. *Where is all this coming from, Jane?* She had opened a tinderbox, she knew, but what had surfaced a few minutes ago had revealed a situation that was rapidly getting out of control, for her at least.

Four

Jane stared at the sun rising behind the curtains of the bedroom window. Mick's steady breathing told her that his sleep was restful, not disturbed like her own. She slid out of bed and went to make a cup of tea. *Five o'clock in the morning and I'm wide awake,* she thought as she curled up in her favourite chair and savoured the hot liquid as it slid down her throat. *I'll call Linda at seven o'clock,* she silently decided. *She'll be up by then and I know she will give me a sensible view of my situation.* She smiled knowingly to herself. *Sensible, down-to-earth Linda... not to mention boring, unadventurous Linda,* she added judgmentally and then chastised herself, knowing full well Linda had been a very dear and loyal friend for as long as she could remember. *She'll be honest with me, if nothing else.*

"Yes, today is fine, but the rest of the week, I'll have no time to spare. My life is hectic at the moment. I'll meet you at the usual place and we'll walk around the cliffs," Linda told her. "Pack a picnic lunch; I'll bring fruit and yogurt for dessert."

~ * ~

"This is the life, Linda," Jane enthused, as they enjoyed their leisurely lunch by the sea. "I never thought I would see the day when I could retire, but here I am, forty-nine years old and my life is just beginning. I love it!" she lied, thinking, *I need to see what Linda's reaction will be. I have to look at it from another perspective.*

Linda was thoughtful. "I don't think a woman can ever retire, Jane," she said with conviction.

"What do you mean?" Jane asked, feeling a bit deflated by her friend's response.

Linda noticed and asked, "What's wrong, Jane? Were you expecting me to jump up and down in excitement for your new life?"

Jane's voice was low. "At the very least, I was expecting a bit of enthusiasm and some agreement, so what did you mean about never retiring?"

"A woman's work is never done, that's what I mean," she told Jane who looked incredulously at her friend.

Jane had to laugh. "A bit clichéd, Lin," she said. "My whole life seems to be that way at the moment—clichéd I mean, but I need to explore this situation with you, Lin, so please listen to my reasoning." She took a deep breath and continued. "I can do what I want, when I want. Mick's always pottering about in the garden, or out on the boat fishing when he's not at work. He loves it and we can give each other space to enjoy our own things. No more clock watching."

Linda looked at Jane with undisguised incredulity. "How can you organise your life if you never look at the time?" she asked. "Have you flipped just because you no longer have to go out to work each day?"

Jane tried to empathise with Linda's reaction. She felt irritated. "I had expected you to offer a few ideas on how I might occupy all the new-found time I have on my hands. What does it matter if we don't eat at the same time every day? I get up around seven-thirty every morning, but it wouldn't matter if I didn't and when the clock says it's eleven, it doesn't necessarily mean that I have to have morning tea. Can't you see that time is flexible, Linda?" She was warming to her own assessment. "I can relax! What doesn't get done today, will still be there to do tomorrow. Can't I convince you that a life like that could be wonderful?"

Linda stared incredulously at Jane. "Jane," she said pointedly. "You have always been so sensible, so organised, so methodical. You've had to be. You are a schoolteacher and it goes with the territory. How can time be flexible? Time is time!" she stated with unusual authority. "It creates routines so you can organise your life. Your husband needs to eat regularly, doesn't he? In my case, it's my husband and my boys. You are starting to annoy me, Jane. You are becoming irresponsible and you never used to be like that."

Jane was becoming irritated. "This is the real me, the one I've kept out of the way until now. I know what you're saying, Lin, but now that Sally's married, I don't have to be tied to a routine and what's more, I don't want that sort of life anymore. I'm allowed to be selfish. I reckon I've earned it. This is my time, my life, my choice!" She leaned back on the bench, the same bench upon which she had sat the previous day as she contemplated her future.

Lunch wasn't supposed to turn into an argument, but Linda was on her high horse and was determined to gallop in at full speed, lance at the ready. "You still have Mick to consider, Jane. There are *always* other people to consider. How selfish can you be?" she said, bristling at Jane's stance.

"No, you're wrong, Lin!" Jane retaliated. "There comes a time when you have to be independent. You *can* be, you know, and still have your family and friends there too."

"I don't agree. You can't be serious, Jane. Just open your eyes." She looked up at the cliff face just ahead. "See those gulls on the cliff? Those brown ones were hatched last year and they still need their parents. They still go back to the nest as a matter of routine. It's where they belong. They still rely on their mother. Life is a cycle. What goes around, comes around. Time takes care of that. You simply can't ignore time and regularity," she emphasised, frustrated that Jane was being so stubborn.

"My, my, Linda, that's deep and very philosophical!" Jane laughed, surprised, but genuinely amused by Linda's declaration. She smiled affectionately at her friend. She couldn't remain irritated with her for long. "Hey, do you remember when Miss Barton told you off for being hare-brained? What did she say?" She mimicked their teacher, *'Linda Stokes, you are the most scatterbrained girl I have ever met!'* I think she'd be pleased with the way you've matured after that little performance!"

"Cheeky!" Linda replied, more relaxed now. "We did enjoy ourselves in those days, didn't we? I remember Miss Weston poking at the food marks on our uniforms. We called them dinner gongs! Miss Weston called them disgraceful!" and they both laughed at the memory. "Those definitely were the best days, Jane."

"They certainly were."

Linda looked at her watch. "Gosh, look at the time. Four o'clock already. I must be off, or dinner won't be ready for Bob and the boys when they arrive home from work. Let's go."

"Oh Linda, you and your routine!" She really wanted to tell Linda that her family wouldn't starve to death if they had to wait for their meals, but she'd rocked the boat enough for one afternoon. What Linda had said earlier had got under her skin. There was something niggling at the back of her mind like that itch she wasn't able to scratch. "I hope they appreciate you," she added amicably.

"Of course they do. I need to be organised to be happy and when I'm happy, they're happy," Linda said as she hugged Jane. "See you next week. Same time, same place."

Jane watched as Linda purposefully walked to her car, checking her watch with the big clock over the surf club door as she passed. She knew that she could always rely on Linda whatever the circumstances and surely that was a good thing, but… and there was a very big but…

~ * ~

The two friends never got around to discussing Jane's future. *According to Linda, I should spend all my time running around after Mick and Sally,* she mused as she drove home. *Well, Sally has her own family now. My job is complete as far as Sally is concerned.* She squirmed at the thought. Sally would always be her little girl, but… *She'll make mistakes with her kids; we all do, but she has to have to the courage to rectify them herself. My mother didn't interfere with my life, but… why are there are so many buts in life?* Her present situation was forcing her to assess her life in general and she significantly recalled the day she had indeed run home to her mum soon after she and Mick had married…

~ * ~

Mick was a very tidy person, a trait Jane found to be extremely annoying in a man. She generally washed up the breakfast dishes before she went to work, but on that particular day, she was running late and left them in the sink. Mick arrived home minutes before she did that day and when she entered the kitchen, he was standing by the sink, arms folded and with a look of revulsion on his face.

"Have you seen this mess?" he demanded, even before Jane had time to put down her briefcase.

"I've just walked through the door, Mick," she told him petulantly.

"There's a congealed mess in the cups and marmalade stuck on the knives, not to mention crumbs all over the sink,' he explained haughtily.

"Oh Mick, don't be so pompous," she said. "I was in a rush this morning..."

"Well, it's disgusting..."

Jane flipped. "Well, if it's a skivvy you're wanting, you've married the wrong person. Tomorrow you can clean up yourself, because I won't be here." She ridiculously stormed out of the kitchen into the bedroom, packed an overnight bag and went home to her mum...

~ * ~

... It all happened so quickly and Mick just stood there and allowed me to go! she recalled silently. *He didn't even run after me and beg me to stay! ...*

~ * ~

... Her mother was aghast. "My goodness, Jane, you haven't been married two minutes and you are running home to Mum!" she said, not hiding her astonishment.

Jane burst into tears. "I can't live with a man who is so obsessed with tidiness. He didn't even consider that I had to get to work and it was the first time I'd left the dishes. If he hadn't arrived home before me, I'd have cleaned up and he'd have been none the wiser."

"You knew what Mick was like before you married him," her mother told her. "Your dad was just the opposite. He left everything lying about the house—dirty socks and underwear on the bedroom floor, keys and loose change on the kitchen bench top, every room in the house was cluttered with tools and stuff when he was doing a job, sometimes for weeks on end. If I'd run home to my mother every time he annoyed me with his untidiness, I'd never have been in my own home."

Jane looked sorrowfully at her mother. "What did you do?" she asked.

"I took a deep breath and thought of all his good qualities. The most important one was that he loved me unconditionally and I knew I loved him, warts an' all! Now he's gone, I miss all that," she said with unmistakable sadness.

Jane was embarrassed when she returned home to Mick. "I'm sorry…"

Mick took her in his arms. "I know, Darl, I know and I'm sorry too."

~ * ~

In an effort to put Linda's philosophy to the test, Jane spent the first few weeks of her retirement leading her life Linda's way. She kept to a strict daily routine. While Mick went to work, she cleaned and cooked, she had morning tea at eleven, lunch at one, dinner at seven. She read books; she went for walks; she watched TV; she read books; she went for walks; she watched TV; she read…

Eventually when she felt almost demented with the mundane, she vociferously decided, "I simply have to do something with my life, or I'll go stark staring mad!"

Five

"I'm going to spend a few days with Sally and Bill," she told Mick the morning after their confrontation about the computer.

"Another *fait accompli*," Mick stated without feeling.

Jane sighed. "I need to get away for a while..."

"From me?" Mick asked. "Just say what's on your mind, Jane. Tell it how it is. I'm really not in the mood for riddles, or euphemisms."

"Okay, I'm getting no support from you at the moment, so I will go away and spend some time with our daughter and her family. She might be prepared to listen to my ideas with a bit more enthusiasm than I'm getting from you. Okay?" She spat out the last bit with unnecessary venom.

Mick finished his breakfast and placed his cup and plate in sink. "You *will* have time to load up the dishwasher before you leave, won't you?" he asked, his words deliberately laced with sarcasm. "And don't be too sure that Sally will take your side. She's too much like you to make a rational decision. She'll react without thinking it through and it might not be how you want it to be."

"Go to work, Mick. I'll leave enough meals prepared to see you through the next few days," Jane told him. Her sense of duty had not deserted her completely and part of her felt guilty about leaving him to fend for himself.

She remained sitting at the breakfast bar, both hands tightly gripping her mug of coffee. Tension showed in the whiteness of her knuckles and she wondered how the coffee mug was standing up to such harsh treatment. *Relax,* she told herself silently. When Mick came behind her and kissed the top of her head, she tensed again, feeling the muscles in her neck tighten.

"Safe journey," he said. "Drive carefully and let me know when you arrive in Coffs Harbour. Give my love to Sally, Bill and the children."

Jane nodded and forced a smile as Mick left. When she heard his car start, she stood up suddenly, momentarily feeling the urge to run to the door and say, *'I'm sorry. I don't want to leave you,'* but she wrapped her arms round herself as protection against the feelings that seemed to be invading her sensitivities from all angles. *Is that what I'm battling?* She thought sadly. *Do I want to leave?* She couldn't bring herself to add Mick's name to the end of the question. She had not even considered that her problems might be unhappiness in her relationship and she was inwardly shocked at the intensity of her thoughts.

She spent the morning busily preparing her husband's meals—pies and casseroles for while she was away. She didn't know how long she would stay with Sally. *It depends on how long it takes for me to be comfortable with myself,* she thought, but she couldn't shake the notion of being unsettled with Mick. *Should I stay and sort it out?* she wondered, *but then I might be opening Pandora's Box...* Again she sighed deeply. *I need to get away.*

She telephoned Sally just after lunch. "Hi darling," she said as breezily as she could muster, "I was thinking of coming to see you for a few days."

"Not a good time at the moment, Mum," Sally told her abruptly. "We have the builders in and we've had what smelt like toxic fumes coming from the old drains. It's been a nightmare and Bill's brother, Jim and his family are coming at the weekend. Sorry."

"Oh..." Jane replied deflated at the unexpected news.

"Is something wrong, Mum? You sound a bit down."

"Nothing wrong. I just feel like a few days away..." She paused then added quickly, "I have time on my hands since I've retired and I can do these things without worrying about what I'm leaving behind; you know, no restrictions now."

"Goodness, Mum, who are you trying to convince? Me or yourself?"

Jane was taken aback. "What do you mean? I don't need convincing about anything," she lied.

"Can I give you a call after the weekend? The builders will be out in a couple of days and our kitchen will be functional again. Jim and Dorothy go home on Sunday evening. We don't see them very often..."

"You don't see your father and me very often either," Jane snapped and immediately regretted it. "Sorry, that was uncalled for. I'll speak to you later then."

Jane flopped onto the lounge completely crestfallen. Her plans had been shattered in the space of a few seconds, but she knew she had to do something to lift her spirits. *How can I expect Sally to understand?* she thought almost wearily. *I don't really understand it myself, but I said I was going away for a few days and that's what I'll do,* she decided. *I've never travelled alone, but perhaps that's what is necessary to give my life some sparkle and, let's face it, it certainly needs some sparkle at the moment.* She hastily wrote a note to Mick telling him that she would call when she arrived. She didn't say where, as she had no idea where she would go, but once on the highway, she could decide where to stay when she saw a sign that appealed. She finished packing the case that had already been started in preparation for her trip to Coffs Harbour and within the hour she was in the car heading north, not south as had been the original plan. "What an adventure," she said out loud and she turned on the radio… the music blared out loudly and Jane joined in enthusiastically. '… *and I'll survive, I will survive.*'

The sign to Noosa attracted her attention just as the sun was setting. She had been driving for three or four hours and her rumbling insides were telling her that she ought to eat. Noosa was fast becoming popular with many Queenslanders and she hoped she would be able to find a place to stay without much fuss. She followed the signs to Noosa Heads and found a quiet resort offering chalet accommodation at reasonable rates.

"I'll check in for three nights," she told the receptionist, a young woman of about thirty, tanned and healthy looking and with a warm, welcoming smile. "If I decide to stay longer, will I be able to do that without too much inconvenience to you?"

"That will be fine, but if you could let me know before Friday, it will be helpful," the young woman told her. "We usually have a lot of weekenders arriving then, so I'll need to know how many chalets I have available."

Jane found her way to her chalet and was very pleasantly surprised to find clean, bright, beautifully furnished accommodation with everything she required. The main room had a queen bed, a dining table with two chairs and a small but perfectly functional kitchen area. The shower room was at the back of the chalet, white tiled with a sea-blue trim and there were white fluffy towels laid out with all the toiletries she would need. "I think I'm going to enjoy this," she said to herself. "Now let's find somewhere to eat."

~ * ~

Mick arrived home just after six o'clock and found a note from Jane about the prepared meals. He looked at his watch and as she said she was only leaving at three, she would probably still be on the road. "I'll give her another half hour or so and then I'll phone Sally if Jane hasn't phoned me by then," he decided. As if by telepathy, the telephone rang. "Jane?" he asked.

"Sorry, but no. My name is Renee and I'm calling on behalf of …"

"Sorry, Renee, but I can't talk now. I'm expecting an important call." He replaced the receiver, cursing that the number of charity calls were increasing and always at inconvenient times.

Jane did call before he had time to reheat his hotpot. "I'm in Noosa…"

"What the hell are you doing in Noosa? I thought you were going to Sally's. This isn't one of your…"

"Just hold on, Mick," Jane said, becoming instantly annoyed again. "Sally has too much happening at the moment, so I made a quick change of plan. I'm going to relax for a few days. I need to do this…"

"*I need to do this*," Mick mimicked. "What has got into you, Jane? I'm beginning to wish you were back at work. At least I could rely on some semblance of normality then."

Jane sighed audibly, her hackles rising, and Mick picked up on it. He bristled as he listened. "Normality? Normality?" Jane shouted and then **realized s**he was attracting stares from the other diners in the restaurant. "I have been trying to create normality for myself since I retired," she said more quietly. "I need my space to work out what I want to do. I do know that the first thing I'm going to do when I come home is buy a computer and your objections to that idea didn't inspire me with confidence at all. I don't know why I asked for your opinion really."

Mick interrupted. "There you go again, Jane. The world doesn't revolve around what you want to do. What's wrong with simple homely pleasures?" He paused and then commented, "You could always help me in the garden. I often need a labourer."

He laughed at his little joke.

"Is that supposed to be funny?" Jane asked, obviously not amused. "You'll have me swabbing the decks of *Hopes and Dreams* next." She paused thinking, *There has to be some significance in that.* "Well, you know where I am. Eden Sands Resort. I am fine and you have no need to worry about me..."

"I'm not worried about you, Jane, but I am concerned about where all this is leading. I'd have to be totally insensitive not to notice that something is developing out of your rash actions. Think about that, won't you, while you enjoy what *you* need." Mick was in no mood for pleasantries and as he put the phone back on the hook, he thought. *This is not my doing. If she wants space, she's got it, but I guarantee she'll come home with egg on her face.* He sighed loudly. "Damn the woman! She's got me talking in bloody clichés now."

Six

Sally and Bill were nearing the end of their kitchen extension and not a minute too soon. Microwave meals were not Sally's favourite way of feeding her family, even though this new piece of technology was one of her most prized possessions. Every breakfast, lunch and dinner had become an unwelcome chore for her. When her mother phoned, she was almost at the end of her tether.

"I don't need her problems on top of my own," she told Bill that evening.

"But you don't know if she has problems, Sal," Bill replied.

"My mother doesn't just decide to come and spend time with us out of the blue. She always has everything planned for weeks. She has problems, you mark my words."

"I think you're wrong," Bill continued. "From what I know of Jane, even if she did have problems, she wouldn't burden you with them. She's the most confident, self-assured woman I know..."

"Excuse me, Bill Mansell," Sally interrupted, "Aren't those traits reserved for me?" She giggled girlishly. "Didn't you tell me that my self-confidence was what you fell in love with?"

"Of course, darl, but like mother, like daughter and Jane sure knows what she's doing. I don't think we need worry about her," Bill stated. "And anyway, your dad knows how to deal with any problems your mum might have."

"You mean masculine wiles?" she asked, smiling at her astute husband.

"Call it what you like, but we men know how to keep our women happy."

Sally grinned. "I'll remind you of that next time you accuse me of being wilful and headstrong. We women also know how to deal with our men!"

~ * ~

Jane lay awake for most of the first night in the chalet. She thought perhaps the state of being alone in her bed after twenty seven years of listening to Mick's gentle snoring beside her was making it difficult to fall asleep. Her mind was full of muddled thoughts and when she eventually dozed off, she dreamed of Mick and computers and Sally and smelly drains. She was sitting at a desk in a strange garden with Chinese jasmine forming a canopy over her head. Mick was shouting to her. "Get that bloody computer away from my plants. The toxic fumes from it will kill them."

"Don't be stupid, Mick..."

"Just hang on until the weekend," Sally called. "Your PC will be okay by then."

Jane looked desperately from one to the other. "I can't hang on. *Hopes and Dreams* is sinking... I can't hang on... I can't..." She woke with a start, breathing heavily and for the next few hours, she tossed and turned until the sun came up.

Strangely, by the time she'd had breakfast, Jane felt refreshed. Being alone didn't make her feel lonely. She greeted the young couple on the next table. "Good morning," she said cheerily. "How are you?"

"We're good, thank you," the young man answered. "I daren't say anything else, considering we're on our honeymoon." He smiled lovingly at his new wife who reached across the table to squeeze his hand.

"Congratulations!" Jane said. "I hope your marriage is long and happy. I suppose it would be a bit trite to say I hope all your troubles will only be little ones!"

The young couple smiled. "Our best man used that in his speech. I guess every best man has to bring it in somewhere and, even though we have heard it at every wedding we've been to, it still gets a laugh!"

"Have a good day," Jane said as she left.

"You too," they told her and they continued to demonstrate their love to the world just in the way they looked at each other.

Momentarily, Jane recalled her honeymoon and how blissfully happy she had been. "Am I still happy?" she asked herself and shivered at the negativity that was still creeping into her mind. She decided to find a quiet spot on the beach so she might collect her thoughts. What had happened in the last couple of days had not been easy. She had felt a tinge of sadness in observing the happiness of the honeymooners. *I remember feeling like that,* she mused. *I hope it lasts for them for many years.* She was finding it difficult to shy away from the looming fact that she felt very uncertain about her relationship with Mick. She tried to focus on the good things about him; tried to recall the reasons she had fallen in love with him all those years before, but all she could think about were the irritations she had noticed recently.

She found the ideal place where she might hide away from the world for a while. Just a short walk from the resort, along a winding beach path, she came across a tiny inlet enclosed by brush on three sides, but with a beautiful view of the turquoise ocean to the northeast. She took out her towel from her backpack and spread it on the soft sand. "Perfect," she said out loud as she sat looking out to sea, knees drawn up and enfolded by her arms. She rested her chin on her knees and listened to the lapping of the waves on the beach some fifty metres away, but there were no people, no birds, no signs of life; no sight, nor sound of civilisation and she felt totally relaxed. As she lay back and felt the warmth of the sun on her body, her mind drifted back to the week before…

"What are you going to do today?" Mick asked as he was leaving for work.

"As if you're interested," she snapped.

Jane squirmed at the profundity of her recollections. *I didn't give him a chance,* she thought guiltily. *Why couldn't I have just been a little more pleasant? He didn't deserve that, so why did I snap?* Making sense of her attitude was becoming more of a problem than she had deemed Mick to be. *What is wrong with me?* She closed her eyes and determined she would sort herself out, whatever it took.

With the sun warming her and the gentle lapping of the waves in her ears, she drifted off to sleep and when she awoke with a start, she was initially confused about her surroundings. Very quickly, she regained her composure and smiled to herself. "I'm where I want to be just now," she said quietly, but was immediately distracted when she looked down at her legs. They were bright red and, looking at each arm in turn, she discovered they were the same. "Oh damn!" she groaned pitifully. "Why didn't I use my sunscreen? I'm going to be pretty sore later… well sore, but not particularly pretty."

Having returned to her chalet mid-afternoon, she showered, doused herself with copious amounts of after-sun lotion and sat on her patio in the cool of the evening breeze. Her legs and arms were warm, but not burning up. She read her copy of *Women's Weekly* from cover to cover, not really taking in what was in print before her. Occasionally she looked abstractedly across the lawn where children were playing and parents were sitting outside their chalets just as she was. The honeymooners wandered hand in hand in the distance and waved to her. "Had a good day?" they called.

Jane nodded enthusiastically and waved back. *Yes, the day has been good, but I'm no nearer to sorting out my life. Maybe tomorrow...* she thought wistfully, *but I am really enjoying my own space. Perhaps Mick and I do need a break from each other.* A huge tear involuntarily trickled down her cheek and she wiped it away quickly before she felt the need to weep properly.

Seven

Mick returned home from work on Friday evening expecting to find Jane there and was surprised when the house seemed lifeless even as he opened the front door. He sighed audibly. "Well, Jane," he said out loud, "you have certainly dug in your heels this time. I ought to have known really. Why did I expect anything else?" He threw his briefcase on the floor by the hallstand, momentarily chastising himself for being untidy, but then with a shrug, he said, "What the hell? It's time I rebelled a bit too." With a flourish, he removed his jacket and threw it on the bed, dropped his shirt and socks on the floor and hastily found a pair of shorts and his thongs. Shuffling into the kitchen, he took the last prepared meal out of the freezer—a chicken and leek pie—and sighed again as he realised that he would have to do some grocery shopping if he intended eating over the weekend. "Bloody woman!" he declared. "Do I need her here?' he questioned logically. "Not really. I am more than capable of looking after myself. Don't ever think I'm dependent on you, Jane Peterson..." He paused as he realised he had not used Jane's maiden name in all the twenty seven years they had been married and now it had just rolled off his tongue as though it were the most natural thing in the world for him to do.

During the next few hours, Mick kept himself busy in an effort to stop from thinking about what appeared to be happening to his relationship with Jane. He regarded the trail of discarded clothes throughout the house and again reprimanded himself for being so untidy. *You are the tidiest person I know, Michael O'Connell,"* he silently said to himself. *Why would you do all this just to prove you don't care if Jane is here or not? She isn't here to see it anyway, and it's so out of character for you...* He retrieved the clothing and placed it in the laundry box ready for washing when Jane came home. He shrugged at the thought that she might not come home for a while. "Okay," he said, "I'll do it tomorrow before I do the shopping. Never let it be said that a man can't fend for himself AND hold down a decent job." He wondered if he should call his errant wife and, with a defiant toss of his head, he declared adamantly, "Certainly not. She can call me when she comes to her senses."

When the telephone rang, he almost ran to pick up the receiver and much to his astonishment, his heart skipped a beat. "Hi darl," he said automatically.

"Hi, Dad. That's a very affectionate greeting." Sally didn't usually call on Fridays as the children were generally at Little Athletics and by the time they were home, showered and in bed, she was just about ready to have dinner and a glass of wine with Bill. Friday nights were the times they looked forward to, so duty calls were rarely on the agenda.

"This is an unexpected surprise," Mick told her. "To what do I owe the pleasure?"

"We're just waiting for Jim and his brood to arrive. They decided to drive up here tonight so we can have the whole day together tomorrow."

"That's nice. Have a good time." Mick loved his daughter dearly, but he wasn't in the mood for small talk and he wondered how much he should tell Sally about the situation that had been developing for the past few days.

He was totally taken aback when Sally asked, "What's up with Mum?"

"Why do you ask?" he answered defensively.

"Because she called earlier in the week asking if she could come to stay with us for a few days. You know as well as I do that she never does things on the spur of the moment and I've been pondering on it for days. Is she there?" Sally had really put him on the spot.

"Not at the moment..."

"Well, when will she be back?"

Mick thought quickly. "She's with Linda, so who knows what time she'll be back," he lied, keeping his tone light. "I'll ask her to call you as soon as she comes in if you like."

"No, it's okay Sally told him. "Jim and Dorothy will be here by then and with four kids running riot, it will hardly be conducive to speaking on the phone. We've let Holly and Jacob stay up longer so they can see their cousins. I'll call after the weekend as I told Mum when we spoke. I just wanted to check she was all right, because she sounded a bit weird... well, weird for Mum, if you see what I mean."

"You know Mum," Mick said deliberately. "I'll still tell her you called, though. Have a good time with the other Mansell clan."

"We will. Speak later. Love you."

"Love you too, Sal. Bye."

Mick replaced the receiver and breathed in deeply. "I lied!" he exclaimed, "I lied to my daughter!" He shook his head incredulously. "What the bloody hell is happening? For god's sake, Jane, sort out this situation before it gets any more out of hand."

~ * ~

That same Friday morning, Jane decided to stay on at Eden Sands Resort for the weekend. She was gradually becoming relaxed, but she had not yet formulated a plan of action. She called Mick just before she turned in for the night. "It's me," she announced as he answered the phone. The sound of his voice made her heart beat faster, not because of the thrill of speaking to the man she loved, but strangely because she felt tense and nervous in divulging her plans to him.

"Oh, about time," he said tersely. "I was beginning to think you'd forgotten where you live."

Jane felt the tension creeping in to every fibre of her being. "Don't start, Mick," she snapped, but then took a deep breath. "I don't want an argument. I'm staying on for another couple of days..."

"Why?"

"I was beginning to feel relaxed and my mind seemed clearer, but now I'm not so sure. Your attitude does nothing to inspire me," she told him.

Mick sighed loudly. "What do you want me to say, Jane? You take off without so much as a by-your-leave; you don't phone for three days and then you tell me you're staying away longer. Are you aware of what you are doing?"

"Yes, I am aware," she said quietly.

"And you think staying away is going to solve the problem?" Mick asked belligerently. "Exactly what am I supposed to think, Jane? Should I be worried?"

"About what?"

"About us. I..." Mick didn't know what to say anymore.

"Don't worry about us," she said. It was a placatory remark and was all she was able to offer just then.

"Just come home and we'll sort this out, whatever it is that is coming between us. I can't believe it's a bloody computer that's causing all this angst," Mick told her. He was desperately trying to say the right thing.

"I'll come home when I'm ready and no, it isn't the computer, although I am still going to buy one," she said. "I need the weekend to sort myself out properly. I'm not expecting you to understand, but at least go along with me for now... please."

Mick sighed again. "Okay," he said, "but I can't say I'm happy about it. Let me know when you're leaving." He replaced the receiver before Jane had time to reply.

Eight

On Saturday morning, Jane found her little inlet had been taken over by two children building impressive sand castles with moats and streams. She smiled at them as she approached. "Isn't this a lovely place?" she said.

"Oh yes it is, and our sand castles don't get washed away by the ocean, but Mummy says we shouldn't talk to strangers," the older of the two boys told her innocently. "She's just over there," he continued as he waved to the lady who was waving back from a few yards away on the beach.

"I'm sorry, but I do understand. Your mummy is very wise," she told them and added as pleasantly as she could muster, "I'll just have to find somewhere else to sit. Enjoy your day."

"We will."

Jane felt fractious. She had claimed that spot as her own for the past week and now the weekend had brought unexpected intrusion. She looked beyond the inlet and noticed that the path wound its way to the top of the headland. Momentarily, she thought she might just go back to the chalet and sit on the veranda, but spurred on by her own determination, she headed off along the winding road. She set a steady pace and found herself singing quietly in time with her steps. *"Tramping the dry, sandy road; tramping the dry, sandy road. Trample, trample, trample, trample—tramping the dry, sandy road...."* She had no idea where it led and she casually shrugged at the analogical significance of the situation. At the top of the headland, she found a rest area with picnic benches under a canopy of honeysuckle and jasmine. It was the perfect sheltered spot, quiet and seemingly uncharted territory for the weekenders. She couldn't believe her luck.

"Hello," the man said. "It seems you've found my retreat. Beautiful, isn't it?"

"Oh, this is your spot, is it?" she asked as she turned to see the new arrival. He was bronzed by the Queensland sun and quite athletic looking for his age. She guessed he might be **about as old as she.**

"I like to think of it as such, but of course, I can't claim it as my own. Most public places are so over-run with tourists these days, and it's difficult to find a place for quiet contemplation," he divulged.

"A man after my own heart," she said amicably. "I needed a place to collect my thoughts and the little inlet I've used all week has suddenly become a building site for prospective developers of sand construction."

He laughed. "I like your descriptive assessment," he told her, "but if you're in need of a time for reflection, I'll move on. I wouldn't like to disturb a lady's peace."

"Please don't go on my account. I think perhaps I might like a bit of company for a while," she told him. "I've done the alone bit for the past few days."

"If you're sure you don't mind. I do love this spot and I won't disturb you," he assured her. "I'm Richard."

"Nice to meet you, Richard. I'm Jane O'Connell."

They each sat in reflective silence for a while. There was no need for conversation. Jane could see the ocean through a gap in the trees and could hear it swishing as the waves hit the shore that was hidden by the rocky headland atop which she sat. She stretched out her tanned legs, crossed her feet and gently rested her clasped hands on her knees. She was very comfortable both in body and spirit. *Perhaps I should take up yoga,* she mused. *I imagine it would lead to feeling like this. Could be the answer to all my problems, I think.*

"You are suddenly looking much more at ease," Richard told her. "This place often works its magic on me when I'm stressed with life's daily pressures."

"I made it that obvious, did I?"

"Not really, but I often sense a person's mood. It comes in very useful at times," Richard stated.

"I find that a bit creepy,' Jane told him. "Oh, but I'm sorry. I didn't mean that to sound rude."

"No offence taken and I shouldn't have been so ready to give my opinion."

They smiled uneasily at each other and, in an effort to ease the tension that had unwittingly crept in, Jane asked, "Do you live locally?"

"Oh so now you're trying to find out where I live," Richard said with a grin.

Jane was going to react to his suggestive remark and tell him to get over himself, but then she saw the twinkle in his eye and the friendly smile on his lips. "You almost had me there," she admitted. "I was just going to tell you where to go!"

"Very smart, Mrs O'Connell... it is Mrs, isn't it? You are wearing a wedding ring after all," Richard rejoined. "Not everybody latches on to my wit immediately. I've been told my sense of humour is a bit weird, but I do like a quick-witted woman!"

Jane regarded the man she had just met with a mixture of interest and intrigue. "In answer to your question, yes, it is Mrs, but..."

"Oh, there's a *but*, is there?"

Jane shook her head slowly. "You don't miss much," she said, "and I was going to say ...but my husband has to work, so I'm taking a break on my own." She didn't feel the need to expound further.

After a brief silence, she looked at her watch. "Goodness, it's lunchtime already," and then she started to laugh.

"What's so funny about lunchtime?" Richard asked, appearing to think he had missed the joke.

"If you knew my friend, Linda, you would know why I'm laughing," Jane explained. "She lives by the clock. Every minute, every second must be accounted for. She will never stray from her routine and her daily rituals never waver. She disapproves of my recent seemingly reckless disregard for time."

"As an observer and purely out of your description of her, I have to say she must lead a very boring existence. I can't imagine never changing my day to day activities," he said. "Time is flexible."

Jane took a deep breath, felt the excitement rising and wanted to run and hug this stranger who had just walked into her life and who was clearly so completely on her wavelength. "I can't believe you just said that,' she told him. "That's exactly what I said to Linda and she told me I was irresponsible and selfish. She doesn't believe that time is flexible at all and she says that regularity in one's life leads to a well-organised and structured way of living."

"I understand that, of course I do, but what is life without a little bit of diversion? When you looked at your watch just a moment ago, did you really think you needed to have lunch because it was twelve-thirty?" he asked.

"Well, if I'm honest, I do feel hungry and perhaps I did accept that twelve-thirty is lunchtime," Jane replied.

"Ah, that goes half way to explaining it. You feel hungry. That says you need to eat and it wouldn't matter what time it was, would it? If you felt hungry at eleven o'clock, for instance, would you make yourself wait until the socially accepted lunchtime before you **ate?**" Richard asked.

"Well, I guess I'd have a snack, but I wouldn't call it lunch. We are ruled by convention, aren't we?" Jane offered, "And it does appear that clocks play some part in that."

"We are, but what's wrong with being unconventional on occasions? I think your friend wouldn't like that, but it's what makes life interesting," Richard added. "Now I must go."

He offered no reason why he should make a hasty departure and Jane thought it wasn't her place to ask. "Okay. Thanks for talking to me. Perhaps we can talk another time…"

"Now that would be too conventional," he said with a grin and left without saying goodbye.

Jane was bemused. *I don't think convention has a place in his life and he is rather opinionated, but he had a weird kind of finesse about him. I quite like that,* she thought as she unpacked her lunch and ate it with relish. "Lunchtime, or not," she said out loud, "I'm starving!"

~ * ~

Mick wondered if he ought to drive up to Noosa for the weekend, seek out Jane and try to persuade her that what she was doing was out of order. *If she has problems, we should be able to fix them,* he thought with rather more than necessary self-assertion. *But Jane is so pig-headed; stubborn at best, stupid at worst. That's harsh criticism, but I think I'm justified in making it.*

He called her on Saturday night. "Come home, Jane," he said bluntly.

"I'll come home when I'm ready," she told him equally as blunt.

"When will that be?"

"Probably on Monday. I'll call as I'm leaving. It's your day off, so you'll be at home." She knew she had to go home and face whatever it was that was making her unhappy. Her time alone had helped her to make that decision at least, although she still had not worked out if it were Mick, or her own insecurity with her new situation.

Mick sighed deeply. "I have nothing more to say just now, Jane. I'd like you to come home. I'm not sure what I think at the moment, but it might be appropriate for you to consider that there are two of us in this relationship. I'll see you on Monday." He replaced the receiver and sighed again.

For the rest of the weekend, he spent his time in the garden during the day and tried watching television as a distraction during the evening. *I can't even be bothered to go out on* Hopes and Dreams. *That's very unusual for me. What on earth is happening?* he thought sadly. Mulling over his present situation, he suddenly shivered at the thought that this might be his life from now on. "Perish the thought," he said out loud, "but I'm not bowing down to her madcap ideas."

Nine

Jane was up early on Sunday morning and set off to walk up the headland again hoping to bump into Richard. He had made a deep impression on her, even though their meeting had been brief. *I think he's the male form of me,* she mused as she wended her way to the idyllic spot Richard had called his own. Her heart was beating fast as she approached the special place, not because she was taxing her physical fitness, but at the thought of seeing this fascinating man again. It felt clandestine and utterly reckless. "What are you doing, Jane?" she asked herself. "You are a married woman and you don't chase after other men." She dared to giggle at her foolishness, but... *I really want to see this man again, to listen to his unconventional views, to see his warm smile and the twinkle in his eye, to touch his sun-tanned hand and feel the thrill of... STOP!* She gasped at her audacity, but still looked around furtively for any sign of his presence. There was nothing, no-one, and she felt instant disappointment. She sat there for a couple of hours intermittently gazing through the gap in the trees at the beautiful view, intermittently opening her book to try to read. She flicked through the pages of Iris Murdoch's *The Sea, The Sea* and picked up on the words about being able to see much more when one looks back. Charles Arrowby, Murdoch's main character, decides to withdraw from the world and dwell in seclusion in a house by the sea. He coincidentally encounters his first love, but she rejects him...

Jane closed her eyes and contemplated her own withdrawal, not so much from the world, but from all that was familiar to her. She had not encountered her first love—indeed that had been Mick, her husband, but she had encountered a person, a stranger who had somehow stirred her innermost feelings as Charles Arrowby had been moved by his adolescent love. She looked out dreamily over the ocean, sparkling turquoise, lapping the shore lovingly. She felt irritated and frustrated that Richard had not appeared again and felt the urge to walk in the direction he had walked when he left the previous day. She sighed. *Use your common sense, Jane,* she told herself, *that is, if you have any left after all this. One twinkle in the eye of a stranger and common sense seems to have flown out of the window... but oh how he made my heart flutter. I haven't felt like that since Shane Boyd kissed me in the cloakroom at school when I was twelve years old. There has never been anything like that first real, grown-up kiss...* She interrupted her thoughts poignantly. *Well, maybe the first time I made love.* That was a swift reminder that she had to go home and face Mick the next day, but she quickly dismissed that thought. *I don't want to think about Mick or sex just now, hmmm, definitely not sex,* and she wandered back to her chalet to shower and change before dinner.

She decided to make her meal that evening a celebratory one. *I'll celebrate the new me,* she thought, *and this is definitely the new me, I'm sure of that.* When the waiter came to take her order, she ordered wine, just one glass to begin with, and having savoured chili prawns, fillet steak with green salad and strawberry

Pavlova topped with fresh cream, she decided to take the rest of the bottle of Shiraz back to her chalet.

The February evening was delightfully balmy and she found a glass in her kitchen cupboard before sitting on the patio outside with the remains of her bottle of wine. She giggled girlishly as she poured her third glass. The one glass over dinner had become two and she was beginning to feel very, very relaxed. She watched the sunset on the horizon and thought she caught a glimpse of a man taking his evening stroll. Shielding her eyes from the glare, she was able to confirm that she had indeed seen the man... "Richard?" she asked herself quietly. "Richard?" she said more loudly now. "Richard," she shouted across the sprawling expanse of lawn in front of her chalet.

The man stopped and looked across at her. He waved briefly and Jane's heart skipped a beat. "Hello again, Mrs O'Connell..." he called.

Jane was taken aback with his formal greeting, but she ran across to where he was standing. "Hello again," she gushed. "Please don't be so formal. My name is Jane and you may call me that rather than Mrs O'Connell."

"But we've only just met," he replied nonchalantly.

"I know, but you only told me your first name, so it would only be fair for you to use mine," Jane told him. Her face was flushed as a result of the wine, but she felt herself blush under the gaze of this dashingly handsome gentleman. "Would you like to share what is left of my bottle of wine?"

"I don't think so, Mrs O'Connell," Richard said. He was being dismissive and Jane wondered if she had said something untoward. She was aware that she was flirting shamelessly with him, but instantly realised Richard was not responding.

"Oh, you don't drink then?" she asked lightly.

"Yes, I do enjoy a glass of wine, but I think you've had more than enough for now," Richard explained kindly. "I like your cocking a snook at convention, but inviting someone out for a drink is still a man's privilege in my book. Please don't be offended. I'll walk you back to your chalet if you like."

"Well, if we're being honest, then no, thank you. I don't think I wish to spend time with somebody who talks to me as though I were a child," Jane said calmly. "I have had three glasses of wine...well, two and a bit to be exact. I left the third when I came across to talk to you. I thought we had so much in common yesterday and an adult after dinner conversation would have rounded off my last day here." She was feeling slighted and it showed.

"I hardly know you, Jane..."

He called me Jane! she thought feeling a rush of the teenage thrill she had felt when they met the day before and she grasped the opportunity to relieve the tension she had caused. "I apologise profoundly," she offered. "I had no right to speak to you like that."

"No offence taken," he assured her, "and I will escort you back to your chalet if you like. We can have our adult conversation as we walk."

Jane smiled albeit weakly. She felt belittled, stupid, embarrassed and wondered if she ought to just go back and finish her wine on her own.

"Don't be embarrassed," Richard said as they set off to stroll back towards the row of chalets.

"I'm not..."

"Yes, you are and it's not just the wine that's making your cheeks red. I told you yesterday that I was able to sense people's moods and I sense you are feeling a bit uncomfortable in my presence at the moment," he told her.

"You're an infuriating man, do you realise that?" she said defensively.

Richard shrugged.

"Has anybody ever managed to penetrate that wall you have built around yourself?" Jane continued unabashed. "You're not the only person who is able to read another person's attitudes. A lesser woman than I would have given up trying to talk to you by now. I spent over twenty years in a classroom and recognising others'mood and demeanour was very important to my being able to carry out my job…"

"Now the teacher is talking to me as if I were one of her pupils," he mocked, but Jane noticed that twinkle in his eye again and was spurred on by it.

Thus undeterred, she went on. "Are you going to answer my question?"

"Which one? The one about being infuriating or the other about piercing my hard exterior."

"Both, if you don't mind," she urged. "I'm going home tomorrow and I'd like to think I made a friend during my self-imposed exile."

Richard dug his hands deep into his pockets as they stopped outside Jane's chalet. "I will have a glass of wine with you," he said when he saw the bottle on the table and he stood framed in the doorway as she went in to find another glass.

Jane felt her heart leap again as she turned and saw his manly silhouette against the setting sun and instantly wondered if he were feeling the same thrill she was. He moved to sit at the table as she returned with the glass and poured out what remained in the bottle. They sat in contemplative silence for a short time, neither wanting to disturb the calmness of the situation. There was something surreal about it and eventually Jane began to feel unnerved. "Well, are you going to answer my question, Mr..?" she asked gently. "I don't even know your name."

"All in good time, lady, all in good time. Is it really necessary to know everything about me? Tomorrow you'll go home to your conventional life with your conventional husband and your conventional friend and I will be just the guy you talked to when you stayed in Eden Sands Resort. Wouldn't it be less conventional not to know who I am? How do you know I'm called Richard?" he asked.

"Because you told me so yourself yesterday."

"But I'm not your conventional bloke, am I?" he stated, that glint in his eye appearing again. "I might have made up the name."

Jane was confused. "Yes, I guess you might have, but yesterday I was certain that you and I were on the same wave-length. Now I'm not so sure. I think you are messing with my mind."

"Ah, well, I guess that partly answers your first question. You find me infuriating...Yes?" Richard said with more than a little confidence. "And I would agree with you that some women would have given up before now and indeed have done so many times previously, so that's a point in your favour in trying to stick it out."

"I guess so, but why are you putting me to the test? That in itself is infuriating and I'm beginning to feel I simply ought to tell you to get lost!" Jane could not fathom this man at all, but instead of bidding him a hasty goodnight, she took a swig of her wine and prepared to go into battle with this intriguing character that had somehow got under her skin. "Now, please explain this impenetrable wall you have built around yourself."

Richard appeared to shift uncomfortably in his seat. "That's only for me to know," he said bluntly. "We only met yesterday and there is no way I would bare my soul to a stranger. Like it or lump it, Jane. I intend to maintain my mystery in the same way you are maintaining yours."

"There is no mystery about me, Richard, or whoever you are. I'm Jane O'Connell, former teacher, taking a break to find myself in my new found freedom."

"Ah, but it isn't that simple, is it?" Richard observed.

"What do you mean?" she asked, her heart thumping in her chest at the thought that he had detected the insecurity which she had not yet found the courage to openly acknowledge and accept herself. She lowered her eyes and twirled her wine glass between her fingers to hide her uneasiness.

"You know what I mean, Jane." He emptied his glass with a flourish and stood to leave. Walking round to her, he took her hand and pulled her up until they were standing only inches apart. Taking her into his arms, he kissed her full on the lips, tenderly and with affection. "Maybe that will help you decide," he said. "Goodnight."

Not another word was spoken and he walked away without looking back.

Ten

As Jane drove home on Monday morning, her mind was a blur. She had fallen asleep with a smile on her face the night before, but wakened still asking the questions about her relationship with Mick. *Have I simply tired of him?* she asked herself. *Have we come to a point in our lives where we don't have things in common anymore? Do we still love each other, or are we just staying together because of convention?* She smiled at the word. The roads were quiet and she enjoyed the drive. She stopped for lunch at Caboolture and called Mick to say she would be home in a couple of hours.

"Shall I make something for dinner?" he offered, "or would you like to go to the Sheraton?"

"My, my, Mick!" she exclaimed. "Why would we go to the Sheraton?" Then she changed her tone. "No, we'll eat in. Have you been shopping?"

Now it was Mick's turn to show his disdain. "Yes, I've been shopping," he said condescendingly. "I'm perfectly capable of pushing a trolley round a supermarket, you know."

Jane sighed. "Good. Okay" she said, not showing her irritation this time. "If we have chicken, I'll make chicken and mushroom pasta. It's quick and we can open a bottle of wine. Not a problem."

"That's fine then," Mick said guardedly. "I'll be glad when you're back."

"Thanks," she replied, but didn't know if she felt the same. "See you soon."

She took longer than she intended drinking her coffee. She was mulling over what had happened the night before, not with the thrill of falling in love again, but with objective, analytical scrutiny. *Maybe that will help you decide, he said. What was his game? Why would he kiss me like that and then walk away? I liked it, oh yes, I liked it and no doubt he knew.* She smiled to herself. *What a strange man; what a fascinating man; what a bloody infuriating man!*

By the time she approached Brisbane, Jane had concluded that her break had not really solved her problems, but she had truly enjoyed the freedom both physical and emotional. *I went away to find myself. Didn't I tell Richard that was my reason for being at Eden Sands? I'm not yet convinced that I know where I'm going, but...* She paused pensively. *One thing I learned from Richard, if that's his name, is to follow your instincts and that's what I intend to do.*

~ * ~

When she drew onto the drive, Mick was nowhere to be seen. *Hmm,* she thought, her mind filled with sarcasm. *He's eager to welcome me home.* She took a deep breath as she opened the door and still there was no sign of her husband. "I'm home," she said very quietly and glanced through the window to see Mick watering the potted plants at the far end of the garden. She went out onto the deck and called out to him louder now. "I'm home!"

Mick looked up and waved, casually, she observed, not enthusiastically. "I'll just finish watering these seedlings and I'll be right there. Put the kettle on, will you?"

Jane went straight to the bedroom and began to unpack her case. She was in the laundry when Mick eventually came into the house. She turned to see him standing in the laundry doorway and she fleetingly pictured Richard standing similarly in her chalet doorway the night before. "Hi," Mick said quietly, but he didn't move to give her a welcome home kiss, not even a hug. "I'll put the kettle on, shall I?"

"If you like. A cup of tea would be nice," she replied and finished loading the washing machine before she went to join Mick in the kitchen. She noticed the chicken in a dish on the counter and thought, *At least he remembered we have to eat.*

Taking her by surprise, he asked bluntly, "Did you sort yourself out then?"

Jane bristled and found it difficult to look her husband in the eye. If he saw the aggravation that still lurked behind her expression, he surely wouldn't understand from whence it came. "I think I know myself better now," she offered.

Mick smiled sardonically. "And you didn't know yourself before you went to Noosa? Give me a break, Jane. You've had fifty years to get to know yourself."

"Don't be sarcastic, Mick," she interrupted. "My life has been turned upside down since I retired."

"What's so diff...?"

"Stop it, Mick! Why can't you just listen to what I have to say without contradicting me all the time?"

Mick threw up his hands in resignation, but his expression was certainly lacking in respect for what she had to say.

Jane continued quietly. "I just need my life to be meaningful. I would like something more than just being at home day in and day out. I have tired of the mundane and I need something to inspire me, to motivate me and to thrill me with anticipation of what is coming next."

"You sound like one of those New Age people, Jane. For goodness sake, listen to yourself," Mick told her. "It's about time you grew up and took life more seriously instead of going off into your fantasy world."

Jane was gaining confidence from Mick's negativity. "You just don't get it, do you?" she stated. "All your unwillingness to accept what I would like to do is not helping us at all. In fact, your stance in opposing me in everything just recently has done absolutely nothing at all to inspire me and I'm beginning to wonder where it will all lead."

"Ah, now we're getting at the truth, aren't we? This isn't about you wanting to carry out your hare-brained schemes at all. It's about us. I knew it! I bloody well knew it all along!" Mick was shouting and his face was flushed with anger.

"Don't assume that you're right about that, Mick, just because I went away on my own, but if you put out suggestions like that, then I might just think *you* aren't so comfortable with *me* anymore." Jane was shifting the emphasis and she knew. She realised in that instant that Mick had already thought it through.

"Look, you've just arrived home. We both know there's more to this than your retirement and a flaming computer. I'm not quite sure how to deal with it just now, but we both have to work out what we need to do to keep this marriage together." He was struggling to contain his animosity.

Jane was momentarily amazed; stunned into silence at her husband's assessment of the situation, but felt the need to add her views. "I know something isn't right at the moment, but I don't know what it is. I'm sorry, but I think we have to bide our time and see what happens. It isn't that I don't love you..."

"Are you sure about that, Jane, because from where I'm standing, it isn't very obvious anymore," Mick said deliberately.

"Surely you aren't expecting the rush of emotion we felt when we were first married, because I think you would be dreaming if you thought that kind of love would last," she told him. "We have to be sensible about this," but then she felt her cheeks burning at the thrill she had found in Richard's kiss.

Mick looked at her almost with contempt and refrained from explaining that he was fifty years old, not fifteen. Jane understood that look.

"All I can suggest is that we try to overcome whatever it is that's causing all this angst," he said. "Surely we can deal with it like sensible adults."

"I'll make dinner," she said. "Did you chill a bottle of wine?" She needed to focus on something else and she busied herself at the counter top doing anything that would be a distraction.

Mick went into the lounge room and turned on the television. He needed a distraction too, but his mind wasn't on what he saw on the screen. He had been mentally preparing for this for days and now the time had come, he didn't know what to do about it.

Eleven

Dinner was a quiet affair and they each ate in silence, mulling over their own situation. Intermittently, Mick gave a nervous cough and Jane asked if he were all right.

"I'm fine, Jane. I just haven't got a lot to say at the moment."

"Me neither," she replied.

"That makes a change," Mick said and couldn't help but smile as he looked at his wife whom he still blamed for this mess. *Where's the feisty girl I fell in love with?* he thought wistfully. *Suddenly she has become disgruntled, dissatisfied and totally disillusioned and I don't feel able to help her. On the other hand, do I want to help her? She's stubborn, always has been, but this time it feels different.*

By the time they had eaten and finished the bottle of Chardonnay, they both felt a little more relaxed and the wine had loosened their tongues, not confrontationally, but in a positive way. Jane was the first to speak after she had cleared away the dishes. "I'm going to buy a computer tomorrow," she announced lightly. "I know you're not keen on the idea, but it's what I want to do. I need a challenge and who knows, it might just be the stimulation I need."

Mick didn't oppose her idea, indeed he embraced it. "If that's what will bring the old Jane back, go ahead," he said. "It can go in the school room."

"It's not the school room anymore," she told him. "But it can now become my office. That sounds better and I don't want to keep telling myself I'm going into the school room and reminding myself of my past life!" She giggled at her little joke.

"I know it's the wine that's making you giggle, Jane, but please try to bring back the girl I married."

Jane looked at Mick. He did appear saddened by the whole situation, but there still remained that defiance about him and it irked her. She considered that his agreement to her buying the computer was condescending, placatory at best, but she'd take it if that's what was on offer. "Look, Mick, the wine has relaxed us both, but it still doesn't solve what is happening. God forbid that we'll need to get drunk in order for us to tolerate each other."

"That's a bit harsh, darl," Mick told her, his tone incongruously agreeable.

"You know well what I mean," she replied, equally pleasantly. "I think I'll go to bed now. All that driving has taken its toll. Goodnight."

There was still no physical show of affection and neither one seemed to care. Mick stayed to watch the late night news and Jane went quietly to the bedroom. Once there, she stood and looked at the marital bed they had shared for twenty-seven years. She slid beneath the doona and felt an odd sense of misplacement, so she lay as close to the edge of the bed as she dared without fearing she'd fall off. When Mick eventually came into the room, she lay stock-still so he'd think she was sleeping. He too kept close to his side of the bed and they each lay there not wanting, nor needing to feel the other's closeness.

~ * ~

When the computer was delivered, she was so excited. The delivery man set it up in her office and asked her if she needed any instruction before he left. "If you just tell me how to switch on and log on to the Internet, I'll be fine," she told him. "I've enrolled on a basic IT course which starts next week, so I'll just play until then. I learned a little bit about computers at my school before I retired, so I don't think I'll do anything wrong. Thank you very much for setting it up for me."

"No worries," he said as he left.

~ * ~

She was working out how to set up an e-mail account when Mick arrived home from work. "Look at this," she encouraged him, "I'm a dot com dot au. How exciting!"

"Oh yes," he ventured unenthusiastically, "and who are you going to e-mail?"

"I'll start by e-mailing my colleagues from school. They'll help me get established. Mind you, I'll have to phone Kate in the technology department to let me have her e-mail address."

"That's ironic, isn't it? You have to use the phone to get an e-mail address." Mick turned to walk away. "Is dinner on?"

Jane sighed. "Yes." She refrained from saying more.

For the next few days, Jane was fascinated by what she could find out at the press of a button and she began to feel that she was in control of her life again. Mick showed little interest, but at least he kept his derogatory comments to himself. He still couldn't see the benefits of a home computer and much less the advantage of spending thousands of dollars on something he thought would become obsolete in a comparatively short time.

The first day of the college course was very exciting for Jane. She sat in a class of about twenty students, most of whom were younger, but there were half a dozen who looked to be the same age as she. They each had a desk that housed a personal computer, but they weren't switched on and one or two of the younger students wondered if they ought to switch on before class. The general consensus was that they should wait until the tutor arrived. Jane smiled at the gentleman sitting next to her. "I bet they think we oldies are a bit backward at coming forward," she said.

"I think we are more patient," he said, "and possibly more polite."

Jane chose not to comment on that. She'd spent all her working life dealing with young people. She'd prided herself on being treated with respect and politeness from her students and she didn't need to tell this man whom she had only just met that to generalise about young people was wrong. When the college principal appeared at the classroom door, there was a shuffling of feet and a rattling of chairs as he approached the front of the class. "The Information Technology tutor, Mr Clemens, is running late," he announced. "He called to say he'll be here by ten o'clock and suggested you all take an early break. Please be back in the classroom by ten."

"I wonder if he's related to the famous Clemens," Jane said to the judgmental man to whom she had spoken previously. "You know, Samuel Langhorne Clemens, the famous Mark Twain."

"Well, he did visit these shores, so he might well be," the man replied. "I'm Larry, by the way. Larry Watson."

"Jane O'Connell. The Twain connection could be very interesting, couldn't it?"

"Do you really think he might be related to Mark Twain?" a second older lady asked as she came over to join them.

"You never know," Jane told her, "although I would have expected a descendant of Mark Twain to be a writer, not an IT specialist."

"I'm Betty and you are...?"

"Jane and this is Larry," as she indicated the man she had just met.

Introductions over, they each outlined their reasons for joining the class. Larry was branching into computer sales after selling televisions for the past decade. "I need to keep up with progress in the technical world," he said. "I'll need to extend my knowledge beyond the basics eventually, but this will be a start. I'm sure everybody will have a PC in the next few years."

"I totally agree about the computer being the future," Jane stated confidently. "I haven't convinced my husband yet, but I think you're right about every home having a PC. I need something to challenge me in my retirement. That's why I'm here."

Betty looked rather coy. "I'm here to prove to my grandchildren that I'm not the old stick in the mud they think I am." She winked mischievously. "I'll show the little devils!"

At five to ten, the class had resumed their positions by the computers and it was a further quarter of an hour before the tutor walked in from the back of the room. "Good morning," he called out cheerily as he arrived at the door. "Sorry for the delay..." They all turned round to see a tall, bronzed man of about fifty, quite athletic looking for his age...

Jane gasped audibly as Betty turned round and winked again, assuming Jane was openly stunned by the handsome features of the man who had just walked in the room. Richard caught Jane's eye, but did not acknowledge her. His composure was intact; why wouldn't it be?

Standing confidently in front of the class, he was every inch the polished performer. "My apologies again for keeping you waiting. Traffic on the road from the Sunshine Coast was very heavy—long weekenders, I guess." He dared to look at Jane who sat wide-eyed, hardly daring to return his gaze. "You are surprised to see me, Mrs O'Connell?"

The rest of the class all looked curiously at Jane. She felt uncomfortable, but she determined not to allow the situation to blur her judgment. "You could say that, Mr Clemens," she declared making sure she emphasised the Clemens and the point was not lost on Richard.

"I'm Paul Clemens," he announced to the class and Jane literally gaped at this infuriating man. "You may call me Paul. We are all adults here, so let us not stand on conventional ceremony. High school teacher title respect need not apply."

Betty couldn't wait to ask. "Are you related to…?"

Paul answered the question for the whole class. "I believe I am distantly related, very distantly, but I'm a person in my own right and I prefer to be respected as such. And you are?" Paul appeared unconcerned.

"I'm Betty Rogers and I didn't mean to be rude." She looked embarrassed and Jane understood her feelings. Paul, on the other hand, merely shrugged and waved a dismissive hand in her direction.

Jane made a hasty decision to take the class as though she had never seen this tutor. She focused upon the content of the lesson, very basic stuff to begin with, but after two hours, she had learned most of the computer terms, could find her way around the QWERTY keyboard and knew the difference between a document and a file. Richard's … Paul's lesson was well planned, she observed, as she thought, *I would never have picked him as a college tutor and yet maybe that's why we had an instant connection.*

At the end of the lesson, Paul made an announcement. "This afternoon we are extending the opportunity for those of you who wish to expand their knowledge of information technology. I will start classes on basic desktop publishing. How many of you would be interested?"

A show of hands signalled that several of the students would like to attend. Jane reserved judgment. She wasn't sure about spending all day with this infuriating acquaintance of hers. It had taken all her powers of concentration not to allow her mind to wander back to that kiss. *What did it mean?* she wondered. *And how could Fate deal this hand so soon after the event?*

"Go and get some lunch," he told them, "if you normally eat at this time..."

Another dig at me, Jane presumed.

"...and Mrs O'Connell, may I have a word?"

As the others filed out of the room and made their way to the refectory, Jane remained seated. Richard... Paul wandered over to her desk and perched on the end of it. "Aren't you staying for the next class?" he asked casually.

"I don't know."

"Not a very decisive answer, Mrs ..."

"Stop it with the Mrs O'Connell. You made a point of not sticking to classroom convention, so what's with the formality all of a sudden?" She was aware that she was gabbling and snapping too. "You know my name, so use it."

"Oh, my, my Mrs O'Connell, feline characteristics do not become you. Why are you being so tetchy?" he asked.

"You mean to say you don't know?" she snapped. "What are the odds of this happening?"

"What?"

"Don't be so infuriating, Rich... or whatever your name is. Would you have told me you were teaching this course if I'd said I intended joining such a class when I left Noosa?" she probed.

"That's hypothetical, but probably not," he told her nonchalantly. "Why should I tell you? You were just some woman..."

Jane stood and faced him, her face only inches from his, but then she pulled back deliberately. "What?" she spat, "Just some woman who what? Is this the real arrogant you, or the one you prefer to display in private? On the other hand, perhaps you're hiding behind that wall again. I give up with you." She paused. "Who are you anyway? Richard, or Paul, or some other persona who shall remain nameless?"

"It doesn't matter who I am. I was Richard in Noosa and I'm Paul here in college. Decide which one you prefer. I told you I didn't bow down to convention. A name is something one is known by in given situations. That's good enough for me and should be accepted by you. Problem solved. Now are you coming to this afternoon's class or not?"

"Why? So you can belittle me again?"

"I never belittled you, Jane. Why would you say that?"

Jane looked down to hide her embarrassment. "You kissed me," she said quietly.

Richard was unfazed. "I did and you didn't object. I detected that you were in Noosa on your own to sort out your feelings for your husband. You didn't have to explain that to me. Your whole demeanour did that for you."

"Excuse me?" Jane asked quizzically.

"You were flirting with me..."

"I was not! I found you intriguing, true, but I wasn't flirting..."

Jane started for the door. "Are you running away from the truth now?" he asked.

"You are the most infuriating, arrogant, opinionated person I have ever met," she told him. "I'm going to have some lunch... not because of the time, but because I'm hungry." She stormed out of the room and marched deliberately down the corridor to the refectory.

"See you this afternoon," he called.

Twelve

Jane did attend the afternoon class, but made sure she sat at the back of the room so as not to be too close to the tutor in more ways than one. She found the classes interesting, enlightening and certainly a challenge. During the following few weeks, she kept a low profile, although her whole being was crying out to spend more time with the man who had touched her heart-strings in a way no-one ever had. Occasionally she caught his eye, but avoided his stare.

She began to accept Mick with more tolerance, merely because he had allowed her to immerse herself in her new found challenge without interfering. "How is the course going?" he asked from time to time.

"Good," she told him without expounding further. She spent her evenings on her computer practising the skills she was learning each week. Bedtimes were tense affairs for her. She didn't feel inclined to have Mick close to her and he didn't seem to object to that. The subject was never discussed. *If we don't talk about it, it's not happening,* she convinced herself.

On the days she didn't have a class, she began to spend in the college library on the pretext she was researching the topic they had covered in the previous lecture. That way she might just bump into Richard—*I refuse to call him Paul,* she thought with a bold touch of childish stubbornness. She didn't feel obliged to inform Mick she was spending so much time there whilst he was at work. "What he doesn't know won't hurt him," she told herself. On his days off, she would say, "I'm just going for a walk. I'll be back in time for lunch, or dinner," as the case may be.

Then Mick became curious. "When you go for a walk, why do you always go in the car?" he enquired.

She needed to think quickly. "I always walk around the headland by the surf club," she told him.

"Maybe I'll come with you next time," he rejoined.

Jane was momentarily caught off guard. "Why?" she asked in an effort to give herself time to work out what she should say next.

"I just thought I might join you in something you obviously enjoy and doesn't involve computers," he said.

"You have never walked round there with me before. Why would you want to start now?"

Mick sighed loudly. "I'm making an effort, Jane," he said, the irritation evident in his tone. "We seem to be at an impasse and I thought going to college and spending all this time on your precious computer, you might at least find a bit of time to spend with me."

"I appreciate that," she said and she meant it, but her confused feelings still haunted her. As long as she was seeing Richard regularly, she became more uncertain of her feelings for Mick. *On the other hand,* she thought sensibly, *Richard gives me no intimation that he is interested. Oh, he drops subtle hints about what happened in Noosa, but nothing I could hold onto as reciprocating my feelings. Maybe I should ask him… or maybe not.* Her embarrassment at her own behaviour made her hold back. The thought of total humiliation left her feeling nothing less than absurdly foolish. *So why do I insist on behaving like a love-struck adolescent?* Her middle-aged mind continued to avoid any semblance of common sense.

Mick walked away in resignation of the fact that his wife did not wish to spend time with him. *Not yet anyway, if ever.* He shrugged. *Do I care? I'm not sure I do anymore.*

Out of the blue, Sally called. "Sorry it's been so long, Mum. Are you feeling better now?"

"I haven't been sick," she replied, puzzled that her daughter thought she had been ill.

"You called me weeks ago saying you needed to come down to stay. You sounded a bit under the weather. You don't usually visit without making plans weeks in advance. I thought it odd that you wanted to come on the spur of the moment and assumed you were feeling out of sorts," Sally explained.

"I wasn't feeling out of sorts at all," she said defensively. "Can't a mother come and see her daughter without making an advance appointment?" She was being rather more aggressive than necessary.

"Hold on, Mum, this is not an interrogation." Sally was becoming suspicious again. "You always plan ahead and anyway, I called when you were out with Linda just after Jim and his crew had been to stay with us."

"Oh?"

"I thought you might have returned my call when Dad gave you the message."

"I didn't get a message," Jane told her, "and I haven't seen Linda for a couple of months…"

"What's going on, Mum?'

"What do you mean?" Jane knew she had not been very astute in her explanation.

Sally decided to be blunt. "There's something going on and I intend to find out what it is. Dad was very cagy too when I spoke to him. Will you come down here, or do I have to come up there?" she demanded.

"There's no need, because there's nothing going on, as you put it, and anyway, I go to college twice a week now. I'm learning how to use a computer," Jane said in an effort to change the topic of their conversation.

"Don't change the subject, Mother" Sally snapped. "And anyway, what on earth would you want with a computer? They're for the young, not the middle-aged."

"My, my. Pardon me for breathing, Sally!" she said with measured sarcasm. "You're as bad as your father. Has he been getting in your ear?"

"No he hasn't, but that gives me the gist of how things are with you and Dad. No wonder you both evade questions. You are both too old to have adolescent tiffs. Get over yourselves and stop fighting." Sally was being presumptuous, but thought she was on the right track.

Jane was becoming irritated. "Look here, young lady, don't you speak to me like that. Your father and I are not fighting."

"Yes you are, otherwise you would call him my dad, not my father. I know you, Mum. There's something very odd happening and I can't say I like it," Sally told her. "I'll come up tomorrow."

"I'm at college all day tomorrow," Jane happily informed her daughter, hoping it would suggest to Sally that she would be driving all that way for nothing.

"I'll meet you after your morning class and we'll have lunch together. Where is the college?" she asked.

Jane felt like a rabbit caught in headlights and she didn't know whether to run, or stay and face whatever was in store. "It's in Southport, but you really don't need to drive all that way. I only have an hour for lunch and then there's another class in the afternoon."

"I'm coming. No arguments." Sally replaced the phone before her mother was able to object.

~ * ~

Jane didn't know how she would react to Sally's interrogation—*And that's what it will be when she gets here, an interrogation.* She spent the morning class duly concentrating on preparing a Word document for assessment. She could not possibly have anticipated what was in store.

"May I walk to the refectory with you?" Richard asked at the end of the class.

"Why?"

"I have something I would like to say. It won't take long."

"I'm meeting my daughter for lunch, so it isn't convenient for me to be seen with you," Jane told him, feeling her face redden at the intimation in her words.

"Ashamed of me, are you?" Richard said, with that irritating twinkle in his eye.

Jane sighed audibly. "What is it, Richard? I'm tired of your games..."

"My games?" he questioned. "You have been playing games with me ever since we met. What do you want from me?"

"I don't want anything from you," she replied, feeling more than a little awkward.

Richard eyed her suspiciously. "I told you at the outset that I'm able to sense people's moods without being told. Somehow, you and I have a connection and I can read you like a book..."

"You don't know me at all," she interrupted, "so..."

Now it was his turn to interrupt. "I know enough to work out that you want me to think you don't care about me, that you are trying unconvincingly to avoid me and yet you turn up at college when we don't have a class hoping to catch a glimpse of me."

Jane was utterly astonished. She felt her cheeks burning and was unable to hide her embarrassment. She admitted to herself that she had been sprung, not only sprung, but also completely humiliated. "I can explain," she offered.

"No need," he told her. "Your problems have nothing to do with me and the whole point of this conversation is to solve your dilemma for you."

"What makes you think I have a dilemma? You have shown no interest in my position since we left Noosa and common sense tells me not to involve you in my problems." She suddenly felt strangely removed from the situation with him.

Richard continued unabashed. "I'm married," he said. "Very happily married. My wife is on a sabbatical in London. She understands me ..."

"She'd have to," Jane quipped sarcastically.

"There's the frightened child reaction again, Jane. You leave yourself wide open to my judgmental opinions and yes, I am judgmental. I know that, but I'm also very astute and, although you might not agree at this moment in time, I do care about people."

Jane suddenly and irrefutably realised she was no match for this person. She didn't feel academically threatened by him, but on an emotional, psychological level, she was left floundering. "I'm not sure I ought to ask this, but why did you kiss me with so much tenderness?"

"You needed to have something to help you see where your heart belonged."

"But you made matters worse than they were."

"Not really. I can guarantee that you went back home and began to assess your situation more sensibly. You are still with your husband, aren't you? That kiss didn't make you try to follow me and had I not turned up here, you wouldn't have had any idea who, or where I might be."

Jane half smiled wryly. "I still don't know who you are, or where you come from," she told him as he shrugged unapologetically. "You are a very intimidating and infuriating person, do you know that?"

"So you said previously. I told you then I was unconventional," he said with that twinkle in his eye again. "I find you fascinating too, Jane, but I'm not about to become the escape route from your marriage. How is your friend, by the way, the one who is chained to her clock?"

"Still running around after her brood, I think, but I haven't seen her for a while. I've had other things on my mind," she said, "but thank you, Richard, if that's your name."

"That's for me to know," he said pointedly. "I'm leaving college today and going to join my wife in London for a few weeks. The classes will continue with a guy called Colin Forrest. I didn't want to leave without informing you personally."

Jane was not surprised by his announcement. "Thank you again, Richard... for everything." She moved forward to kiss him on the cheek and he hugged her warmly.

~ * ~

Sally drew in to the car park just as Richard and Jane were saying their goodbyes. "Oh my god!" she exclaimed.

Thirteen

Heart pounding in her chest, head whirling, Sally drove out of the car park and headed for her parents' house. "My mother is having an affair!" she exclaimed and tears welled up in her eyes. She pulled over to the side of the road and quietly wept. Questions of *why* and *how long* began to creep into her shocked brain. *Does Dad know?* she thought wildly. *Oh my goodness, the poor man and I haven't been there for him. What can she be thinking? No wonder she was evasive. I can't believe it, but I know what I saw.*

Sally sat for almost an hour trying to collect her thoughts as Jane waited in the car park for her daughter to arrive for lunch. After thirty minutes, she concluded that Sally hadn't managed to drive up to meet her after all and she had to admit that she was relieved.

~ * ~

Sally rushed to her parents' house and found it locked up for the day. *Damn!* she thought. *Dad will be at work.* She tutted loudly and threw up her arms in disgust. *Makes it easy for Mum, doesn't it? While the cat's away, the mice will play.* "Good analogy, Sal," she said out loud. "What a sneaky, conniving, little mouse she has been." She sighed. *It just shows... you never know what goes on even in your own family... and...* she gasped at the thought... *not even with my own mother.*

She sat on the doorstep for a while contemplating what she should do next. *Do I tell Dad? Do I confront HER? She can't deny it when I tell her what I saw. Oh Mum, what are you doing? What have you done? No wonder she was evasive when I asked her what was wrong,* she said to herself for the umpteenth time in the past half an hour. *Poor Dad...*

After an hour and there being no sign of Jane returning, Sally decided to drive home, removing herself from the situation. Slowly, her mind was clearing. *It's nothing to do with me,* she assured herself. *I know they are my parents and I care about them, but they are grown people—adults—and for the moment, I'll leave them to it. Surely they will tell me if and when it becomes necessary.* With heavy heart, she returned to Coffs Harbour and the security of her own family and her own home.

~ * ~

Jane went into her afternoon class with a much more open mind. Richard's sudden departure, and indeed the explanation of his bizarre actions, had pointed her in the right direction. *I know I behaved like a love-sick teenager,* she thought as she drove home at the end of the afternoon. *I didn't really think I could have an affair...* Her thoughts halted abruptly *...Or did I?* She was embarrassed at the idea. *I did feel good, though, at the thought of falling in love with a stranger. That really was very naughty of me.* She shrugged, not out of nonchalance, but more out of acceptance that she had been a little bit foolish. *BUT,* she thought with concern, *it still doesn't solve the problem of Mick. I don't know how I feel about him anymore and that's the difficulty just now. It has to be dealt with.*

~ * ~

"Can we talk?" she asked him as they finished dinner that evening.

"What do you mean, can we talk?" Mick asked incredulously. "What is the matter with you, Jane? We've been together for almost thirty years and you're asking can we talk?" He stared at her, his eyebrows raised in disbelief.

"If you are going to ask me what's wrong every time I try to have a discussion with you, then it looks like we can't talk—civilly anyway," Jane told him pointedly. "I need to…"

"Oh I see! YOU need to talk. Well that makes it official then, doesn't it?" he replied scathingly. "Jane needs to talk. Drop everything, Mick. JANE NEEDS TO TALK." His voice was very loud and laced with the unmistakeable sarcasm he had used in several contretemps recently.

"If I didn't know better, I would say you'd had too much to drink," she said as she stood and walked away from the table. It was the table around which family and friends had gathered on numerous occasions, where conversations had been light and sociable, where discussions had often become heated yet remained friendly. Now she felt she could no longer discuss anything with the man who was her husband and whom she did not know anymore.

"Is that what you think? That I need a drink to be able to face up to you?

She stood still with her back to him.

"Go on, Jane," Mick continued. "Walk away when the going gets tough."

She turned deliberately and looked at him with undisguised disdain. Shaking her head slowly, she said, "That's the reason I needed to talk to you. You have become pompous and ridiculously supercilious…"

"Oh have I?" he interrupted caustically. "And what about you? What have you become, Mrs Perfect?"

"I know exactly what I have become," she told him honestly. "And that was another thing I wanted to talk to you about. I have spent the last six months analysing myself..."

"And what gems of information did you come up with?" Mick scoffed.

"You'd be surprised, Mick," she said. "Even you don't know me as well as you think you do."

Mick stood up from the table, not threateningly, but more demanding she pay attention. "You appal me, Jane. You are the most self-centred, opinionated, egocentric person I have ever known and you have the gall to call me pompous and supercilious?"

She wanted to tell him that self-centred and egocentric meant the same thing. *Typical scientist,* she thought with a sigh that appeared to come from the depths of her soul.

"We'd better not continue this conversation tonight, otherwise we both might say something we'll regret," he dared to say. "I'm going to tend to my plants. At least they don't talk back."

Jane remained silent. *Just go, Mick. I can't take any more of this today.*

Fourteen

As the weeks passed, Mick began to relish his time at work away from the tension and the uncomfortable atmosphere at home that enveloped him as soon as he walked through the door. His thoughts weren't hostile; he was desperately trying to be tolerant. *I didn't start all this. She will have to solve the problems she has. If she continues with this stand-off, then... I refuse to think further on the situation.*

At work he was happy. His colleagues were pleasant and completely unaware of his errant wife. He liked Samantha best as she was at an age when girlish silliness was replaced by the common sense that recognises humorous situations with decorum. *Somehow she has retained a sense of fun without being ridiculously childish. I guess she must be mid-thirties... forty at the most.* Samantha caught him smiling at her occasionally and said cheekily, "Hey, Mr O'Connell. Get on with your work or the boss will be on you like a tonne of bricks."

"I *am* the boss, Sam, so watch what you say, or I might just replace you with a serious, silent type!"

"Yes sir, Mr O'Connell, sir," she replied, "but you wouldn't enjoy your job half so much if you did that. Just think how tedious the day would be without me to keep you on your toes."

"Just get on with your work, Sam," he said laughing with her. *She certainly does brighten the day*, he thought.

Because of the very nature of his position, Mick was necessarily the last person to leave the building. He started to stay late to avoid going home to the frosty atmosphere that awaited him. Most evenings, he did the paperwork ready for the next day. Other nights he would go for coffee at Frankie's Patisserie next door and try to unwind a little before facing the wife with whom he could no longer communicate in a civil manner. It was Friday, the day before his weekend off. He walked slowly along the rear corridor on his way to the car park. As he passed the ladies' room, he heard something. Curious, he stopped and listened. *Somebody is crying*, he thought as he crept nearer to the door to make sure he wasn't imagining things.

The sobs were quiet, but plaintive. Mick put his ear to the door. He knocked gently. "Hello. Who's in there? Are you all right?"

The crying stopped momentarily.

"May I come in?" he asked.

"Please yourself," she said, although her words weren't antagonistic.

Mick cautiously opened the door and peeped inside. "Samantha! Whatever is the matter?"

Samantha began to cry again and he went to comfort her, to hold her, to show she was not alone, whatever it was that was causing her such grief. She clung to him like a frightened child and his fatherly intuition was to hold her until the crying subsided. He stroked her head gently and whispered in her ear.

"Sh-sh-sh, baby. Don't cry. It'll be all right, you'll see. Come on, sweetheart. Sh-sh-sh."

They stood enfolded in each other's arms for a little while until Mick led her to the staff lounge room and she sat quietly while he made a cup of tea. "Do you want to talk?" he asked as he gave her one of the two cups he was holding and sat beside her.

She took the cup from him slowly and sipped the tea delicately. "I'm not sure talking will help," she said, her voice still broken by her sadness.

"I don't wish to pry," he assured her. "God knows there are things we all would wish to keep private and believe me, I know that very well."

Samantha looked at him through sad eyes. "My partner called just as I was leaving work…"

"I didn't hear the phone," Mick said, puzzled that his office phone hadn't rung in the past hour.

"Oh, no," she explained. "I have one of the new mobile phones…"

"My goodness, Sam! What is it with all this new technology? I don't know where it's all leading us."

Sam smiled weakly. "My partner bought it for me so he could contact me when he works out of the city. Sometimes he can't get to a landline and these mobiles are very handy in such circumstances. Now I wish I hadn't got the blasted thing," she said with more than a little venom in her tone.

Mick looked at her questioningly.

"He isn't coming home… ever," she revealed as the tears welled up in her eyes again.

"What do you mean?" Mick asked.

"I mean he's left me and he's living with an ex-girlfriend in Toowoomba. I knew there was something odd when I left this morning. He was hanging around in the house instead of going to work. He always leaves before me, but today he seemed to be dawdling. When I asked him why, he said he didn't have to start until ten o'clock and I was naive enough to take his word."

Mick looked at her with understanding and took her hand in his. "I think I know where this is going," he said. "He packed his things when you left and then called to give you the news. The bastard!"

Samantha began to weep again, but soon recovered enough to assess her situation rationally. "You know," she conceded, "talking *has* helped. These are tears of relief, not sadness. I have felt for a while he and I were growing apart anyway. I knew it wouldn't be long before it ended. You do know, don't you, when things aren't right?"

Mick nodded slowly and deliberately in agreement. He was still holding her hand. She leaned forward and kissed him on the cheek, but she allowed her lips to linger longer than was appropriate in the circumstances. Mick took her tear-stained face in his hands and held it close to his. His thoughts were running wild. *What are you doing, Mick? Don't do anything you'll regret. I want to kiss you, Sam. I need to kiss you, Sam. You aren't moving away and your eyes are telling me to do it...* She took his hands from her face and held him close. Her lips found his and she kissed him with a longing and passion he hadn't felt for a long time. He responded with a tenderness that befitted the situation.

"Oh Sam," he sighed. "Sam, Sam, Sam..."

Suddenly he pulled back and stood up with his back to her. "I'm sorry," he said, his voice croaking with emotion.

"You mean you didn't enjoy it?" Samantha asked, bewildered by his reaction.

"Oh I did enjoy it... too much," he admitted as he turned to face her again. "But I'm your boss and I have absolutely no right to put you in such a position."

"But *I* put *you* in that position," she told him adamantly. "I'm not usually so forward, but it felt right. I wanted you to kiss me; I needed you to kiss me. Have I offended you?"

Mick sighed. "Of course you haven't offended me. What man wouldn't be flattered when an attractive woman wants to kiss him? Oh Sam, can't you see where all this could lead? You're a sweet, sweet girl and any man would want to be with you, but …" He paused deliberately. "…I'm your boss."

"Does that really make any difference when two people are attracted to each other?" she asked with genuine concern. "I wouldn't put you in a position where you'd lose your job…" She blushed, her cheeks were burning. "I like you, Mr O'Connell." She laughed at the incongruity. "Please may I call you Michael?" she asked.

He laughed with her. "Of course; that's my name and only my mother ever called me Michael, but I'd like it to be your name for me."

"Thank you," she said, happier than she had been half an hour earlier.

"Now, do you think you might be able to drive home safely?" he asked. "I'm concerned that if you cry again, your vision might be impaired."

"I'm fine now… and thank you, Michael," she told him. She smiled at him, the most disarming smile he had ever seen in spite of the traces of sadness that still lingered in her eyes.

It was a spur of the moment decision. "Look," he said. "I have the weekend off. Why don't I pick you up tomorrow and we'll go out for the day? It will take your mind off things and I know I'll enjoy it too."

"Are you sure? Won't your wife mind?"

Mick was taken aback. *My wife? I never gave her a thought through all this.* "That won't be a problem, I assure you," he said with confidence. *I don't need to expound further at this point.* "I'll pick you up at ten. Where would you like to go?"

"Surprise me," she told him, with a hint of excitement in her voice. "I love surprises."

When Mick arrived home, Jane was nowhere to be seen. He didn't feel the need to call out and he wandered into the kitchen to find a note on the table.

I thought I'd better let you know I'll be away for the weekend. I'm going to Noosa again. Not that you'll be interested, but I can relax there. I didn't make dinner. I think you might like to eat out.
See you when I get back.
Jane

"Typical," Mick said out loud and decided to get changed and go to the golf club for dinner. *I'll have male company in the members' bar without women in attendance.* He smiled. *Jane, I have to say, you have a little bit of common sense after all! Maybe you're psychic and understood I didn't want your company tonight.* As far as Jane was concerned, sarcasm filled his mind. *Have a good trip, dear.*

Fifteen

He was up bright and early on Saturday morning. He showered, dressed casually in shorts and tee-shirt and packed a picnic hamper. He drove the short distance to Samantha's house and was there on the dot of ten o'clock. She was waiting at the front door as he drew up.

"I wasn't sure you'd turn up," she said, observing the ruggedly handsome man as he got out of his car.

"Why wouldn't I turn up? A date is a date. Only the most ill-mannered of people wouldn't turn up when he said he would."

Samantha smiled shyly. "Well...you know..." She stopped. She seemed at a loss for words.

Michael gently took her hand. "Don't worry about last night," he said. "We have all day to talk, to laugh, to enjoy. I'm looking forward to it."

"Where are we going?" she asked, relaxed.

"You said you wanted me to surprise you..."

She laughed. "Well, you've done that already by just being here."

He nudged her playfully. "Get in the car," he instructed as he led her round to the passenger side.

"Yes, sir! Right away, sir!" she said and then they were on their way to Jacob's Well.

"I've never been to Jacob's Well," she told him as they approached the village.

"It's a lovely place, but we're not staying here. Last night, I ate at the golf club and one of my golfing friends offered me his boat for the day…"

"Wow!" Sam enthused. "What luxury!"

"You haven't seen the boat yet," he informed her. "Are you up for rowing?" He inclined his head to the dinghy moored at the jetty.

"You have to be joking!" she said with uncertainty.

"No, I'm not. Come on! Grab your things and I hope you've brought a sweater. It might be a bit chilly bobbing about in a rowing boat in the middle of the Broadwater."

She climbed gingerly into the rowing boat and appeared to be very unsure of what she had let herself in for.

"I'm not expecting you to row." Michael grinned at her. "What sort of gentleman would ask his lady to provide the muscle power?"

She sat demurely at the stern and watched as Michael rowed masterfully out to open water. "You steer me in the right direction," he instructed. "Aim for that island just behind the yacht that's anchored to your port side."

"Speak English, please Michael. Port side?"

He laughed amicably. "To your left. You are facing forward so port is on your left; starboard on your right."

"You're very knowledgeable," she told him. "I'm impressed."

He smiled knowingly. "Let's just drift slowly towards the yacht and look how the other half live," he said.

He gradually drew closer to the stern of the yacht and secured the dinghy to the ring that she supposed was made for the job.

"What are you doing?" Sam asked.

"I'm going to have a look on board."

"You can't do that! It's trespassing."

"There's nobody here, so who will know? Come on. Don't be chicken," he coaxed.

"I really don't know about this, Michael," she cried. "But I don't like the idea of being left on my own in this little boat either."

He climbed on the ladder at the back of the yacht and held out his hand to her.

Cautiously, she stood and stretched out her left leg and placed her foot on the first rung while holding tightly on to Michael's hand. "Grab hold of the sides of the ladder with both hands," he instructed and he climbed onto the yacht as she did so.

He was waiting quietly for her as she falteringly climbed aboard. He took both her hands in his and looked directly into her frightened eyes. "I haven't been totally honest with you," he divulged. "This yacht—*Hopes and Dreams*—belongs to…"

"Your friend from the golf club?"

"No," he continued. "It belongs to me."

Samantha gasped and allowed her jaw to drop in astonishment. "How come you never mentioned it at work?" she asked wide-eyed. "If it were mine, I'd be telling everybody about my weekends on the water. Oh Michael. How wonderful!"

"Not my style, Sam, and anyway, why would a fifty year old man want to brag about his boat unless he wanted to impress somebody?" he said pragmatically. "This is my haven, my get-away, my man's shed on the water."

"I wouldn't call it a shed," she commented. "It's beautiful."

"I like it and I spend most of the time fishing when I'm not pottering around in the garden at home," he told her.

"What about your wife?" she dared to ask.

"Let's go out to the Broadwater and then we'll drop anchor at lunchtime."

His swift dismissal of her question couldn't be hidden, but she didn't pursue it further.

~ * ~

Sam stood beside Michael as they sailed through the beautiful turquoise waters towards the Broadwater where they dropped anchor. Michael familiarised her with the basic techniques of sailing before he produced a picnic fit for a princess. "Lunch is served," he said, smiling broadly at the lady who glowed in the midday sun. "Stay in the shade," he advised. "Remember only mad dogs and Englishmen…"

"This is wonderful. Thank you," she said quietly and squeezed his arm in appreciation.

They ate well: garlic prawns, smoked salmon, green salad with sun-dried tomatoes and pine nuts, pâté and rice crackers, fresh fruit and cream, wine —just one glass since Michael was very mindful he was in charge of his boat.

After lunch they sat at each end of the enormous couch as they watched the sea birds swooping and diving for food. A flock of pelicans flew over and Michael remarked that they were on their way to Labrador for their daily feed at a locally renowned seafood retail outlet. "They feed the pelicans at one-thirty every day except Monday," he told her. "It's quite a sight. I'll take you sometime."

Sam sighed. "That would be lovely, but…"

Michael pre-empted her. "You want to know about Jane, don't you?"

She nodded.

"Jane and I are living separate lives albeit in the same house," he admitted, "but I don't want you to think that's why I've brought you here today."

"You can't blame me for wondering."

He shifted to make himself more comfortable, both physically and emotionally. "When I invited you out last night, it was a spur of the moment thing. You were unhappy and I'm not in what you would exactly call a deliriously happy situation either. However, it seemed like a good idea for both of us to get away for a little while."

"You really don't need to justify yourself," she told him. "I'm a big girl..." She smiled the same disarming smile that pulled at his heartstrings the night before. "I'm thirty-nine years old, never married, but just coming out of a long-term relationship," she revealed. "I like you; I like your company. What's wrong with that?"

"Nothing wrong with it per se, but I am still married and I really shouldn't be giving you all this personal attention," he said. "I might be putting myself in a very invidious position. If Jane should find out, she'd have a field day. Separation and divorce haven't been mentioned yet, but I think it's only a matter of time. She has pushed me away and I can honestly say she's caused much of the angst in our household, but there isn't another man involved. I think I can be sure of that. I don't wish to imply that I am blameless or that I'm bitter and twisted about it. I've resigned myself to the fact these things happen sometimes. When things aren't right between a man and his wife, all one can see in the other is negativity. It's very difficult to see what we thought was good in the beginning. Everything Jane does at the moment annoys me and I know for a fact, I annoy her. We are at a stage where neither of us wants to be the one to make the final move. I'm not sure Jane realises that just now. She's too caught up in thinking she is always right and everybody else is wrong."

She breathed in deeply. "I understand, Michael," she said gently. "If you want to take me home now, I don't mind." She paused again to choose her words carefully. "On the other hand, I'm happy to spend time with you, whatever you decide to do after today. I promise all knowledge of this day out stays strictly between you and me. I won't chase after you if you decide not to ask me out again. You can trust me, but you have only my word on that. I don't know what I can do to convince you."

Michael moved closer to her. "You know," he said quietly. "Something tells me that I *can* trust you. I just have this strong feeling, a connection like I've never felt. How can I explain it when I don't understand it myself?"

"Sh-sh," she whispered and it was her turn to move across the couch to be closer to him. "Kiss me again," she urged as she crawled on hands and knees across the settee, her face invitingly close to his. "Please…"

His heart was beating fast. His thoughts were pressing, urgent, carnal even. *I want this woman; I need her, but I mustn't use her to satisfy my own sexual needs. I'm better than that. I'm really not that sort of bloke, but…* "Are you sure, Sam?"

She nodded in answer to his question and stretched out towards him until they were lying side by side. They kissed long and tenderly and the closeness of their bodies overpowered their sensibilities. "Please, Michael. Please… please," she whispered huskily.

~ * ~

Afterwards, they lay in the cabin, totally relaxed, satisfied, happy. "You are amazing, do you know that?" His voice was still hoarse with passion.

She smiled. "You're not so bad yourself…"

"For a fifty year old, you mean?"

She tapped his arm playfully. "Age has nothing to do with it," she reassured him. "Maturity speaks volumes. I could very easily…" She stopped abruptly.

Michael was aware of some tension creeping into her limbs. "Very easily what?" he asked.

"Don't go there, Michael. Just let's enjoy our time together."

"I'm all for that," he said happily and he rolled over to scoop her into his arms again. "Let's stay the night with *Hopes and Dreams,*" he suggested.

"Perfect," she agreed. "Now where were we?"

Sixteen

The atmosphere in the O'Connell house was cold—icy in fact. Jane went out for her daily walk before Mick was up and didn't return until he had gone to work. They had slept in separate beds for the past four weeks and neither seemed to feel the need for any show of intimacy between them. The longer time moved on, the more difficult it became to broach the inevitable subject of their relationship and more to the point, their marriage. Mick started coming home late from work. He didn't appear as though he'd been drinking, but Jane noted there was often a healthy glow about him when he arrived home.

Maybe he's going to the gym, she thought, but didn't dwell on the matter. She was still making dinner for two, but she was eating hers before he arrived home so the bitterness in their feelings for each other didn't make life any more unpleasant than it was already. Generally she was working on the PC in her office, so some days, they didn't see each other at all. The novel she had only previously mused about, was unexpectedly taking shape and she absorbed herself in it. It was entitled, *Finding Ben,* about an orphan boy going in search of his roots. Ben was discovering much about his own character as his investigations progressed and coincidentally, Jane was discovering things about herself too.

~ * ~

It was Wednesday morning when Linda called. "Are you free for lunch?" she asked cheerily. "It is ages since we had a girlie chat."

"Well, excuse me, Mrs Johnson, whose fault is that? Every time I called, you were too busy to spend time with me, so I stopped inviting you for lunch. I have so much going on in my life just now. I'll have to consult my diary..."

"You are joking... aren't you, Jane?" Linda asked, unsure of what to detect from Jane's attitude.

"Well, yes and no," Jane told her. "I am busy; I do have a lot going on in my life. I have started a new venture..."

"Hold on a minute, Jane O'Connell. Last time we spoke, you wanted ideas for how you might use the new-found freedom you had. What's changed? Have you and Mick started a business?"

Jane shivered involuntarily. These days, the mere mention of Mick's name made her shudder and in a paradoxical sort of way, she hated herself for it. "That's what I want to talk to you about," she said quietly.

"Wow! A new business!" Linda said, jumping to conclusions. "What are you doing? Are you selling Mick's garden produce and your wonderful home-made pies and cakes? How exciting!"

"Linda," Jane said with a sigh, "Give me a break. Just meet me for lunch and I'll fill you in then. I'll see you at Gino's at twelve-thirty."

~ * ~

Linda was gushing when they met. "Jane, dear friend, tell me all about your new venture. It sounds very exciting. Whose idea was it? Is it bringing in an income and more to the point ...?"

"Stop, Linda!' Jane interrupted. "There is no new business. Where have you got such ideas from?

Linda gave Jane a look of disdain. "From you! You said..."

"No, *you* said, Lin, not me. You jumped to conclusions."

"Well, you didn't correct me."

"You didn't give me chance, but I'm correcting you now. There's no business and no plans to start one, but I *am* writing a novel," Jane told her. "The computer course I have been doing has made it easy for me to put my ideas down and I have lots of ideas for an interesting story."

"I don't understand. How can learning how to use a computer give you ideas for a story? It doesn't make sense to me," Linda added. "You talk in riddles sometimes, Jane."

Jane sighed. "I didn't say the course had given me ideas, Lin. Why don't you listen to what I'm saying?"

"I can't see the point of home computers anyway. They are just a trend at the moment and they'll disappear in a couple of years, you mark my words."

Jane sighed. "You should get together with Mick. His attitude is the same. He sees no good in anything I do at the moment."

"Trouble at mill?" Linda asked lightly, trying to imitate the northern English accent of the big mill owners during the Industrial Revolution.

Jane looked down at her hands in her lap. "Let's order lunch first and then we'll have our discussion when we've eaten."

After they'd eaten, Jane said, "I need to talk, Lin, but not here. Can we go for a walk along the beach?"

Linda looked at her watch and Jane was quick to notice. "Look, if I'm taking up your precious time, forget I asked. I would hate to interfere with your stupid routine. You are my best friend, Lin, but I have to say, you don't give me much of your time these days. What do I have to do to convince you that your family won't collapse if they have to look after themselves occasionally?"

Linda was taken aback. "My, my, Jane. Don't hold back, will you? How I run my life is really my affair, not yours and I'll thank you to keep your opinions to yourself. What is wrong with you?"

Jane felt contrite. "I'm sorry. My life is a mess. My marriage is a sham and I don't know what to do."

Linda was shocked. "Have you talked to Mick?"

"Oh yes, I've talked to Mick—about three months ago! I hardly see him these days and you know what, Lin, I'm happy with that. It suits my needs at the moment. I think I don't love him anymore. I've grown apart from him. We don't enjoy the same things and he contradicts everything I say. Nobody in my family ever got divorced and the whole prospect of starting divorce proceedings fills me with dread. The biggest obstacle is Mick. I know he still loves me. I can tell, because he does make some effort occasionally to put things right."

"What sort of effort?" Linda asked, still quite dumbfounded at Jane's revelations.

"Only little things like asking me how the course is going, offering to go for a walk with me, suggesting we go to the Sheraton for dinner..." She paused poignantly and looked at Linda who was clearly flabbergasted at what Jane was revealing. "Actually, I'm deluding myself. It must be months since he asked me anything. He stays at work late, goes out on the boat more often than he used to, doesn't do half as much in the garden as he did previously and I've noticed he's looking healthier than he has looked for a long time. It could be his weekends on the boat and he might be going to the gym, or playing golf, but I think he just doesn't want to be in the house with me. Maybe he's just proving a point; I simply don't know anymore."

Linda appeared to be confused. "You are still living together, aren't you?" she asked.

"We are living in the same house. We sleep in separate rooms..."

Linda stopped walking and held on to Jane's arm to prevent her from walking away from her. "Jane, we have been friends forever and I don't want to spoil our friendship, but I can't condone what you are doing. You are behaving like a spoilt child. Go home and sort things out with Mick. If he loves you, he's probably waiting for you to come to your senses. What I know of Mick, he doesn't suffer fools gladly."

Jane regarded Linda through shrewd eyes. "You really haven't been listening to me, Lin. I have fallen out of love with Mick. Meeting somebody else in Noosa made me realise that."

"Excuse me?"

Jane related the whole story of Richard, admitting to her silliness too, but making sure that Linda understood there was no affair taking place. "He was the most infuriating man I had ever met. Irritating, condescending sometimes, but clever and witty and very attractive. I didn't fall in love with him; I just fantasised about being with him. Mind you, he set me straight and I appreciated that. He's gone to London now to be with his wife so I'll never see him again."

Linda was aghast. "How could you, Jane? You, a married woman, flirting with a complete stranger? What does Mick know of this?"

"Don't be so supercilious, Lin. Mick knows nothing, because there's nothing to know. Richard, in his weird way of looking at things, made me realise I no longer love my husband. Now I have to find a way of telling him. The prospect of that fills me with fear and trepidation. I keep putting it off, but as long as we aren't seeing much of each other, it's easy just to carry on as we are."

"And live a lie, you mean?" Linda asked judgmentally. "You astound me, Jane. I can't believe you are behaving this way. Have you told Sally?"

"No. She doesn't need to know. She and Bill haven't been to see us for months. Sally was supposed to meet me for lunch one day when I was at college, but she didn't turn up. I haven't spoken to her since and I have to say, I don't want her involved in what's going on with Mick and me. I know I'll have to tell her sometime, but not yet."

"I don't understand you at all anymore and I'm inclined to be with Mick on this one. It seems the problem is yours, Jane, not his," she said pointedly. "Sort yourself out, or you'll alienate yourself from all your family and friends. I don't want to be involved and it's too hard for me to see you changing so much. Much as I value our friendship, I don't want to see you again until you do the right thing." She turned and walked back in the direction from which they came.

"What price friendship, Linda?" Jane called out. "Just go then. I don't need you. I don't need anybody." Tears coursed down her cheeks, but her inner resolve made her determined to retain some semblance of normality... *Whatever normality might be*, she thought and she boldly called out to anybody who might be listening as she strode off into her uncertain future. "Come hell or high water, I'll survive. Just you see if I don't."

Seventeen

Linda's parting gesture was a rude awakening for Jane in spite of the disappointment she had felt at her friend's reaction. She decided she ought to visit her daughter and put her point of view before Mick had chance to canvas her support. *Why should I have to keep on justifying myself?* she thought. *Why can't people see my point of view? I know I have to sort myself out, and I will, but is it too much to ask for a little bit of understanding?*

She called Sally before Mick came home from work. "Hi, darling," she offered tentatively, somehow feeling awkward because of the long silence between them.

"What do you want?" was Sally's cool reply.

"Goodness, Sal, how about—*Hi Mum, how are you? Good to hear from you.* It must be months since we've heard from you and I think you owe me an explanation why you didn't keep our lunch date." Jane was a little irritated by her daughter's attitude.

"You didn't call and ask me at the time, did you? Apparently you weren't bothered whether I was there or not. Have you got something to hide?" Sally asked calmly.

"What are you talking about, Sal? I'm always pleased to see you, you know that."

Sally went quiet.

"Are you still there, Sal?"

"I'm here, Mum, but I don't know how to deal with this. I saw you…" she dared to say.

"Saw me when?" Jane asked, confused.

"The day I was supposed to meet you for lunch," Sally informed her. "Don't deny it, Mum, because I know what I saw."

"What did you see? I have no idea what you are talking about."

Sally was becoming irate. "Oh, you would say that, wouldn't you? Anybody who has an affair behind her husband's back will always deny it…"

"Affair? I haven't had an affair. Where on earth did you get that idea?"

"I saw you in another man's arms on the grounds of the college. To enjoy a prolonged embrace from another man is not acceptable for a happily married woman. It's not appropriate and it was shocking for me, your daughter, to witness your clandestine goings-on."

Jane realised Sally had witnessed her goodbye to Richard. "That was my tutor and he was leaving that day to go to London to join his wife! How stupid can you be, Sal?" she explained. "I wasn't having an affair with him!" *But she doesn't need to know all the implications of my friendship with Richard. That would only complicate things, especially since she's hell bent on dishing the dirt at the moment.*

"I don't believe you. Does Dad know about this tutor who passionately embraces his students when he leaves?"

"Of course, he doesn't know. There is absolutely nothing he should know and anyway, he has no interest whatsoever in anything I do, and for your information, Mrs Jump-to-conclusions Mansell…” She was gabbling and hated herself for sounding so defensive. “I called you today because I need to talk to you about something personal regarding your dad and me,” Jane revealed. “Life is not great between us…”

“I knew it,” Sally said emphatically. “You have both been evasive for months. Why didn't you tell me before? But you were too busy with the dirty goings-on between you and your tutor…”

“Stop it, Sally!” she snapped. “You are wrong; totally wrong and I'm not going to argue with you over something you know nothing about. Get off your high horse and just listen. I didn't tell you before, because I thought it would all blow over, but it seems to be going from bad to worse…”

“No wonder if you're having an affair. Poor Dad…”

Jane was fast becoming angry. “Don't *poor Dad* me! Since I took early retirement, he has given me no support whatsoever. He is against everything I do and the whole situation has made me realise I have nothing in common with him anymore.” It sounded futile when put into words, but she continued regardless of that. “We have grown apart. I hoped you would give me a little support… I'm your mother!”

“I can't take sides, Mum,” Sally told her, “and you shouldn't ask me to take sides. I have to go,” she said through her tears.

With that, Jane heard the telephone click and Sally was gone.

~ * ~

Mick arrived home just as Jane was about to go to bed. “Have you a few minutes to spare?” he asked.

“Why?” Jane snapped and then, “Sorry. I didn't mean to snap. Will it take long? I'm tired and my head aches from staring at the PC all day.”

“What do you expect, Jane? Those things can't be good for the eyesight…” he paused. “Please let's not get into an argument about home computers again. It's becoming tedious.”

Jane looked him in the eye for the first time in weeks. *He is actually wearying of this situation. There's no fight left in him. Oh my goodness! I can't believe how I feel. I actually feel sorry for him. My heart is going out to him...* "I'm listening," she said quietly.

"There is perhaps too much to discuss if you are tired. Go to bed now and I'll get up early in the morning. We can talk before you go out for your walk. Goodnight," he said and went to his room without another word.

~ * ~

Jane lay awake for what seemed like hours after she heard Mick switch off the light in the room next door. Her thoughts were clear and she planned what she would say when she and Mick had their heart to heart chat. *Planning what I am going to say isn't the right thing to do really. It never comes out as one plans, but I do have to be clear in my mind. I'll admit that I've been confused, about my life, about my decision to retire early, about my feelings...* She sat up in her bed. *Will it be wise to admit I thought I didn't love him anymore? Maybe not, because he's bound to ask me to try again and at this moment in time, I want to, I really want to. My heart fluttered when I looked at him just now. I saw a longing and yearning in his eyes that hasn't been there for years. What have I done to him? Do I ask for forgiveness? Do I tell him about Richard?* She shifted uncomfortably. *I guess not. What he doesn't know won't hurt him, so I'll leave Richard out of the equation.* She shifted again as she silently reasoned, *Is that the right way to rekindle our feelings for each other?*

She plumped up her pillow and made herself comfortable. *Mick was such a lovable guy when we met. I want to find that guy again. We had so much fun. We were soul mates. We could read each other's thoughts. Just recently we have been so far apart and it's been impossible to know what the other has been thinking. Can we ever return to the closeness we used to have?*

She snuggled under the doona and closed her eyes. *It won't happen straight away. We'll need to do a lot of soul searching, but we'll try, darl, won't we? We'll try...* And she drifted off to sleep with a smile on her face.

~ * ~

Mick lay in the darkness of his lonely room for a long time. His mind was clear, clearer than it had been for months. *I can't go on leading this double life. It isn't fair on anybody. I am still married to Jane and I did promise for better or worse.* He sighed. *In this day and age, we don't have to put up with the worse bit. There is a way out. I certainly have to do what is right for us all—for Jane, for Samantha, for me. Please Lord, give me strength.*

Eighteen

He was already in the kitchen making their morning cups of tea when Jane appeared. "You haven't done that for a while," she commented.

"Done what?" he asked, making a bold effort not to react to her sarcastic observation.

"Made tea for us both," she told him.

"Well, the situation hasn't lent itself to amicable breakfasts just recently," he stated. His thoughts were clear. *I must make this as easy as possible for both of us. Jane does tend to get the wrong end of the stick sometimes. I need her to know exactly where we stand if our lives are to be happy and meaningful again.* "Shall we sit on the deck?"

Jane smiled and nodded. *Good start anyway,* she thought as she opened the sliding doors for him.

Mick placed the cups on the table—on opposite sides. Jane was confused. *He's sending mixed messages. First he makes the tea and then makes sure we aren't sitting side by side.* She sat facing outward, looking towards the garden as Mick walked round to face her, his position significantly looking away from what had thus far been his retreat, his sanctuary.

Holding his mug in both hands on the table, he stared at it for a while before he looked directly at Jane. "I don't want this to turn into an argument, Jane," he said gently.

She looked at him and said. "Okay. I understand." *I can see that vulnerability in his eyes again. He feels the same as I do. He wants to start again, to put the past few months behind us.* She took a deep breath and waited expectantly for his plea.

"I want a divorce."

For Jane, time stood still. With her shocked eyes telling him exactly how she was feeling, the only word she was able to gasp was, "What?"

"Our marriage is obviously over. You have pushed me away for long enough. I don't know you anymore, Jane, and any love there was between us has gone. I'm not going to go over the same old ground again. You know what's been happening between us as well as I do..."

"You can't be serious," she interrupted. "I know I've been a pain, but I still love you, Mi..."

"Stop it, Jane." It was his turn to interrupt now. "We have been living separate lives for over a year. Oh yes, we were in the same house..." he paused deliberately. "...but we could hardly call it a home. You have been doing your thing; I have done mine. Neither of us took much interest in the other's existence; we didn't eat or sleep together and we didn't object to the fact that we were becoming more and more estranged. That is not my idea of a good marriage."

"But all marriages go through their bad patches..."

"Bad patches, yes, but not for over a year. A guy has to be made of stone to put up with the rejection I've suffered lately," he told her. "I don't love you anymore, Jane. I'm sorry."

Jane's emotions were in turmoil. She felt shocked and sad, but her anger was rising and was about to erupt. "Rejection? Rejection?" she shouted. "I'll tell you about rejection. You have rejected everything I set out to do since I retired. You treated me like a stupid child who didn't know her own mind. You pooh-poohed the idea of the computer and you showed no interest in what I was doing because you didn't approve. Don't tell me about rejection, Mick. I've had it in bucket-loads."

Mick remained calm. *I knew she'd react like this. Never her fault; always mine.* He sighed. "Jane, can't you see there have been faults on both sides? We have grown apart..."

"That's exactly what I told Linda..."

Mick was surprised. "Oh I see," he said. "You discussed the situation with Linda, but you couldn't discuss it with me. And what pearls of wisdom did she come up with?"

"If you must know, she was appalled at what I was doing..." She halted abruptly. *Oh dear,* she thought, *watch where this goes, Jane. Richard has no place in this conversation. He mustn't have any part in this. It's complicated enough without him.* "She told me to sort it out and refused to discuss it. She said she was with you on this..."

"My, my! Linda on my side? Things are looking up," he commented. "Her views and mine are usually poles apart. What appalled her? The computer or your attitude?"

Jane shifted uncomfortably in her seat. She stared out into the garden, looking neglected since Mick had chosen not to spend so much time in there recently. "She simply disapproved of me and what I was doing," she offered. "You know Linda. If everything isn't planned and organised at the right time, she thinks the world is ending." She managed a half smile, but had to concede that Mick's expression was frustratingly unfathomable.

"It all sounds a bit vague to me," he said, "but Linda has nothing to do with what has been happening here. This is between you and me and I have to say, I have come to the point of no return. I'll pack up my things during the next few days and leave."

"But where will you go?" she asked plaintively. "Don't do this to me, Mick, please don't do it." Tears coursed down her cheeks and she desperately brushed them away.

Mick sighed loudly. "I've made my decision," he said without showing his innermost feelings. "I've seen Rob Spence. He'll sort out the divorce papers. Let's keep this as amicable as possible."

"All a *fait accompli* then," Jane said with a hint of sarcasm in her tone. "And you had the gall to tell me I presented you with done deals. Touché, Mr O'Connell."

"What's good for the goose…" He stopped as he realised he was slipping to Jane's cliché-ridden ways. "I have to go to work now. I know I've shocked you, but you have to admit, it's been coming for months. We both have a lot to think about and discuss later." And he left without another word.

~ * ~

Jane sat in her favourite place on top of the cliff, looking out upon a sparkling blue ocean, calm today , the very antithesis of the turmoil she felt inside. Tears ran down her cheeks. "I thought I could make my marriage work," she said out loud. "I was going to tell Mick…" She paused significantly. "…*ask* Mick if we could start again, but he had already made his decision." Alone and very lonely, she tried to unravel the tangled thoughts that were spiralling around inside her head as she thought back to earlier when Mick had dropped the bombshell.

She looked out to the horizon and half-smiled again, realising through her tears that the distance was significant and wondered where she should go next. Her mind was full of tangled thoughts, but she did admit to herself that she knew what she had done. *I know exactly where it all began. It began with my decision to retire early. Why couldn't he tell me he didn't want me to retire? He could have been forceful for once in his life.* She brushed away her tears with the back of her hand. *He did try to warn me, I guess. I just didn't listen... same as always, Jane. When do you ever listen? I have alienated myself from everybody who means anything to me. Mick, Sally...* She paused and took in a deep breath while she continued her self-assessment. *I even told Linda I didn't need her friendship, well as good as...* She sighed; a long, meaningful sigh from deep within her soul and remained sitting staring out to sea in complete silence, unaware of anything that surrounded her.

~ * ~

Michael went work with mixed feelings. As he drove along the highway, he made some effort to assess his situation now that he had taken the first step to his future. *I'm sure I've done the right thing. I don't love Jane anymore and I am totally besotted with Sam, but I need my own space for a while. Sam will understand why I can't move in with her straight away...* He smiled to himself. *She and Jane are so different and I can't believe I have fallen in love again at my age. That's why I have to take my time...*

When he arrived at the pharmacy, he went straight to his office. "Good morning!" he called cheerily as he passed through the shop.

There was a chorus of '*Good morning, Mr O'Connell*' and he acknowledged it with a nod of the head and a smile. Samantha mingled with the crowd and tried desperately not to show her excitement. "Samantha?" he called from the door of his office, "I'd like a word with you, please."

"Oh dear, what have you done, Sam?" her colleague, Patricia, asked.

Samantha shrugged. "I don't know, unless it was the stack of scripts I didn't file before I went home last night," she said casually.

"Well, he didn't sound too pleased," Patricia continued earnestly. "I wouldn't like to be in your shoes. Good luck."

She went in the office and Michael closed the door with a flourish as the staff looked at each other questioningly. "That'll keep 'em guessing," he said and he took her in his arms, hugging her tightly and kissing her tenderly. "Sit down," he said. "It will look like I'm interviewing you if anybody should come in." He looked her squarely in the eye. "I told her," he said quietly, yet confidently.

"And?"

"She was shocked. I really couldn't read her reaction at first and she surprised me by saying she still loved me…"

"Oh dear. I don't like the sound of that. I don't wish her any harm, but you have to be sure you are doing what is right, Michael, for yourself, not for me. I love you, but I won't be a marriage breaker and I don't want to be labelled as a *femme fatale*. If she wants to try to save your marriage, I'll stand aside…"

Michael was taken aback.

Samantha continued earnestly. "I won't like it and I don't want to be your bit on the side. I'm not making threats or demands, but please think carefully before you take the next step." Samantha was desperately trying not to cry, but the tears involuntarily trickled down her cheeks.

He reached across the desk and took her hand to reassure her. "I have taken the next step, Sam. Don't worry. Your name wasn't mentioned. I don't see the need to complicate matters and she has no idea that we have been seeing each other. I can't say I like the thought of keeping you a secret, because I want to shout it from the hilltops that I love you, but what I need to explain to you at the moment is, I won't move in with you just yet. I'm going to inspect a unit after work and I'll rent for a while. The house will have to be sold, but it won't happen immediately. My guess is that Jane will stay there just out of bloody-mindedness. She has the right to do that if she chooses. These are apparently all the things I have to consider when I get divorced. It's pretty daunting." He paused and looked at her lovingly. "But you're worth it."

"I just need you to be sure, darl. We can carry on as we have been doing for the past few months," she said. "It's not ideal, but I'll wait. Now I'd better go and face the music out there."

Her tear-stained face drew sympathetic glances and only Patricia dared to ask, "What's wrong, Sam? Was it the scripts?"

Samantha shook her head. "Leave it, Tricia, I'll be okay," she said sharply and she busied herself with the batch of new prescriptions that had accumulated while she had been in the office.

~ * ~

Jane sat for hours just staring out across the ocean. Her tears subsided and she began to think more clearly. *That's it then,* she thought resignedly. *I had convinced myself I didn't love Mick long before he turned the tables on me, the ba.….. * She breathed in deeply. *Maybe I shall enjoy being on my own for a while. Perhaps I'll travel. I could go to London. I've never been to the UK and maybe Richard and his wife will show me around.* She tutted loudly and chastised herself. *Jane Peterson, behave yourself. He's married; he doesn't need you and your bumptious attitude to interfere in his life again.* She laughed at her stupidity. *But he was a challenge, wasn't he? And a tease... ah well, if only... no use going down that road now, but the travel idea is very tempting. I can't believe how practical I feel and suddenly very positive. If this is how divorcees feel, then bring it on!* She suddenly thought of her daughter. *Perhaps I ought to call Sally.* She stood quickly totally in panic, realising that Sally had misinterpreted information she would prefer not to be unearthed again. *Oh my goodness—Sally!* She pressed her lips together tightly and breathed in deeply. *Well, maybe not. She can call me when she's ready. I still feel very angry with her.*

~ * ~

Michael decided to call Sally from work. "Hi Sal," he said quietly. "How are you?"

"Dad!" she cried. "What are you doing calling at this time of the day? Shouldn't you be at work?"

"I am at work," he replied, "but I need to have a word with you. Can you talk for a few minutes?"

"Of course I can," she told him. "Now what is it you need to talk about?"

~ * ~

The atmosphere in the O'Connell house was chilly, but not as icy as it had been for the past year. Somehow, the heated discussion earlier had cleared the air and released some of the tension. *I have learned a lot today,* he thought as he returned to the house and prepared to pack up his belongings. *Sally surprised me—nay, shocked is more appropriate and any reservations I had about leaving Jane have certainly been dispelled.* When he heard Jane's office door open, he went to confront her.

"When were you going to tell me?" he asked, not hiding his annoyance.

"Tell you what?" she asked.

"Don't act the innocent with me, Jane. I spoke to Sally today..."

"Ah, I see, but I hope you haven't taken her seriously," she said knowingly. "I guess it's no use telling you she's got it all wrong, but she has and big time. She has no idea what she's talking about. But if it makes you feel better about walking out on a wife who was ready and willing to give our marriage another try, then go ahead and think what you like. I don't care."

"Typical," he told her. "Make it look like I'm the guilty party. You have an affair behind my back and expect me to take the blame for our marriage breaking down. Grow up, Jane." Then his conscience got the better of him. *How can you stand here and say that?* he asked himself silently. *Whether Sally's version is true or not, you have absolutely no room to talk, Michael O'Connell.* He smiled inwardly. *Michael? Yes, Michael. I love you, Sam, and Jane has absolutely no need to know about you.*

Jane stood and faced him confidently. "You know best, Mick," she said with an air of sarcasm, "so just revel in the fact you are free to lead your own life without me hindering you. I was devastated earlier today when you chose to walk away from this situation, but I'm not sad anymore. The fact that this whole damn business has been festering for almost a year has made it easier for me to sort out what I'm going to do. I'm going to pack up too and leave. Decision made. I'm going to London and I'll finish writing my best-seller. I know you won't understand, but *Finding Ben* is certainly a cathartic exercise in helping me to find myself. I shall travel alone; there is nobody else involved. Maybe this adventure is what I have been looking for; in fact, I'm suddenly very excited about it. I fly out on Thursday week...Thursday's child has far to go, a good omen, I think."

"Don't you think you should speak to Sally before you leave?" he asked as pleasantly as he could muster. "I think you owe her that, at least."

"No, I don't," she replied firmly. "She accused me of something that didn't happen. She hasn't called since and it is she who owes me an apology. I'm sure you'll tell her I'm leaving so that's all that matters. It's very sad, but it doesn't stop me loving her. Perhaps I'll shoulder much of the blame, but I can't allow my daughter to cast aspersions against me. I tried to explain to her, but she just went off on her high horse. However, she's a grown woman and will decide what she wants to do as regards our relationship. My attempt at explaining failed. I'll miss her terribly, and the children too, but I'll cope. When she's ready, she'll know what she needs to do."

Mick nodded slowly as if in agreement although his eyes reflecting the sadness he was feeling. "You know, Jane," he said gently. "I never thought we'd become a statistic in the failed marriage records and I'm sorry about it, but we have to agree that we've come to the right decision. We couldn't go on as we were. You know as well as I do, we were merely existing, not living." He had to laugh. "That's what you said about your life when you retired. Well, you certainly made sure I understood what you were talking about!"

"Still dishing out the blame, Mick," she said matter-of-factly.

"If the cap fits... bloody hell," he exclaimed. "You've passed on the clichés too. Thanks for that!"

"Don't mention it," she said light-heartedly. "Do you mind if I give you a hug?"

"Not at all," he told her, but when they came close, there was a tension between them that clearly confirmed they didn't belong together anymore.

"Good luck, Jane," he said. "I really mean that."

"Thanks and the same to you."

Jane left as planned and Michael decided to stay on in the house until it had been sold. Jane's half of the monies would have to be forwarded to her to help fund her self-imposed exile. It was going to take almost a year before the divorce would be finalised. Not until the deal was done would he feel free to move in with Sam.

Nineteen

Jane arrived in London very early on a cold, wet October morning. She was tired and had not prepared for the drastic drop in temperature. It was a shock to the system and the first decision she made when she had checked into a motel near the airport, was to buy some winter clothes. Having done that, she spent the week recovering from the jet-lag before she became the typical tourist. The next four weeks saw her around Buckingham Palace, Windsor Castle, The Palace of Westminster and the famous Big Ben, Downing Street, Hampton Court and Harrods, each given equal priority, and an ambition realised was going to the theatre to see *The Mousetrap*.

"Do you mind if I join you?" the woman asked.

Jane looked up from her newspaper and saw that she was laden with shopping bags and was looking for a place where she might put down her cup of coffee. A quick scan of the café made Jane realise the only empty place was at her table. She nodded and said, "Not at all. Feel free."

The two women smiled at each other and Jane asked, "Do you live in London?"

"I do, but not in the City—far too expensive."

"I can see that," Jane replied as she gestured with her newspaper open at the property page. "I'm looking for a base, something cheap and clean, but even shoe-boxes cost an arm and a leg," she continued light-heartedly. "Where's the best place to live, would you say?"

The newcomer took a sip of her cappuccino and leaned across the table to see what Jane was reading. "Wow!" she said smiling. "Chelsea? Properties there are likely to be too expensive, unless you own Harrods. You need to look farther afield—you might try Crouch End. It's an up and coming area, but has a lot of student accommodation. I heard recently that many of the bedsits have been renovated for yuppie types..." she paused. "You're not exactly a yuppie, are you?"

"Yuppie?"

"Young Urban Professional."

"Well, I guess not, but I don't mind mixing with students. I'm an ex-teacher and would relish the intellectual atmosphere," Jane explained. "Surely, students wouldn't be able to afford these rents." She pointed out an advertisement she had spotted as they talked.

"My goodness, no," her companion declared. "Four hundred pounds a month! You might be better to share if you don't mind living with someone else."

Jane looked pensive. "Maybe later, when I have settled. I have only been here a few weeks and I need to put down some roots somewhere." She didn't feel the need to make this stranger party to her life story, much as she had been very friendly and helpful.

"Try Crouch End then. There might still be a few good places that won't make you sing for your supper," she said amicably. "But look, take my number and if all else fails, you can have my spare room. My husband works away a lot and I'd really enjoy the company." She scribbled her telephone number on the top of the page on Jane's newspaper. "I'm Barbara, by the way."

"I'm Jane, and thanks Barbara. I might just call you if I can't find anywhere. The Ibis is fine temporarily, but I would like to have some of my stuff sent over from Australia and I can't do that until I find a place to call my own."

"I thought I detected the accent," Barbara said. "I've often thought I might go to Australia. My husband has been several times on business."

"Many of them do these days," Jane replied almost dismissively. "Sorry, but I need to go and chase up these agents. Thanks for all your help."

~ * ~

Weeks later, Jane moved into her newly renovated bedsit just before Christmas with just the basic furniture. Early in January, with the festive season well and truly over, she tried to call Mick. The old home number was unavailable. *That's odd,* she thought. *Don't tell me he is so small-minded as to change the number after I left. Pathetic, Mick! I'm ten thousand miles away and you are still irritating me six months on. He said the house sale was going through when he wrote, but I still haven't received my settlement. I'm going to have to call Sally, but I can't say I relish the thought.* With her heart beating wildly in her chest, she dialled the number.

"Hello?" It was Bill, not Sally.

"Hi Bill, this is Jane ..." She paused taking a deep breath to calm herself and to gauge his reaction.

"Hi Jane," he said. "What a surprise!"

"I know I'm calling out of the blue, but things were so strained between Sally and me and I was waiting for her to contact me before I did anything further to upset her," she said, not without a touch of regret.

"Sally isn't here at the moment..."

"Isn't, or doesn't want to be?" Jane asked bluntly.

"No, truly, Jane, she isn't here. I don't think I would be talking so freely if she were here," Bill informed her.

"My name is still mud, is it?" she asked pointedly.

Bill coughed. "Jane, I don't want to get involved with whatever it is…"

"I understand, but please allow me to say that Sally's version of events is wrong and she didn't even call me when her dad told her of the split. What am I supposed to gather from that?" she said pointedly.

Bill sighed audibly. "Look, Jane, I'll never understand why a mother and daughter can't freely communicate in circumstances such as yours, but I'll tell her you called. Have you a number she can contact?"

Now it was Jane's turn to sigh. "Not at the moment. I think I'll have to buy one of the new mobile phones, but it will be expensive, anyway, for Sally to call the UK. Do you have Mick's number, please? The stupid man has changed his landline number so I can't contact him. It's important. I don't want to bother him at work."

"He's moved house…"

Jane was stunned. "Oh," was all she was able to say.

"You'll have to speak to him for the details, but he has one of the new mobile phones…" Bill informed her.

"You are joking! Mick with new technology! My goodness!" she exclaimed, thinking, *Why on earth couldn't he embrace progress when I was there?* "Just let me have his number please, Bill. I'll call him later."

~ * ~

Calculating the ten hour time difference, Jane called Mick the following Sunday afternoon Australia time.

"Michael O'Connell," he answered brightly.

Michael? Jane thought disparagingly. "It's me," she said without ceremony. "I need some of my things, if you might send them to me..." She paused, but remembering her manners, she added, "Please."

"Well, this is a surprise. Your things are in storage. You packed them up yourself. If you want them, you're going to have to give me specific instructions. I don't know what the boxes contain." His attitude was curt and Jane noticed.

"Look Mick... or Michael, if that's what you're calling yourself these days," she said with an obvious snigger, "If you tell me where you are, I'll write down the instructions for you. Would you have told me you had moved house if I hadn't needed to speak to you? And then there's the little matter of my settlement now that the house is sold..."

Michael took a deep breath. "I only moved out yesterday. The transfer will be dealt with tomorrow as soon as the bank opens. Your details are recorded in my diary and the money should be with you in a couple of days..."

"Michael, who is it?" Samantha called from the kitchen.

Jane was taken aback. "A-ha," she said. "It hasn't taken you long, has it? Have I been naive, or are you shacking up with somebody you've just met?"

"It has absolutely nothing to do with you, Jane, but no, I am not *shacking up* as you put it with somebody I have just met. I have known Sam for a long time..."

Samantha peeped round the door and mouthed, "Sorry!" He waved a *no problem* gesture in her direction.

"Are you telling me you were seeing her before we were divorced?" Jane continued not trying to hide her dismay.

"No, I am not telling you that." Michael was thinking on his feet.

"Well," Jane said through a deep exhalation of breath, "And you had the gall to accuse me..." She stopped before the conversation grew ugly. "I'll send the instructions to work. Thanks for looking after my things, but I have no longer any desire to talk to you. Goodbye."

~ * ~

That night she lay in bed staring into the darkness. Being alone in bed at night were often lonely times. Her thoughts were yet again confused. *I can't believe it. Was he really having an affair behind my back? He didn't actually deny it, but he didn't admit it either.* She pushed herself up and sat resting her head against the padded headboard. *The wily old fox. And he had the gall to accuse me on Sally's say-so. I thought I knew him and let's face it, I thought he would come back to me eventually.* She shuddered as she felt a tear trickle down her cheek. *Don't you dare cry, Jane Peterson. You are stronger than that. I'll show, Michael O'Connell and all the bloody rest of you who condemned me. I have a life to live and I'll do it my way.* She had to smile. *I sound like a broken record. I'm certainly doing Gloria Gaynor and Frank Sinatra proud.* Still, in spite of all her positive thoughts, she wept into her pillow that night until she fell into an uneasy sleep.

Twenty

When Jane's belongings eventually arrived, she spent a whole day setting up her apartment and reminiscing with each package she unwrapped. She had instructed Mick to sell the furniture unless he wanted to keep certain pieces and the sale of her computer would pay the shipping fees for the few packing cases she would need to be sent.

'*I have bought another computer here,*' she told him in her letter of instructions. '*I have all my work on several floppy discs which I brought with me anyway. Why you can't see the value of this technology puzzles me since you are supposed to be an intelligent, forward-thinking man of the world.*' She needed to get her dig in as some sort of revenge for what she considered his very insensitive actions. '*Maybe your new lady-friend has more influence over you than I ever had. I see you now have a mobile phone—alleluia!*' She had smiled as she sealed the letter. "Up yours, Michael O'Connell. See if I care."

~ * ~

She planned her days around writing her novel and making sure she had time to socialise as often as possible. She formed a friendship with Barbara, the lady who had pointed her in the direction of Crouch End and whose husband often travelled to Australia on business. They usually met in a bar that was walking distance from her apartment. *The Dog and Partridge* was frequented by a motley crew and that suited Jane down to the ground. "And what brought you to London?" she asked the extraordinarily dressed gentleman who asked if he might join them after furtively contemplating for several nights whether or not he should be bold enough to talk to the two classy ladies at the other end of the bar.

"Hello there," he replied with typical eighties' swagger to cover his nervousness. "I had to come and sample the big smoke. A country boy like me needs to find out what this new era is all about…"

Jane stopped herself from smiling too broadly. *This guy is priceless,* she thought. *Just look at him. Long hair—clean though, and his jacket sleeves rolled up. He must be my age, but he's trying too hard to be one of the in-crowd. Not my type, but certainly an interesting character. I just wish he'd cover his chest and the medallion really isn't doing much for him.*

"Do you come here often? Sorry I didn't catch your name," she asked amicably.

"Freddy," he told her. "I wish I could claim Mercury, but it's …" He paused sheepishly. "Actually it's Smith. Not very imaginative, is it?"

"Popular though," she said with a grin.

Much to Jane's surprise, the evening was surprisingly pleasant. "Thanks for your company," Freddy said as they were leaving the bar. "Can I see you home safely?"

Barbara discreetly left the two alone and had called a taxi a few minutes earlier.

"I live only a couple of hundred yards away—literally," she informed him.

"In that case, it will be my pleasure," and he took her arm and guided her through the door.

~ * ~

"Well, here we are," she told him as they arrived at the door of the apartment block.

"Wow, you actually live here?" he asked in awe of the situation.

"I do."

"I wanted to rent one of these, but my wage wouldn't allow it," he admitted.

"What do you do?" she asked, genuinely interested in this gentleman's position.

He looked embarrassed. "I'm a security guard at Harrods. It's kind of responsible and the rules and regulations are very strict. One wrong move and I'd be out."

Jane sensed he was uncomfortable. "Look, Freddy," she said amicably. "If you are happy with your life, that's all that matters."

"Oh, I am happy with it. I do feel I'm responsible for protecting the public and the company. If we nab shoplifters, we are doing the store and the public a service and I believe, protecting the villains from themselves, if you see what I mean."

"I *do* see what you mean," Jane agreed. "I actually understand exactly what you are saying." *This guy has an endearing quality about him.* "Why don't you come in for a nightcap?"

They walked up the stairs rather than taking the elevator. "I'm on the first floor," she informed him. "I always walk up the stairs, my daily exercise. When you get to my age..." She stopped abruptly. *Don't tell him your age, Jane. Let him wonder about it.*

"Your age?" he asked. "I'd say you were similar to me... early forties."

"Close," she said, "but that's all I'm saying." She smiled amicably. "This is it. Come in."

She ushered him into her lounge and invited him to sit down. "Tea or coffee, or would you like something a little stronger? I have wine and a small selection of spirits. I'm not a big drinker, but my new friends pop in sometimes and like a nightcap. Personally, I like red wine…"

"Slow down, Jane," Freddy said laughing. "You are babbling…"

She giggled girlishly. "Am I? Well, it's not every night I bring a man back to my apartment."

"Do you live alone? Is there a Mister Jane around somewhere?"

Jane shook her head. "I'm single." *No need to tell him the truth.* "I had a big falling out with my best friend so I could probably blame that for my being in London. It seemed the best thing to do, get the hell away from any agro."

"Good move," he replied. "I was married once. My wife died of cancer ten years ago."

"I'm sorry," Jane told him.

"Thank you, but it's okay. You learn to live with it, but I've never fancied getting married again. Too painful when it ends."

"I understand, but if you're happy with your life… Did you say what you would like to drink?"

"I'll have a glass of red with you if that's all right. Thank you."

She poured two glasses of Shiraz and handed one to him. She sat next to him on the sofa. "You said you came from the country," she reminded him. "Where exactly?"

He took a sip of his wine. "Nice drop. Australian?"

"What else is there?" she said laughing.

"I was born and brought up in Ambleside in the Lake District," he told her. "Not a lot happens there except for all the day trippers, campers, caravanners and fell walkers invading the area all summer and most weekends during the rest of the year. It's a beautiful place, though, just on the edge of Lake Windermere."

"The Lakes are on my wish-list," she told him. "I intend to move up there sometime. I'm a…" She paused deliberately.

"A what?" he asked.

She looked sheepish. "I was going to say I'm a writer, but I can't really claim that distinction yet. I'm writing my first novel..."

Freddy grinned. "Wow! I never knew a writer. Will you let me have a signed copy when it's published?"

She inched closer to him and offered her glass to make a toast. "I will indeed. Let's drink to that," she said as they clinked their glasses and sipped simultaneously. Their eyes met, a meeting of needs at that particular time. Placing their glasses on the breakfast bar, she led him to her bedroom.

~ * ~

When she woke the following morning, she was alone in her bed. She looked at the pillow next to hers. It was plumped up and it appeared that no head had rested there. *I'm sure I didn't dream what happened last night,* she thought as she got out of bed. "I'm naked," she said out loud. "I never sleep naked unless..." Catching sight of herself in the mirror, she was embarrassed. *Oh my goodness! I'm not as sylphlike as I thought I was. If Freddy saw me like this, no wonder he took flight.* She placed her hands on her rounded abdomen and grimaced. "You need to lose weight, girl..." *But I'm not a girl, am I? I'm a fifty year old woman who lured a forty-something man to her bed.* She dared to look at her reflection again. *Well, if I'm being totally honest, I'm not that bad for a fifty year old. If I cut out the wine and the chocolate, run up and down the stairs several times a day and generally eat more healthily, I can shed a few pounds.* "I'll do it," she declared and silently made a pact with herself. *Diet starts today.* As she showered, she tried to make sense of what had happened. *I have no idea why Freddy disappeared, but I can't deny I liked what he had to offer before he left.* She smiled and shrugged. *We didn't do anything wrong. We are both consenting adults. I'll try to make him understand when I see him again.* Her mind went back to the conversation they had before their carnal instincts took over.

He's a widower, poor guy. Maybe he had remained faithful to his wife's memory until I came along. Help! What have I done?

Throwing on her dressing gown, she padded into the kitchen and saw the two glasses they had hastily left on the breakfast bar the night before. She breathed a sigh of paradoxical relief. *I knew I hadn't dreamt it. The emotions I'm still feeling are too strong. Goodness, Jane! Had you really missed that side of your life so much?* She felt her cheeks burning and busied herself making breakfast as she attempted to overcome her confusion.

She looked back later and wondered how it had happened. *I wasn't particularly attracted to him,* she thought, not with regret, but more as an exercise of self-assessment. *He was pleasant enough, not very worldly-wise, but certainly entertaining. Did the drink have anything to do with it? Perhaps...*

Twenty-one

Jane didn't go to the Dog and Partridge for several days. Somehow she felt she wasn't quite ready to face Freddy after their little fling. She had no idea how he'd react when they came face to face again. She worked on *Finding Ben* and realised her reckless behaviour had fuelled her creative fire. *I love this,* she thought. *It's the catharsis I knew I needed and Ben's character is surely developing through me. I'm beginning to love the little guy.* When her phone rang, she was startled. "Hello. Jane Peterson."

It was Barbara. "Jane!" she called almost deafeningly. "Where are you? I have been ringing your bell for days. Has the intercom stopped working?"

"I've been busy, Barbara. I turned off the intercom and my mobile because I needed to work undisturbed. Sorry."

Barbara continued unabashed. "I missed you at the D and P. Freddy hasn't been in either. I have no idea what's happened to him. Have you heard from him? You and he were getting along well when we were last together."

Jane took a deep breath in order to compose herself. "I haven't seen him after that night. He walked me home and that was that," she fibbed. *No need to let Barbara into our little secret.* "He's not my type, Barbara, so I won't be sorry if I don't see him again. How are you anyway? Anything happening at the D and P?"

"I'm fine thanks, and I'm glad you're okay. You might like to go and see the group that's on in the pub at the weekend. The Country Boys. They are supposed to be very good and the lead singer is an Aussie from Broome. You might know him."

Jane laughed. "Barbara, Broome is just about as far away from where I live as you could get. It's at least a four hour flight. Just think about it. In four hours you could fly to Greece or the Canary Islands from here. Would you know anybody who lives in those places, or do you know anybody in John o' Groats, for instance? At least it's on the same land mass."

Barbara laughed with her. "But Australia looks quite small in the atlas!" she said.

"Australia is vast, believe me," Jane informed her. "I might try to see the group, though. A country boy from Broome, hey? Sounds interesting. Will you be there?"

"No, my better half is home now for a few weeks so I won't be around. We have a lot of catching up to do, if you understand my meaning."

Jane gasped audibly for effect. "Whoa there, girl! Too much information," she said light-heartedly. "Give me a call when you feel like a night out. See yer!"

Barbara's call had added to Jane's guilt as regards Freddy. *Well, it seems I really scared off the poor guy if he's stopped going to the Dog and Partridge. I feel really bad now. All we did was to fulfil a need in each other,* her conscience told her. *He doesn't have to go to ground just because we...* Try as she might, she could not dismiss the thought that she might have tarnished the memory of his dear wife and she genuinely felt very guilty about that.

~ * ~

The Country Boys were well worth the price of the ticket. For five pounds she was entertained for three hours and by her own countrymen. She shamelessly sat close to the dais erected in the bar for the performance and smiled provocatively at the lead singer. In her mind, she convinced herself that a bit of harmless flirting didn't hurt anybody. *He's a good looking guy and Australian to boot.* "On yer, Aussie!" she called out as the applause echoed round the room.

The lead singer winked at her and called back, "How yer doin', sheila?"

"Good, mate!" she called. Her thoughts were happy. *He's nice. Not too young either. Might be late thirties... can I pass for a younger woman? Maybe he likes older women.* She took a sip of her wine and caught his gaze again.

"Catch yer later," he mouthed and she nodded.

At the end of the performance, he joined her. "I'm Bruce..."

She laughed as she shook his hand. "You'd have to be, wouldn't you?"

"What do you mean?" he asked.

Jane offered him the empty seat at her table. "I'd guess every Australian man in England says his name is Bruce," she told him. "Come on, mate. What's your real name?"

"Bruce," he said with a grin. "Bruce McIlroy. And you are?"

"Whoops," she said coyly, her cheeks flushing with embarrassment. "Sorry, Bruce. It just sounded so typically Aussie; I thought you were milking the situation. I'm Jane."

Bruce grinned again. "Is that your real name?" he asked cheekily.

"Touché, Mr McIlroy," she conceded. "But it's so good to hear an Aussie accent. It's funny the things you miss when you're away from home."

"Have you been away long?" Bruce asked, somehow showing he understood.

"Just over six months, but I love what I'm doing…"

Bruce scrutinised her expression. "You aren't very convincing. Anything I can do to help?"

She smiled and reached across to touch his arm. "No, but thanks. I acted very impulsively when I came out here and I do love London, but I'm getting to the point now where I need to move on. City life is too hectic. I'm thinking of going to the Lake District."

Bruce looked at Jane's hand still resting on his arm. "Are you flirting with me?" he asked pointedly.

"What on earth makes you ask that?" She was startled by the direct question.

"Because your hand is seductively resting on my arm and you have a look of longing in your eyes."

Snatching her hand away, Jane had to admit to herself that she was embarrassed. *I am indeed flirting with a complete stranger. Maybe the description of typical female divorcees is true. Could it be that I'm desperate for attention? Do I need to prove that I'm still attractive to the opposite sex?* "I'm sorry," she said almost shyly.

Bruce took her hand. "I understand more than you think," he told her. "I have been touring for over a year now. My wife is in Melbourne. She has a high profile job and she travels around Australia extensively. We decided our marriage would become an open one while we are separated. It's the only way our relationship will survive. I don't ask what she's up to and she doesn't ask me."

Jane was stunned. "And it actually works?" she asked wide-eyed.

"It does for us," he reiterated.

"Would it rude of me to ask how old you are?" she enquired.

"We are late thirties—not young, but certainly not old," Bruce explained. "I'll be forty next month when, according to legend, life begins. I'm not fazed by it. In fact I'm quite looking forward to it."

Jane smiled affectionately. "You'll enjoy it," she told him. "My fortieth is long gone, but I still feel twenty-five in my head. I refuse to be old."

"You are wearing well, Jane," he complimented her. "I'd have put you at about my age, flattery intended! Are you married?"

Jane nudged him playfully. "And flattery will get you everywhere," she joked.

"I hope so," he jested in return.

"But in answer to your question, no. I'm single. I hope I didn't make it obvious; you know, kind of desperate, because I'm not desperate."

Bruce leaned over so that his face was close to hers. "It wasn't obvious, but a woman as attractive as you should not be single, or be in here alone," he whispered.

"My friend couldn't make it tonight and the usual crowd I meet must have other places to be," she told him.

"No need to explain," he said. "And I'm not going to ask why you are single. It's none of my business, but I am attracted to you. You have a spirit about you that is very interesting, captivating in fact."

"Whoa there, baby," she interrupted. "I might be old enough to be your mother."

"Ah, but you're not. I'm a pretty good judge of age and character and I say you will allow me to walk you home and we'll take it from there."

"Confident, aren't you?" she said, but the flattery was beguiling and she was encouraged by it. "I might not let you into my apartment, though, and how do you know I'm not just a tease?"

"I'll take that risk," he said as he stood and signalled to his mates that he was leaving. "Come on,"

He put a protective arm around her as they walked the few hundred metres to her flat and they chatted amicably about the home country. They had an easy rapport and when they arrived at Jane's door, he took her in his arms and kissed her tenderly.

"Are you going to invite me in?" he asked.

Jane looked him in the eye. "Are you sure you want to do this, because I'm not sure at all," she said bluntly, but secretly thinking, *I am so thankful I took on that exercise regime. If I hadn't, there is no way I would even consider allowing this man to see my naked body.* "You can come in for a nightcap and we'll see what happens."

"Tea? Coffee?" she asked with a grin.

"I'll have a beer, please, if you have one. I haven't had a drink all night. Booze and singing don't go together, not for me anyway."

She handed him a bottle of *Four X* and poured herself a glass of red.

She put on some soul music. "I like this," she told him. "It really is good for the soul."

"How come you came to listen to us then? This and country are poles apart."

"Not really," she explained. "Music is always good for the soul, regardless of genre. It's a bit like literature. If you can relate to it, then it's good. Your music reminded me of home; it was earthy and meaningful. It touched my heart. Maybe that's why I am allowing you to be here just now."

He moved closer to her. "And that's why I'm going to make love to you tonight knowing that you will respond in the way you want to and need. There'll be no strings attached and no regrets. We'll part in the morning having made beautiful music together."

Twenty-two

The boy stared long and hard at the door that closed on him. Destiny had brought him to this place, fate dealing some very cruel blows during his young life. A wealth of experience had been packed into his nineteen years. He thought that nothing could touch him anymore, but when the door slammed, he felt a wrench in his heart as never before, a new and desperate sensation—hurt, regret and isolation all rolled into one great, black cloud which enveloped him.

Jane's main character was facing a crisis in his young life. She immersed herself in solving his problems. She spent much of her time trying to solve Ben's crises rather than her own. Bruce had left that morning, a smile on his face as he bid her a fond farewell.

"See yer, Jane Peterson, woman extraordinaire, soon to be best-selling author. I'm glad I met you. I'll sew you into the seams of my memory. Thank you. You are amazing."

"You are the biggest bull-shitter I have ever met," she said light-heartedly. "Enjoy the rest of your tour and don't leave it too long before you go home to that gem of a wife of yours. She must be one in a million." *And please God, don't ever let me meet her, because I might just tell her what a fool she is to let loose her charismatic husband on unsuspecting females wherever he might be. A more naive girl than I is likely to expect much more from him than a one night stand. The implications of what all that might involve don't bear thinking about.*

Guilt, this time, was not on her agenda. The fact that she had willingly had sex with two strangers in the space of one month, surprised her, but didn't fill her with disgust. *I am a hot-blooded woman,* she told herself. *Mick did nothing for my ego during the final year of our marriage. I didn't love him; I didn't like him; I didn't want him to touch me. The thought of his naked body next to mine repulsed me.* She rested her head in her hands as she endeavoured to dissociate her own life from her main character, Ben's.

"Tell me," the old man said, "What brings you to my house?"

Ben didn't answer immediately. He hardly knew where to begin. He thought carefully for a few seconds before he offered, "I found this address in an old book."

"So what?" the old man interjected, not fully comprehending the need to make the visit just because of that. He inclined his silver head towards the boy as he rocked back and forth, back and forth, each movement giving a strange, eerie continuity to every passing moment, a bold emphasis that time does not stand still.

Ben looked into the old man's eyes. They were grey and sad, but there was a paradoxical spark of interest which spurred Ben on and he continued, "I found the book in an old chest. Someone had written 'Outcast' on it, which I thought was extremely appropriate under the circumstances." He hesitated, because he thought he noticed a change in the countenance of the old man.

"What do you mean 'appropriate'?" the old man asked.

"We never belonged," the boy went on…

She looked up from her writing and cleared her mind yet again of the thought that at the age of fifty, teenage promiscuity seemed to be taking over her life...

"We never belonged," the boy went on, "Our hut was at the edge of the village. People turned away when we went to the pump for water." He lowered his eyes, sadly remembering the white woman who had collected him from the orphanage in Leopoldville and taken him in, the woman who had devoted her life to protecting him from the intolerance of narrow-minded bigots. 'Bastard' they had called him, or 'brown boy' when they were feeling more hospitable, but they never gave him his proper name. That way they never had to admit to his acquaintance. The woman had never talked to him about the past and she lived by her own rules—cope with the present and be ready for the future. "What's gone is gone," she had said. "We cannot change it."

"Indeed we cannot change it," Jane said with feeling. "Tomorrow I shall give notice on the apartment and move on."

~ * ~

Three months' notice seemed to last forever, but it did allow Jane to explore the possibilities of places where she might best be inspired to continue her writing. The Lake District was top of her list and she went up there for several weekend visits during her lease-enforced stay in London. It was easy to feel the tranquility wherever she went. She avoided Ambleside, unrealistically thinking she might bump into Freddy if she went there. *After all, he hasn't been seen in the Dog and Partridge since that fateful night and I even ventured into Harrods to see if I could get a glimpse of him, all to no avail.* She squirmed at her own pathetic attempt at dealing with a situation that really didn't need fixing at all. *The guy did a runner. We could have talked it through if he had a problem.* She had been in Cumbria for only a couple of days and she really didn't want to be thinking of a man who couldn't face the realities of life. *Anyway, I doubt if he'd have high-tailed it back to The Lakes. After all, he said himself there was nothing really going on up here. But...*

Her thoughts were directed to the little cottage she'd seen earlier in the day. She'd visited Wordsworth's place, Dove Cottage; had seen the hills and vales described in his daffodils poem, but it wasn't Grasmere that took her fancy. It was Coniston Water, where John Ruskin, the nineteenth century art critic, writer and philanthropist retired to spend his later years observing nature until his death in 1900. Jane felt at peace there more than anywhere she had visited. *Bracken Cottage* at the north end of the lake was perfect and it was for rent.

Once settled, she wrote to Sally.

My dear Sally,

This place is a little bit of heaven on earth and I'd like to share it with you. The peace that I'm feeling just now prompted me to write to you, to break the long silence that has blighted our lives for the past eighteen months. I am not making demands of you, Sal. I sincerely hope we can put the past behind us and be friends again.

I know your dad has moved on and I'm happy with that. Our life together had run its course. It happens. I am aware that my attitude acted as catalyst in a situation that was already simmering beneath the surface. Having time on my hands after I retired only served to make me see the flaws that were occurring in our marriage, imperfections that both your father and I had ignored, maybe for longer than we'd care to admit.

Having said that, I can tell you from the bottom of my heart that I did not have an affair with my tutor...

Jane stopped writing. *I haven't thought of Richard for ages. Maybe that tells me he meant nothing in the whole scheme of things. I can well do without all the hassle of his unconventional views.* She smiled to herself. *BUT he did point me in the right direction in a roundabout way. I'll forgive myself that little contradiction in terms! Back to Sally, though...*

She sucked the end of her pen in contemplation... *I don't know how long I shall stay away from Australia. My life here is very different and whilst I enjoy the different culture, I do miss the Gold Coast weather. I don't think I have ever felt as cold as I did that first winter in London. I needed thick woolly socks and a hot water bottle in bed at night to stop my feet from freezing. Even in summer, the sun struggles to perform as I know it can!*

I miss you all very much ...well, not your father, but I know he'd expect me to say that and if I'm being honest, I do think of him often when I'm assessing my position in life just now. I have no regrets. I wish him and his new lady all the luck in the world. The most important part of our life together will always be you. You were made of our love and even though that love has gone, individually we love you every bit as much as we ever did— stronger and deeper if truth be known. As we grow older, we appreciate our children more. Always understand that, Sal.

And now, before I get too emotional for my own good, I'll stop. Please write to me, Sally or if you have ventured into twentieth century technology and bought a computer, you might like to e-mail me. My e-mail address is <u>ontherun@peterson.com</u> I miss you.

With fondest love to you all,
Mum

~ * ~

She found a little teashop in Hawkshead that she frequented every Friday afternoon. She discovered what it was that bound English ladies together – afternoon tea in China cups with cucumber sandwiches and little cakes on tiered stands. She spent the first two occasions discreetly observing elegantly dressed ladies of varying ages as they greeted each other and chatted light-heartedly about the weather, the craft shops in the village, the next flower show and the welcome onslaught of the summer visitors. On the third Friday, she was already seated at her usual table when the first of the ladies arrived.

"Good afternoon," she said, as she caught the lady's eye. "You are the first to arrive, I think."

The younger lady smiled. "It looks like it, doesn't it? I usually come with my mother, but she has an appointment she can't miss, so I'm here alone—well, at the moment anyway. Are you new here?"

"Comparatively new, I dare say," Jane ventured. "I'm renting Bracken Cottage on Coniston Water. This is my weekly treat. I find it deliciously English."

"You are Australian, I guess," the young woman said. "What brings you to The Lakes and to Hawkshead in particular?"

Jane looked at her companion with surprised eyes. "Surely you know what brings colonials to the Lake District. You live here. You must know its fascination to visitors, particularly those of us who claim to have more than a passing connection to the United Kingdom."

"Yes, I understand," the young woman continued. "I'm sorry. I didn't mean to sound patronising. I simply wished to make your acquaintance. Would you care to join me for tea? I'm Victoria Smith."

"Hello, Mrs Smith. I'm Jane Peterson and I ought not to have been so rude. It is I who should apologise. I'm sorry."

"No need to apologise, and yes, I'm Mrs Smith." Victoria emphasised the 'Mrs' and smiled proudly. "Very newly married, but for the second time around. Love is definitely lovelier the second time around."

"Well, congratulations. I hope you'll be very happy," Jane told her and continued,

"Are there many Smiths in these parts? I met somebody a short while ago whose name was Smith..." *Me and my big mouth again. I had no intention of enquiring about Freddy, especially not so close to where he was born and bred. Could it be that he came back home and re-married? Help! Claw your way out of this one, Jane,* she silently instructed herself.

"Not very imaginative, is it?" Victoria said shyly.

Oh my goodness! Where did I last hear those words? That's exactly what Freddy said. "I guess there are Smiths everywhere around the world. It might be interesting to research the origin of the name. I'm sure it's something to with a blacksmith." She was gabbling, but taking a deep breath, she steered the conversation away from the topic. "When do the daffodils begin to show?" she asked.

"Oh, not until spring... March, or it could be April, if the weather has been bad during the winter. You really must stay until after Easter to experience the full splendour of the spring flowers."

The other ladies in the group didn't arrive for some reason. Victoria was puzzled, but not unduly so. "It only takes one to say she isn't coming and the others follow suit," she explained to Jane. "The word sheep springs to mind, but I mustn't be judgmental."

Jane put her at her ease immediately. "Look," she said cheerily, "you are talking to an Australian. We take people as we find them and go with the flow." Her thoughts were self-critical. *My, my, Jane! You are the most judgmental person on this earth. Using Victoria's turn of phrase—two-faced springs to mind!* She smiled at her companion and thanked her for her company. "If you are ever in the vicinity of Bracken Cottage, please feel free to call. I'm usually home and often need an excuse to leave my work for a while."

"What do you do?"

"I write."

"Oh, how wonderful!" Victoria enthused. "I've never met a writer, but you are certainly in the right place for inspiration."

"My sentiments exactly," Jane agreed. "You aren't the first to say so." *And wasn't that what Freddy said? She must surely know the guy. They are so similar in their expression. Just be careful, Jane,* she silently advised herself again.

"Thank you for inviting me," Victoria said as she left the tea-room. "Perhaps when my husband returns from London, we'll come to visit you together. Goodbye and see you again sometime."

Stunned into silence, Jane smiled to hide the astonishment she felt inside and nodded as Victoria went through the door.

Twenty-three

Jane again immersed herself in Ben's story...

There followed a momentary silence. The boy looked through the window at the setting West African sun, veiled by the dust on glass that had apparently never been polished. The old man rocked backwards and forwards, the old chair creaking, creating a surreal, unnerving atmosphere in the gathering gloom. The boy shivered involuntarily and looked at the old man again. The aged African was staring blankly into a space somewhere between the present and the future and his black eyes were extraordinarily clear. He wondered what was going on behind his stare. Then he vividly remembered the advice of the old white woman. "Don't worry your head, little one. You'll be fine. There is nothing in this life that needs your concern. Just be yourself."

"What was her name?" the old man asked, "The woman you speak of."

"*Nan... everybody called her Nan, even the village Headman. He visited her occasionally, out of duty, mind you, certainly not affection. He was a hard, harsh man. He told her she wasn't welcome in the village, but he had always been ready to take her money when she offered a fair price for a roof over her head. 'He's not yours,' he would say, and I would go outside trying not to listen to him.*"

She stopped typing as a tear trickled down her cheek. Brushing it away with the back of her hand, she felt sad. *It's almost like I'm living his sad life,* she thought miserably. *It's only when I get into Ben's head that I feel miserable. Could I be transferring my inner feelings into him? Perhaps so, but I'm not sad for myself; perhaps more unhappy that I'm alone when I still have so much to offer a close relationship.* Inwardly she wrestled with conflicting views. *I like my own space and I often enjoy being alone, but...* Another tear trickled down her cheek. *...I miss regular company and yes, I miss male company. Oh, not the sex, although I'm not past it just yet* ...She felt her mouth twitch, forcing a smile and she returned to her typing...

The old man looked at Ben with affection. "You're a lot like me," he told him. "Think yourself lucky. From now on you have a friend."

"Thank you," Ben said, grateful that suddenly and remarkably he didn't feel totally alone anymore. "If you are my friend, what do I call you? You didn't tell me your name."

"I don't hold much store by names. I can be whom I like, when I like," the old man said pointedly. "Seeing that I'm growing old, you can call me Old Joe. Would you like that?"

"I would," Ben told him. "It will be like having a family. I had Nan, but I never had a family..."

"You need friends; everybody needs friends," the old man continued.

Ben nodded in agreement.

"What you need is a girlfriend," Old Joe suddenly announced with a knowing smile.

Ben felt his cheeks burning at Old Joe's suggestion, but when he met Elizabeth a few weeks later, he discovered feelings and responses he had never before experienced.

Jane stopped writing again, thinking back to her first sexual encounter. *Ben's first sexual encounter must help him to understand a part of his character he hasn't noticed before. This is where I need to draw upon as much sensitivity as I am able. Time for a break, I think.*

~ * ~

Just as she was sitting having a welcome cup of tea, there was a knock on her door. Suddenly, her brain went into overdrive. *Please God, don't let be Victoria and her husband, please, please. If she's with Freddy, I can't handle it.* She opened the door to a stranger and visibly relaxed.

"Sorry, ma'am, I didn't mean to startle you," the gentleman said. "I have walked right around the lake and now I'm looking for somewhere to stay. Can you please direct me to the nearest bed and breakfast place?"

Jane smiled. "I'm not really startled. It's just that I wasn't expecting anybody to knock on my door. I guess you'll need to go back towards the village to find accommodation."

The man looked disappointed. "I was hoping I could find somewhere out of the village. I like quiet evenings and just at the moment it's very busy down there."

Jane shrugged, not nonchalantly, rather more out of understanding. "It's September so the crowds will be dispersing soon. I'll drive you down there, if you like. There's a converted farmhouse that does B and B and that's a little way off the beaten track. I'll drop you off there."

"Oh no, I couldn't ask you to do that," he said.

"No problem. I need a break anyway. Sometimes the brain can get overloaded with an incredibly weighty and far too vivid imagination..."

"You're a writer!" he said with feeling.

"I am!" Jane agreed enthusiastically. "And I guess it takes one to know one, but what's an American..."

"Canadian," he corrected.

"Whoops, sorry. I never could tell the difference in the accents, but to continue, what's a Canadian writer doing walking round lovely Lake Coniston without booking accommodation in advance?" she asked amicably. "But come on, we'll talk in the car. I'm Jane and I apologise in advance for the jalopy. It comes with the rented cottage, so beggars can't be choosers."

He smiled. "Indeed they cannot," he agreed. "I'm Brad Courtney. I'm a journalist on a commission to find what it is this place offers to inspire those with creative pens and imaginations."

Jane laughed. "Very eloquently put, Mr Courtney, even if it is slightly elaborate. Mind you, your description does have an interesting turn of phrase. I do like the thought of creative pens."

"Would you mind being a part of my research, Jane?" he asked. "An Australian—you are Australian and not from New Zealand?" He grinned.

"Ha ha, Brad. Good point," she acknowledged.

"Well, an Australian writer renting an idyllic cottage on the edge of Lake Coniston can only be looking for the inspiration of Wordsworth, Coleridge, Ruskin and the like. You'd be a fascinating resource. Please say you will let me interview you."

"I rather liked Beatrix Potter and Arthur Ransome," Jane added, "And I do believe Keats and Tennyson loved the place too. Who wouldn't be inspired walking in their footsteps?"

"Well, what do you say?" Brad asked eagerly.

"I say, here we are at Coniston Hall Farm. Seems there are caravans and tents available too. You shouldn't have too much trouble finding a bed for the night."

Brad looked disappointed that she didn't respond to his request. "Point taken, Jane. I really shouldn't have been so insistent, but at least say you'll think about it. Journalists have to grasp every opportunity that comes their way."

"I'll think about it. Let me sleep on it. You may call at the cottage tomorrow if you have nothing else planned," she told him.

"Nothing that won't keep," he replied, "so see you tomorrow." He winked at her.

"Nothing decided yet, Mr Courtney. I'm not sure I want my views plastered all over Canadian newspapers."

"Oh, nothing like that," he assured her. "Just a tiny article in a little suburban rag!"

"Like I said," she reiterated. "Nothing decided yet."

~ * ~

Out of the blue she received an e-mail from her daughter. Her heart skipped a beat when she opened it: *Hi Mum,* it said. *Thanks for getting in touch. I don't know where to start. We've been along a rocky road, you and I, but I don't want us to be enemies. I'm not going to go over old ground. I will say, though, I'm sorry and hope you'll accept my apology. I have missed you, still do. I hope that your self-imposed exile won't last forever, even though it sounds wonderful in the English Lake District.*

I'm not sure you'll want to hear this, but I think you should know that Dad re-married last weekend. Sam is very nice; younger than Dad and they appear to be very happy. I got his permission to tell you, so please don't be mad at him. I want you to know Sam will never take your place; you have to believe that.

Holly and Jacob have been asking where you are and why you have gone so far away. I placated them by saying you needed to find a good place to write your book—Dad told me you'd started a bestseller—and all good writers need peace and quiet to be able to concentrate. They didn't question why you couldn't find peace and quiet here, but they're happy for now. Don't leave it too long, Mum.

Lots of love from us all,

Sally

Jane wrote back immediately, simply to tell Sally that the world is a small place these days with e-mails and telephones. *Just you wait, Sal. Soon we'll be able to see each other when we phone. Technology is the future, you mark my words!* She clicked on *send* with a very satisfied feeling lifting her spirits.

~ * ~

She was singing at the top of her voice when Brad arrived at her door. "Wow, that's one happy lady!" he exclaimed.

"Hi Brad. Yes, I am a happy lady this morning."

"Does that mean you've decided to answer my questions?" he asked excitedly.

"Come inside and we'll talk," she invited. "Would you like a cup of coffee?"

"Yes, please. White with two."

She showed him into the cosy sitting room where there was a log fire burning merrily in the grate to take away the late September chill. "This is what I love about English country life—cosy rooms, log fires, oak beams—the stuff of dreams for me. How could one not be inspired to write of love and happiness in such surroundings?"

Brad laughed. "And I haven't asked you a question yet!"

Jane gave him a mug of steaming coffee and went to sit opposite him by the fireside. "Let's just talk and see what evolves," she suggested.

"Sounds good to me," he replied. "Where would you like to start?"

"Tell me, why is a Canadian journalist wandering around Cumbria alone in what can only be described by somebody from the tropics as freezing cold?" She wanted to say pointedly 'middle-aged journalist,' but felt uncharacteristically awkward.

"This isn't cold, dear lady," he offered. "Cold is minus twenty-five degrees in Interior Alaska."

"I can't even imagine what that would be like. I live on the Gold Coast in Queensland. We think it's cold when our winter daytime temperature drops below twenty Celsius. We have Poms who think it's summer all year round when they first arrive. One year in and they're rugging up with the rest of us!" Jane was happy talking about home.

"Tell me about you," Brad urged. "Who is Jane, the Australian writer hiding away in a tiny cottage on the edge of Coniston Water?"

"You didn't answer my question," she reminded him. "I asked first!"

Brad shrugged resignedly and sighed deeply. "I can see I've met my match here," he said good-humouredly. "What do you want to know?"

"You are alone, willingly wandering around Cumbria, supposedly commissioned to write a literary article for a suburban newspaper..."

"And you don't believe me?" Brad asked pointedly.

She shrugged now. "How would I know? It's unusual to see a..." she paused.

"A middle aged man travelling alone?" he added.

"Well, pretty much so," she said.

"I could say the same about a lady who is not of such tender years, if you'll forgive my bluntness, living alone in such a remote place too," he said observantly.

She breathed in deeply and exhaled slowly. "We are playing games, aren't we? Let's cut to the chase. I really am trying to write my first novel. I'm a former teacher who is divorced and who needed a complete change." *No need to go into detail at this point,* she thought.

Brad put his cup on the hearth and leaned forward with his elbows on his knees. He studied the hearthrug for a few seconds before he spoke. "I'm sorry, Jane. I really have no right to that information. It's your private life and I'm not here to find out about that." His voice was gentle.

"Not a problem," she said confidently. "It is good to speak openly about my situation. I have been in England for almost a year now, have met many people and made new acquaintances, but you are the first I have told about my divorce. If they asked, I just said I was single. Many middle-aged women don't marry. Being a career-woman seems to be the in thing these days."

"I'm not convinced they'd believe you, Jane," he told her. "You are wearing well for..." He paused deliberately before he said emphatically, "middle age."

Jane couldn't help smiling. "Thank you," she said, "but that's enough about me. Your turn."

"Well, before I disclose all," he said light-heartedly, "I note that you spoke only of acquaintances; does that mean you have not made friends?"

Jane shifted in her chair to make herself more comfortable, not just physically, but also psychologically. "Friends are very close, intimate on a subconscious level," she offered. "Whilst I have valued their company and appreciated their time, I do not yet know them well enough to call them friends. For instance, I don't think I would feel comfortable at this point in telling my innermost secrets to the acquaintances I have made."

Brad eyed her closely. "I think you are a very complex, enigmatic woman, Jane. For one thing, I only know you as Jane and we've been in each other's company for a few hours now."

Jane smiled. "There's nothing enigmatic about me. What you see is what you get. My name is Jane Peterson. I assume that one of my ancestors was Peter and his son acquired the name as a natural course of descent."

"Now you are toying with me," he said.

"Not at all," she told him. "I'm relaxed and quite a lot of the real me is coming to the surface. I haven't felt like this for a while.

It's obviously the Coniston air that has a wonderful effect on me. That must answer one of your questions at least. Relaxation makes for well-crafted writing. My creative juices have been flowing well since I came here."

"Do you reckon there is a spiritual connection with this place?"

Jane sighed deeply. "It all depends what you mean by 'spiritual connection,'" she said. "I doubt it. It is my belief that one is in charge of one's own destiny. If I find the Lake District inspirational, it's because I am at peace with myself, not because there are spirits of Wordsworth and Coleridge floating around."

"That's quite a statement, Jane Peterson," Brad affirmed.

"I guess this place is having a similar effect on me as it did on them, but I can't see that the writers themselves have anything to do with the way I feel."

Brad continued with his interview in an indirect way. "Thanks for that, Jane. Do you realise we've been talking for three hours? You have given me much food for thought and I'm sure I can come up with an interesting article about you. I'll let you see the draft before I e-mail it to my editor."

"Oh, the joys of this technological age," she enthused. "Every time I sit at my PC I marvel at it, but it also makes me think of the detrimental effect it has had on my life." She paused as she collected her thoughts. *Skeletons in the cupboard that need to be aired.* "Maybe I'll share that little bit of information with you, Brad..."

"I'm very flattered that I might have become your friend," he told her. "Not long ago, you were saying you hadn't divulged any of your innermost thoughts to your acquaintances."

Jane smiled at him. "I'm comfortable with you, Brad. Perhaps we can be friends and the thing is, all this new technology which fascinates and excites me began the rift in my marriage."

"How come? I'm not sure I understand that. It doesn't make sense," he said.

"My ex-husband had no time for such radical moves in technology; he called them a flash in the pan and a complete waste of time and money," she explained. "Truth was, we weren't on the same page anymore and neither of us realised it for a while. We just kept fighting over the most ridiculous things. He blamed me and my computer; I blamed his pompous attitude and his unwillingness to embrace progress."

"Are you sad about it?" Brad asked gently.

Jane thought for a moment before she answered. "Well... I'm sad that we had to go through all the angst before we split, but I'm not sad that I'm not with Mick anymore. We had run our course. He's moved on and has a new partner; wife actually. I guess it's important to him to have someone in his life and I wish him well; I genuinely wish him well."

"And what about you, Jane? Will you move on?" Brad asked.

"I don't know," she replied honestly. "I felt very vulnerable for a while. It's quite a blow to the female ego when she is rejected." She silently checked herself. *Don't say anything about your promiscuous behaviour, Jane.* She felt her cheeks burning. "I guess life doesn't stop when one gets divorced, but I wouldn't know where to start looking for another available guy." She paused again. "I know some hot-blooded guys are on the look- out for people like me."

"What do you mean?" Brad asked.

"Divorced women are often considered to be easy. I understand that more than you will ever know, but the kind of guys who just want a bit of fun really aren't my type at all." She was feeling uncomfortable with the thoughts of her behaviour in London. "I guess I'll just settle with being on my own from now on."

Brad took her hand. "Thanks for sharing that," he said quietly. "I hope we can be friends for a long time."

Jane smiled at her new friend. "Me too. But what about you, Brad Courtney? The journalist in you kept me talking about myself. You haven't told me anything about you in spite of all my questions. Is there some dark secret you're hiding?"

She noticed that Brad visibly paled as he let go of her hand. "Sorry," she said. "I hope I haven't overstepped the rules of friendship already."

Brad breathed in deeply. "Not at all. I'm just being a bit sensitive. First of all, I have to say I'm not ashamed of who I am," he said with confidence. "I'm never too sure how people will react..." He paused poignantly. "...when I tell them I'm gay."

Jane tried desperately not to look shocked.

"See what I mean?" he continued amicably. "I shocked you, Jane. I don't want you to be shocked."

"Please, will you change shocked to surprised?" she asked.

"Okay, surprised, but why are you surprised? There are lots of us around these days. It's difficult to lead a normal life when people feel awkward in one's company and don't know how to respond. I'm a human being like everybody else..." He paused and laughed a little. "Well, not quite like everybody else, but please don't let this spoil our new friendship, Jane."

"It won't," she assured him. "In a way, it cements it. I feel safe with you."

"Thank you," he said, his words filled with emotion. "I lost my partner a year ago. I came on this trip to focus on something other than my consuming grief. It has helped tremendously. Oh I miss him dreadfully, but I know I'll survive. Like you, I'm not sure I'll move on, but who knows?"

Jane took his hand now as a sign of her friendship. She kissed him on the cheek. "I like you," she said.

"And I like you."

Jane cocked her head to one side and said, "How would you like to stay with me for a while? We'll go and get your things. I have a spare room just crying out for company."

Brad grabbed hold of her, swept her off her feet and swung her round in his arms. "Do you mean it, Jane? Do you really mean it?"

As he set her down, she nodded vigorously. She winked as she said, "What a waste, Brad! Some woman would love to have a handsome guy like you by her side."

He nudged her arm playfully. "You say all the right things, Jane; extremely silly, misguided things, but very flattering. Thanks for being my friend."

Twenty-four

Having Brad as a house guest was good for Jane. He was unobtrusive during the day when she was working and good company in the evening when they relaxed in front of the fire, or watched a bit of television.

"I don't watch much TV," Jane explained soon after Brad had moved in. "But I have become hooked on *Call My Bluff, The Krypton Factor* and *The Darling Buds of May*. There must be no talking when those programmes are on."

"I'm fine with that," Brad agreed. "We don't have to be talking all the time, but I guess we have been rabbiting on a bit since I moved in."

"Rabbiting?" Jane asked laughing. "That's a good old British term I've heard a lot since I came here, but I wouldn't have expected to hear it from a Canadian."

"Why not? I don't think the Brits have the monopoly," Brad joked, but their jocularity was interrupted by a sharp knock on the door.

Jane looked across the table at Brad. "Strange," she said. "Who would come up here at this time of night? It's pitch black outside."

"I'll go," he said. "A man answering the door might be best in this instance." He winked and Jane grinned at his poking fun at himself.

He opened the door to a burly policeman thrusting his warrant card in Brad's face to identify himself. "Oh, good evening officer, is there something wrong?"

The policeman wasn't quick to answer and furtively looked around before he spoke. "May I come in?"

By this time, Jane had appeared at Brad's shoulder. "Yes, come in. All this is very disconcerting, though. Can I offer you a cup of tea?"

"No thanks, ma'am. I can't stay, but I need to inform you that a prisoner has escaped from police custody. It's very embarrassing for us, but we need to find him before he does any more damage to persons or property. Have you seen anybody lurking around here?"

Both Jane and Brad shook their heads.

"I advise you to lock all doors and windows, especially your garage and any other ground floor facilities," the policeman said. "If you see or hear anything suspicious, call nine-nine-nine immediately.

"What does he look like, this escapee?" Brad asked. "We get a lot of fell walkers up here during the day."

"Teenage boy, blue jeans, blue anorak and was last seen wearing a black, red and white knitted hat, the sort you see at football matches."

"He's just a kid then. He doesn't sound dangerous to me," Jane commented.

"You never know what he might do when he's cornered," the policeman answered. "Just do as I ask and please be careful. Goodnight to you both."

With the policeman gone, they decided to lock up as requested. "I'll lock the garage and you check the back door and the downstairs windows," Brad suggested.

"It all seems very cloak and dagger," Jane said light-heartedly, "But I guess we should do as we were asked. We don't want to wake up dead in our beds."

Brad gave her a look of disdain. "Jane!" he declared pointedly. "Don't joke about such matters."

"Sorry," she said contritely. "But I have never yet allowed a teenage boy to get the better of me and I have confronted a few in the classroom more times than I care to remember."

"Desperate times call for desperate measures," Brad said, "so let's just do as the policeman advised. Better to be safe than sorry."

"Okay, but take a torch with you," Jane advised. "It's pretty black out there."

Brad went outside armed with a torch and locked up the garage, not without feeling nervous at the thought that a young thug might be lurking behind the bushes waiting to pounce. He hurried back to the security of the cottage. "All done," he called out as he closed the front door.

"That just about put paid to *Call My Bluff*," Jane said with a sigh.

"There's always next week," Brad consoled her. "I think I'll go up to bed now. I'll read for a while. Goodnight, Jane. See you in the morning. Sweet dreams."

~ * ~

Jane sat at the computer for a while after Brad had gone to bed. The policeman's visit had stirred up her nervous energy; the adrenalin was flowing and she needed to channel her energy into something constructive. She focussed her mind on Ben. Her main character was about to face challenges he had not previously encountered in his young life...

~ * ~

The boy pulled his blue anorak round him and snuggled down on the back seat of the car, grateful for the plaid rug he'd found in the vehicle. He was tired; as soon as his head rested in the leather upholstery, he was asleep.

~ * ~

Ben shot bolt upright when he heard a door bang shut. Elizabeth lay beside him, naked. He took hold of her arm and shook her gently to wake her.

"What's wrong?" she asked sleepily.

Ben signalled to her to keep quiet. "It's him," he whispered. "Walter. He's back."

Elizabeth grabbed her nightgown. "Hide ,at once" she instructed Ben as she quickly covered her naked body. "If my father finds you in my bed, he'll kill us both."

Jane leaned back in her chair and stretched to relieve the tension she was feeling in her neck and spine. She crept into the kitchen to make a cup of tea and took it back to her desk. Placing the cup next to the keyboard, she smiled as she once again thought of Richard. Her mind harked back to the classroom in Southport in Queensland, Australia...

"One of the basic rules when you are using a computer is never to have food or drinks anywhere near it. Most of you would argue that you aren't likely to spill anything, but you must never take that risk."

She picked up the cup and went to sit on the sofa. *Richard... Paul Clemens, whoever you are, you keep forcing your way into my mind. I don't want to think of you; I'm over you; get thee behind me!* She looked at the clock—twelve forty-five. "Time for bed, Jane," she whispered. As she said the words, she suddenly felt nervous. *Am I whispering so as not wake Brad, or do I think someone else might be listening?* She shrugged. *Overactive imagination, Jane. Just go to bed and stop thinking about criminal teenage boys lurking outside.* But she checked that Brad had locked the door before she ventured upstairs and ridiculously looked under her bed to ensure that nobody was hiding there.

~ * ~

After only a few hours' sleep, Jane rose early. She had tossed and turned for what seemed to her all night, struggling with Ben's predicament. She'd left him in Elizabeth's bedroom with a drunken man downstairs who was likely to beat them both to death should he find out what was going on. When Brad appeared, she had had her first cup of coffee and was about to have another.

"Good morning," he greeted her. "Did you sleep well?"

She looked directly at him. "Do you want the polite answer, or the brutally honest?" she asked with a distinct touch of weariness in her voice.

"Oh dear, was it so bad?" Brad asked sympathetically as he poured his first intake of caffeine.

"Well," she began, "I was working out how my main character might get himself and his lover out of a potentially violent situation, but my mind was invaded by teenage boys lurking outside and more than once I was convinced I heard noises outside my window."

Brad grinned. "I slept like a log..."

Jane laughed, albeit half-heartedly. "Good one, Brad."

He looked at her quizzically.

"Logs and the land of your birth," she explained. "I guess all Canadians sleep like logs. There are enough logs around in Canada to lead the way."

"Oh my goodness, Jane," he retaliated. "You've got to do better than that if you want to be a woman known for her finely tuned use of the English language. And anyway, it's too early in the morning for me to even try to understand your jokes, especially weak ones like that."

"Okay, I concede defeat. I'm just trying to rustle up a bit of enthusiasm," she said. "I sure do feel lacklustre this morning."

Brad finished his coffee. "I know what we can do," he said enthusiastically. "Let's do the typically Australian thing and go out for breakfast. That should cheer you up."

Jane pondered on it and then said, "You know, I think it might. Let's do it."

Half an hour later, they were ready to drive into the village to have breakfast at the little country cafe Jane had often visited for afternoon tea when she didn't feel like going to Hawkshead. Brad grabbed the garage key from the hook on the back door, remembering he had locked up the night before on the advice of the policeman.

"You drive," she instructed Brad. "I feel like being chauffeured today." She walked round to the passenger door... "What the hell is this?"

The boy stared bleary eyed at the woman who had disturbed his sleep. Brad had the presence of mind to activate the integral locking system so the kid couldn't do a runner. The boy slowly dragged his knitted hat off his head to reveal shoulder length fair hair, untidy, but clearly well-coiffed. Jane gasped. "He's a girl!" she exclaimed and noticed the girl's eyes fill with tears that spilled down her face, leaving clean lines on grubby cheeks.

Brad was about to reprimand the girl, but Jane stopped him with a shake of her head and a hand gesture that told him to keep quiet. She offered the girl a tissue to dry her eyes, but the girl kept sobbing almost silently. "What's your name?" Jane asked tenderly.

The girl remained silent.

"We can't help you if you won't speak to us," she continued, keeping her tone gentle.

Taking a deep breath to try to control her emotions, the girl spoke softly. "Alison, Alison Jones."

"Well, Alison Jones," Jane coaxed, "What do you say about going into our cottage and having some breakfast?"

Alison nodded slowly and Jane asked Brad to unlock the car doors.

Inside the house, Jane showed the girl to the bathroom where she might clean up a little while she and Brad made breakfast.

"Not exactly a violent criminal," she whispered.

Brad wasn't so sure. "How do we know what she might do?" he asked furtively. "You are too trusting, Jane. She might be climbing out of the bathroom window as we speak."

"No I'm not," Alison said as she entered the kitchen. Her tone wasn't aggressive, more restrained than anything else.

Jane noticed the change in her demeanour and signalled to her to take a seat at the table. "Are you feeling better now?" she asked.

"A little."

"Would you like a bacon sandwich and a cup of tea?" Jane continued, in an effort to make the girl feel more at ease.

Alison nodded.

Brad was becoming irritated at the lack of response from the girl. "Yes please," he said pointedly.

Alison turned round to look at him. "Sorry," she said. "Yes please."

Placated, Brad deigned to smile, only a half smile, not nonetheless friendly. "And now, you know what, Jane," he announced suddenly. "I think I'll take my breakfast to my room and leave you two girls to chat."

"Okay," Jane said appreciatively. "I think we might like that."

Alison displayed the hint of a smile and tentatively took a bite of her sandwich. "Thank you for this," she said quietly. "I..."

"Eat first and we'll chat later. There's no rush."

~ * ~

"I know you want to know why I'm running away from the police," Alison began. "I saw the cop I kneed in the groin when he came to your door."

Jane was wide-eyed. "You assaulted a policeman?" she said with astonishment.

Alison looked very embarrassed. She pressed her lips together in a thin line. "I panicked," she offered.

"But that's no excuse," Jane told her. "What had you done to be arrested anyway?"

"Nothing."

Jane looked directly at the girl, who was once again becoming distressed. "People don't get arrested for nothing," she told her pointedly.

"But I did," she cried.

"Tell me about it," Jane coaxed. "I want to help you, but I need to know what's going on."

Alison sniffed loudly and Jane gave her the pack of tissues she had opened earlier. "Why would you want to help me?" she asked. "You might as well just hand me over to the police."

"I am used to dealing with young people and I know that behind all this cloak and dagger stuff, there is a very frightened girl."

Alison moved uncomfortably.

Jane tried to make her feel at ease and spoke with a tenderness that only an experienced, caring mother could genuinely convey. "Start at the beginning, love. I'm listening."

They moved into the living room and sat on the settee, one at either end, but sideways on so they were facing each other. Jane recalled momentarily that this was how she and Brad had sat during her interview, but she mentally noted that the circumstances could not be more different. "Tell me about yourself first," she encouraged the girl.

"I'm Alison Jones, like I told you. I didn't make it up, honest," she began.

"I believe you, but why are you saying this?" Jane asked.

"Because I gave the police a false name so they think they are looking for Bobbie Walton," she explained. She looked directly at Jane and said, "I'm in deep trouble, aren't I?"

"Maybe, but continue, please."

"I'm sixteen years old and I was born in Ulverston. I have just left school and I need a job. I don't want to go back home."

Jane thought it prudent at this point not to ask why. "What would you like to do for a job? Have you any qualifications?"

Alison's face brightened. "I have ten subjects on my GCSE and I'm very proud of myself for getting them. My lowest grade is a C in Home Economics, but I don't want to be a chef, so that's okay. I'd really like to be a tour guide here in the Lake District. I can speak French and Spanish, so I could take foreign visitors around all the tourist attractions. I already know loads about this place. I love it. My mum used to bring me every summer until she ..." She shivered.

Jane suddenly felt the urge to take her hand to reassure her that she wasn't alone.

"Mum passed away six months ago, just before my exams. That's why I'm proud of what I did. I did it for her." Tears sprung in her eyes as she recalled the traumatic time she'd had. "My dad just drank all the time, saying the booze would ease his pain and he wouldn't listen to me. We'd had talks in school about alcoholism, but he kept saying he didn't have a problem and he just carried on. He threw up every morning and then drank all day. He wouldn't eat anything and he picked up with all sorts of women, real tramps, and he'd bring a different one home every night. I locked myself in my room and tried to block out what I heard coming from my mother's bed... *my mother's bed.*"

Her tone was changing and Jane felt the tension in her hand and heard it in her voice. "You have every right to be angry, Alison, but please don't torture yourself with something which is beyond control," she said.

Alison composed herself again and continued. "I packed up my things a month ago and hired a caravan at Coniston Farm. My *devoted* dad didn't even bother to say goodbye. He stood at the door with one of his floozies and said *'Good riddance'*."

Jane gasped.

The girl continued. "He told me his marriage was already over before my mum took ill. I thought he'd just started drinking when mum was sick, but I understand now what she said the day before she died. She said, *'Don't allow your dad to bring drink into the house.'* When I asked why, she had fallen asleep and she never woke up after that."

"Poor love," Jane said as she gently squeezed the girl's hand. "But what happened with the police?"

"My best friend from school stayed in the caravan with me for a couple of weeks. She's great and it was good to have some company. Her parents were okay with it at first, but they decided it wasn't good for her to be responsible for me. I understood where they were coming from, but she was only keeping me company and we weren't doing anything wrong. It was like playing house when we were kids, but this was real. Most of the time we played music and did jigsaws—I love doing jigsaws—but Beth's parents made her go home. The night before last was the first night on my own. I didn't want to stay on my own all day and all night, so after lunch I walked into the village. On my way there, I saw some lads with spray cans doing this fantastic art work on an old barn."

"Do you mean graffiti artists?" Jane asked.

"Exactly. They were brilliant at it and they said they had permission from the owner to paint the old barn. They were making it blend into the countryside instead of being an eyesore. I stood and watched for a while and when I was leaving, one of them threw an empty can to me and asked me to throw it away."

Jane shifted in her seat. "I think I know where this is going," she said.

"I didn't see a waste bin, so I carried the can all the way into the village. Suddenly, just as I was approaching the top end of the main street, this police car pulled up and the guy jumped out and grabbed hold of my arm." She demonstrated how roughly he treated her. "*Got yer, you little toe rag,* he said. He asked me my name and I told him Bobbie Walton. He thought I was a boy. He said he'd seen all the tags I'd put around the village. I told him it wasn't me, but he wouldn't listen and all the time he was pulling me towards the car to take me to the police station. That's when I kneed him in the groin and ran. He couldn't follow me because ...well, you know why."

"You must have taken off like a whippet," Jane said not trying to hide her amusement. "We are three miles away from the village."

Alison, too, saw the funny side of it. "I know all the pathways inside out and a car couldn't possibly follow me. When I saw your cottage, I hid under that upside down wheelbarrow when the cop pulled up. He didn't see me and I think he was still hurting from what I'd done, so he didn't even search."

Jane took hold of the girl and gave her a hug. "Thank goodness we found you this morning. Don't worry anymore. We'll sort it out. I'll just call Brad..."

"Is he your husband?"

No, he isn't," Jane told her with a smile. "Just a friend, but he's very knowledgeable and he'll know what to do."

Twenty-five

Jane lay in bed and thought over the events of the past couple of months. *This has to make a good story sometime,* she mused. *Brad and Alison just happened in my life and here I am with a life-long friend and a temporary daughter who has shown strength and resilience in the face of adversity. She'll be fine, I know. I think I'll give Ben some of her qualities, including the vulnerability she has that makes her endearingly fragile on occasions. How lucky she has been in finding an apprenticeship with English Heritage and she'll be seconded to complete her further education until she becomes fully qualified. Her mother would be very proud.* She turned over and plumped up her pillow. *Brad knew exactly what to do in order to exonerate her from the little incident with the police. The village policeman was really very understanding eventually. His ego was bruised...* Jane had to laugh *...as well as a certain part of his body, but he had a heart of gold and let Alison off with a warning to keep well out of trouble in the future. I don't think there is any danger* *she'll ever get in trouble again. She's a nice kid and a real credit to her mother. I hope I can give her a little bit of stability until she feels able to step out into the big wide world alone.*

~ * ~

By Christmas, Alison had settled well into her new life. Jane had made up a bed in the loft with the cottage owner's permission and having a young person around was enlightening and illuminating. Both she and Brad enjoyed Alison's company and hearing a daily account of her new life with English Heritage. She was made aware that being a tour guide would only be part of her job initially, but she would train to become a marketing manager of historic sites and buildings and might be placed anywhere in the country. "Not only that, my boss told me I would be an asset because of my French and Spanish qualifications. I'll be able to do promotions overseas. It's all very exciting and they'll sponsor me while I do my A levels," she told Jane. "Thank you so much for becoming my unofficial guardian. I'll never be able to repay you."

"No payment necessary," Jane told her. "To see you happy and smiling is all the recompense we need."

~ * ~

Brad came home one evening with the news that his office in Vancouver needed him back.

"Oh bugger, Brad. I have got so used to you being around. Do you really have to go back?" Jane bewailed.

"Sorry, babe," he said with a wry smile. "We have to say goodbye early in the New Year."

"*Au revoir*, darl," she insisted. "Not goodbye. I demand that you come to see me as soon as possible whether I'm here in the UK or back in Australia."

Alison paled. "Are you going back to Australia?" she asked.

"Oh baby, don't worry. I'm not even thinking about going back yet. My work here isn't done. I'm still only forty-five thousand words into *Finding Ben* and, as your surrogate mother, I shall be here for as long as is necessary," Jane explained. "But..."

"Oh my goodness, there's a but," Alison groaned.

"Yes, there is a but," Jane reiterated. "You won't be in The Lakes forever, you know. English Heritage could send you anywhere in the country, or by your own admission, overseas, and that's what you want, isn't it?"

"Well, yes it is, but…" She grinned as she found her own 'but' this time. "But I don't want to leave you."

"You just wait till you meet the man of your dreams," Brad interjected.

Alison grinned. "Well, seeing that you mentioned it…"

Both adults gaped in unison at what seemed to be an announcement that their ward had a new boyfriend, but a sharp knock on the door stopped them in their tracks.

Jane was quick to quip, "You haven't been at it with your spray can again, have you, young lady?"

They all laughed, but a more urgent knock made them realise it wasn't time for jokes. "Just a moment," Jane called out. "I'll be right there."

"Hello, Ms Peterson," Victoria Smith said breezily. "I hope we haven't come at an inconvenient time."

We? Jane thought as she scanned the driveway for another person. *Oh please God, don't tell me my worst nightmare is happening.*

"My husband is just parking the car. He'll be along in a minute," Victoria said.

At the sound of Victoria's voice, Alison approached the door to confirm her assumption that she knew the speaker. As she crept up behind Jane, still out of Victoria's sight, Mr Smith appeared and he was walking towards them with a definite spring in his step.

Jane almost died; Alison cried out in shock—it could hardly be described as surprise. "Uncle Freddy! What are you doing here and with Victoria Bradford?"

Jane couldn't believe her eyes. *This is the guy I met, but he isn't the Freddy I recall*, she thought. *The guy I knew in London was an overdressed, over exuberant wannabe who was desperate to be in tune with the era. I can't actually say I knew him, because I didn't. We just fulfilled a need in each other at that particular time. It all seems so long ago, but my word, just look at him now.*

In front of her was a confident, dapper man in a suit, with an attractive wife by his side. He even dared to look Jane in the eye as he spoke. "Hello, Ms Peterson," he greeted her. "My wife..."

Didn't he pronounce that a little too emphatically?

" ...has told me about you. Australian, are you?"

"I am indeed. Nice to meet you, Mr Smith," Jane replied, rather too formally. *Might as well join in his little game for now.* "Won't you come in?"

The Smiths entered the cottage and Brad invited them to sit down. Freddy glanced over at Jane, who sensed the questioning going on his mind. "This is my dear friend, Brad Courtney, a Canadian journalist. He is due to leave England next week. We shall miss him terribly."

Alison had stood by watching and listening to the small talk. "What are you doing here?" she asked pointedly, "And when did you marry Victoria? It's weird that you and Mum's best friend should be together. I never thought you'd marry again after Auntie Marian died. You always..."

Jane felt the need to stop this conversation in its tracks. An investigation into the whys and wherefores of Freddy's marriage to Victoria might not be appropriate. "Put the kettle on, Alison. Let us at least show your uncle we are civilised. Tea?" she asked them collectively.

"That would be lovely, Jane ...you don't mind if I call you Jane?" Victoria asked politely

"Not at all."

They made themselves comfortable while Alison busied herself in the kitchen.

"Didn't you say your husband worked in London?" Jane asked Victoria and then to Freddy, "What do you do?" she continued, still going along with the charade, but feeling rather irritated that she and Freddy were being underhanded with everybody and particularly with each other.

She actually thought Freddy looked sheepish. "I work in a bank dealing with corporate finance."

Jane felt her jaw drop, but tried to hide her surprise. She stared at the man in front of her, who had certainly pulled the wool over her eyes previously. "Oh," she offered, knowing full well she must sound uninterested.

"Not interesting enough for you, Ms Peterson?"

"Jane, please," she insisted. "On the contrary; very interesting. May I ask if it has any connection with retail and security?" she said as she tried to draw out a bit of the Freddy she had met in London.

"Hardly," Freddy informed her. "I guess big business and retail in some instances might be associated, but not in my field."

Jane was out of her depth. "If I might change the subject," she said. "Is it by coincidence that you are here as far as Alison is concerned? It is almost beyond belief that you are visiting now that I have been given caring rights for her until she completes her education and training—I don't think there's any legal terminology to cover that situation. Social Services have allowed me to be her unofficial guardian while she is still following a course of study."

Freddy took a deep breath. "Don't worry about legalities. It is coincidence pure and simple," he said. "I had no idea she was here. Victoria wanted to go for a drive and suggested we called in on you since it had been so long since you and she had met."

"So what now?" she asked. "I should hate to upset our arrangements. She has settled so well and ..."

"I have no objection to her being here," he replied. "I appreciate what you appear to be doing, but I don't think it necessary at this point to discuss private family matters with you, if you'll pardon my bluntness. She is my niece and as her official god-father I realise I ought to take responsibility for her well-being, since her father has relinquished his responsibility, the waster."

"Why have you come to interfere now?" Alison interrupted. "I'm sixteen and can leave home if I want to. I don't need permission from you, and anyway, I'm happy here. Jane has been like a mother to me. Where were you when Mum was sick? I didn't see you coming up from London to make sure I was all right then." She was becoming angry and distraught.

Freddy looked uncomfortable and Victoria took hold of his arm to give him support. "Your father told me to stay away," he said. "And anyway, I knew Uncle George was here if you needed him."

"Wrong!" Alison spat. "He cleared off to London too, to chase the bright lights. What a waste of space he is, a try-hard middle-aged man who thinks he's an eighties' icon. You should see him—open necked shirts, fake tan—the embarrassing proverbial medallion man! Works at Harrods and thinks he's god's gift to society!" They were harsh words, but very profound coming from a teenager who had been left to fend for herself when she most needed her family around her.

"That's pretty much below the belt, Alison," Freddy told her as Victoria squirmed by his side. "My twin has a lot to answer for, but I don't think you should speak of him like that."

Jane stood by and began to piece together the jigsaw. *Oh my god,* she thought. *Identical twins and I had to meet the deluded one who takes on his brother's persona when he is in a delicate situation. At least he didn't say he was a banker.* "Perhaps we should leave you to discuss this privately," she suggested. "Brad and I will go for a walk. We'll be back in half an hour. Alison, please be polite to your uncle."

Alison half smiled and nodded. "Sorry, Jane," she said sheepishly. "I lost it for a moment then, but I won't let you down."

~ * ~

Alison, Freddy and Victoria talked calmly through the situation without the previous animosity and concluded that nothing should change. When Jane and Brad returned, they were having a second cup of tea and reminiscing about Alison's mother.

"All's well that ends well," Jane commented gaily, momentarily recalling with a wry smile her cliché ridden life before she left Australia. She managed to catch Freddy's eye. "May we speak in private?"

They went into the kitchen, leaving the others to carry on their reminiscences. Once alone, Jane made her feelings clear. "As you said earlier, we don't need to be party to your family affairs," she told Freddy, "but I do need to know that you approve of your niece being here. There has been no formal agreement drawn up, but Social Services are aware that Alison is with me. At sixteen, she is apparently allowed to leave home if she so wishes."

"No problem," Freddy told her. "I am happy she knows what she is doing. Her mother would be very proud of her. My sister, Valerie, and I were never very close, but we always respected our family ties. That's how it is with my twin brother and me, even though for identical twins, we break the mould. We don't think alike, or act alike in spite of how much we look alike."

"I met him in London," Jane revealed.

Freddy raised his eyebrows. "I bet that was a riveting experience," he said sardonically.

Jane smiled. "He told me his name was Freddy. Can you imagine how I felt when you arrived at the door?"

"Not really. Why would I need to do that?" Freddy asked, somewhat bemused at Jane's question. "But my imagination is working overtime and I am wondering just what happened between you two that would invite such an enquiry."

Jane took a deep breath. "That's for me to know and for you not to ask," she said with a grin, "but at least he had the good grace not to say he worked in a bank. He did tell the truth about his job… well I think it was the truth, but in light of what you have told me, how would I know if it was the truth or not? He said he worked in Harrods' security. I think that might be true in view of Alison's comments."

Freddy nodded and then added, "Yes, but did he tell you he never married? I know for a fact he never liked people knowing he was single. In one of our few adult conversations, he said he was always awkward in the company of women and he would say he was married."

"Lie number two then. He told me he was widowed. Now I realise it is you who lost your wife. I'm sorry for your loss," she said sincerely, but thought: *Georgie boy certainly wasn't feeling awkward after a couple of glasses of wine!*

"Thank you, but I'm happy now. I never thought I would find such love after Marian passed away, but Victoria has shown me how to live again. Now I have to persuade her that life in the capital is wonderful and encourage her to move down there to be with me all the time."

"I'm sure she'll follow you to the ends of the earth," Jane told him. "As far as George is concerned, he disappeared from the scene almost as soon as we met. I really thought you were him when you appeared and as such, I assumed it was he who had re-married. How weird is that?"

"Typical of George, I'm afraid. He causes a stir and then runs from the scene. I can only hope he never commits a crime," Freddy said, with the hint of a smile on his lips.

"I never said he caused a stir," Jane corrected. "But he did come over as quite an odd character—odd, but interesting in a way. Is he still in London?"

Freddy shrugged. "I guess so, but who knows? He only gets in touch when he wants something and since he's been in regular employment, he has had no need of handouts. That might sound harsh, but it's the way it is."

Jane smiled her best understanding, appreciative smile. "Thank you for sharing that information with me. I appreciate it. Now I think perhaps we should get back to the others," she said. "I know we are on the same page as far as Alison is concerned."

"Indeed we are," Freddy agreed. "Thank you, Jane. Please feel free to contact me if the need arises."

Twenty-six

Brad left in the middle of January amidst tears of sadness. In the few months that they had been together in the most platonic sense of the words, he and Jane had become the closest of friends. They had told their secrets to each other, had not judged one another and had found a profound closeness that any man and woman could experience without the encumbrance of sex. "Thank you, Brad," she said sincerely as he went into passport control at Manchester Airport.

"No, *thank* you," he told her. "You are one of the most understanding people I have ever met. I shall miss you terribly, dear Jane, but we'll e-mail and telephone and we'll meet again as soon as it's possible."

Jane sniffed and wiped away the tears that were trickling down her cheeks. "I'll be here for the next six months at least, I guess," she informed him, "and then maybe I'll make my way back home. I'd like to go via the States, but I'll see when the time comes. Go now before I flood out the place!"

They hugged closely and Brad went through the sliding doors. He didn't look back because he didn't want Jane to see he was crying too.

That night, she sat staring at her computer screen trying to put all her emotions into Ben. Alison was out with her boyfriend, Gary—the one whom she had hinted about just before her uncle arrived at the door. Jane found Ben where she had left him, hiding in the wardrobe in Elizabeth's room...

Ben tried not to breathe. His heart was beating so wildly in his chest he felt sure Elizabeth's drunken father would hear it if he came into the room. Most of his clothes were still in his hands, but he had managed to scramble into his pants before he pulled the wardrobe door closed. Suddenly, he heard the heavy footsteps on the wooden floor as they approached Elizabeth's room. The door swung open and Walter swore. "Wake up, you little whore!" he shouted. "Where's the bastard who took you?"

Elizabeth stirred in her bed as if she were just waking. "What is it?" she enquired with simulated sleepiness.

Walter staggered across the room to the open window. The curtains were open and they wafted in the cool night breeze. "Gone out through the window, eh?" he said and returned to the side of Elizabeth's bed. Grabbing hold of her arm roughly, he yanked her up and bent over until his face was close to hers. "I know what you've been up to, trollop, and I'll kill that half-cast bastard if I see him anywhere near this house again."

Elizabeth kept quiet. The stench from this man's breath almost overpowered her. She stared wide-eyed at the man whom she instinctively knew had killed her mother; proving it was another matter and, if he saw the fear in her eyes at this moment, he would certainly exploit it...

Jane felt all the desperation of her characters, the hate for the drunken father taken from Alison's abhorrence for her own father; the desperation of Ben who was powerless to help, the fear of both the young people who felt totally alone even though they were together. She had felt that loneliness when she lay on the edge of her bed while Mick, in the same bed, was as far away as he could possibly be, both physically and emotionally. She had to find a way out for them...

Her emotions appeared to be in turmoil. While she sensed Ben's fear, she also felt the strength in Elizabeth's character and knew she would always be there for her first love. Her own thoughts weren't quite so clear. *I thought I was strong like Elizabeth. I never anticipated that my love for Mick would disappear. How can we know what is in store for us? I have a lot of love in my heart still, but not for Mick, I know that now.* She squirmed at the thought of her one night stands in London. *What were you doing, Jane? Did it prove anything to you?* She sighed deeply. *No harm done really, but I have to admit, I feel a sense of shame that I lowered myself in order to prove a point of self-esteem.*

Thinking of Brad, she smiled in recognition of true friendship. *Brad was my soul mate if only for a few months. When people like him come into one's life, it has to be a blessing personified. No problems wrought by sexual attraction, just pure, unadulterated friendship.*

Out of the blue, she pictured Richard framed in the doorway of her chalet at Eden Sands. *How handsome he was,* she recalled and realised she was smiling flirtatiously. *Oh boy! What did you do to my emotions, Richard? You still keep invading my mind, uninvited, but I guess that's you to a tee. You seemed to make your presence felt in the most unconventional ways. Nobody has ever had such an effect on me, not even Mick. Oh, I loved him with a passion in the full flush of youth, but he and I never had the intellectual connection I had with you. I wanted to take it further at the time and yet I didn't know how to deal with you.* She shrugged amidst her memories. *Your wife must be one hell of a woman to command your love and attention...*

"We're home!" Alison called out.

Jane literally roused herself from her reverie and went to greet them in the living room. "Did you have a good time?" she asked.

"We did," Gary told her. "You really must see *Die Hard*. Bruce Willis is fantastic."

"I don't think it's my scene," Jane said. "Violence scares me and so do psychological thrillers. Anything that smacks of insanity gives me nightmares. *Fatal Attraction* gave me the heebie-jeebies."

Alison laughed. "You're showing your age, Jane!" she quipped. "We love anything scary, the more blood and guts, the better. But I know you'll like what's on next week. It's called *Rain Man* with Dustin Hoffman and Tom Cruise."

"Oh yes, I've read the promos about that," Jane said. "I think I might go to see that one. Will you join me?"

Alison looked questioningly at Gary. "You go with Jane," he said. "We're not joined at the hip!"

"That's agreed then," Jane continued. "But never let it be said that I stood in the way of young love. Hot chocolate?"

~ * ~

As the weeks went by, Jane discovered a measure of contentment in her life. There were moments of self-pity when she thought of the people she missed: Sally, Bill and the children particularly, but in an odd kind of way, Alison compensated for some of that. *She reminds me of you on many levels, Sal,* she wrote in her monthly e-mail. *Mind you, she will never be my daughter. Only you can have that treasured distinction. She is intelligent like you, loving like you, extremely well-organised like you and, dare I say it? She is so bloody wilful and stubborn like you at times!* Jane grinned as she typed. *And before you say it, it takes one to know one! She actually drew my attention to my age a couple of weeks ago. We were talking about movies and I realised I just wasn't on the teenage wavelength as regards tastes in films. But thinking about age and time and things, when I assess what has happened in the past eighteen months, it's incredible. This time last year, I was in London and rapidly becoming tired of city life. Now, I feel as though I'm part of the landscape here and my novel is really taking shape.*

And then there was Brad; dear Brad with whom she connected immediately. Her thoughts strayed again. *Not like the connection with Richard …Damn you Richard… and I still don't know your name. I miss Brad's wit, his ability to see situations way beyond the superficial appearance, his friendly laugh and above all, his caring nature. I know we'll be friends forever even though we live at opposite ends of the earth. We telephone and e-mail—thank you God, for giving me the wisdom to embrace technology. Even though it became the catalyst in the break-up of my marriage, it was only a matter of time before the split would have happened, regardless of my determination to snub Mick's views.* She sighed. *That was exactly it. I snubbed Mick on every level. I can admit that now.*

She returned to her main character, Ben. She needed to give him the courage to stand up to Walter, but it was a difficult task, not just for Ben, but for her. The easy way out would be to run away. Isn't that what she had done in fleeing to England? But back to Ben…

…It was the stuff that nightmares are made of: confronting what appeared to be the impossible, facing what life had thrown at him, accepting with courage something so alien to him. He loved Elizabeth and he considered that she was worth any hardship, even violence, he might have to endure. Confusing thoughts invaded his brain. Who in his right mind would accept this challenge without question? Who would walk blindly into a situation knowing he might get hurt, or worse? Walter was completely unknown to him apart from the snippets of information Liz had divulged in moments of vulnerability.

He remained hidden in the wardrobe until he was certain Walter was long gone. Elizabeth had not called out to him; perhaps she was too scared, perhaps she thought he had slipped out through the window in the darkness. He tried to summon up the courage to venture out of his little prison into the boiling cauldron they had undoubtedly created. He knew he had stepped into the adult world when he sampled the delights of passionate love-making for the first time. He closed his eyes and trembled at the thought, his knees turning to jelly as he recalled the desire that had swept through his whole body and filled him with a feeling of urgency like he had never previously experienced. When Old Joe told him he needed a girlfriend, he didn't warn him that falling in love might lead to this. Old Joe's relationships must have been easy by comparison...

Jane stretched and looked at the clock. It was midnight and she hadn't noticed how late it was. Neither had she noticed when Gary had left. He must surely have gone home by now. She went upstairs to the loft and saw that Alison's door was shut. Gently, she knocked. "Alison," she whispered. "Are you awake?"

There was no sound. Thinking she ought not to waken the girl who had to be up early for work in the morning, she went to her own room and got ready for bed herself.

Behind the loft door, Alison had signalled to her bedfellow to keep quiet. She knew Jane would not enter her room without invitation. That was Jane's way of ensuring her ward's privacy. The two young people snuggled close and drifted off to a completely satisfied sleep.

Jane lay awake for ages contemplating Ben's next move.

Twenty-seven

Alison had left for work before Jane rose. There was nothing unfamiliar about that. Jane's late nights often led to her sleeping in. It seemed her imagination worked best in the wee small hours of the morning. On that particular morning, there were two cups and two plates left in the sink. *Oh dear,* she thought. *If this is what I think it is, I'm dealing with something so personal I have to question whether or not I should interfere.* She considered making house rules. *It will be like shutting the stable door after the horse has bolted, but it is my house after all.*

~ * ~

"Alison, we need to talk," she said as soon as the girl came home from work.

"That sounds ominous," Alison commented.

"Well, it might be," Jane told her, "if we aren't on the same page."

The girl looked worried. "Have I done something to upset you, Jane?" she asked.

"Depends," was the reply.

"On what?"

"On whether or not you think sleeping with your boyfriend would upset me," Jane explained.

Alison paled. "I'm seventeen next month and sixteen is the age of consent," she said weakly.

Jane pressed her lips together and sighed deeply and loudly. "I'm not here to tell you what you should, or shouldn't do, Alison. I offered to allow you to share my home because I liked you and you needed somewhere to stay. However, I do feel you have overstepped the boundaries a bit..."

"Sorry, but..."

"Let me finish, please," Jane said firmly. "I think I am mature enough and worldly-wise enough to give you advice. I have to ask if you feel ready to accept the consequences should you continue to have a sexual relationship."

Alison looked at her wide-eyed.

Jane continued unabashed. "You are very young, on the brink of starting a wonderful career, a career that will inevitably involve a lot of travelling. It isn't very long ago that you were over the moon about the prospects of your new job."

Alison nodded in agreement, but while her eyes questioned what Jane was saying, her thoughts questioned her own judgment. *What was I thinking? I was scared and Gary was desperate...*

"How would you be able to travel with a baby in tow? It could happen, you know. Did you take precautions?"

Alison felt her cheeks burning. "It was my first time, Jane. Gary said it would be all right."

Jane was aghast. "And so he would!" she exclaimed. "Don't you realise that men, young men in particular, are ruled by what's between their legs? Sorry to be so plain-spoken, but it's true, I'm afraid. These days it seems to be the done thing to hop into bed with a boyfriend. At the risk of sounding like my own mother, in my day a girl kept herself for the man she was going to marry." She stopped abruptly. *Pan calling kettle, Jane,* she thought. *How dare you question promiscuity when not so long ago you chose to hop into bed with anybody who was willing and able?*

"And did you?" Alison dared to ask.

Jane shrugged. "I didn't wait until I got married, if that's what you are asking," she divulged honestly, "but my husband was the first and I knew at the time we would marry."

"Gary has been asking me to sleep with him for ages," Alison revealed, "but I always said no. He kept saying I didn't love him if I didn't have sex with him and I thought he would finish with me if I didn't do as he wanted. I love him, Jane. He's my first real boyfriend and it would break my heart if he left me."

Jane moved close to the girl who looked so vulnerable at the moment and took her hand in hers. "Look, darl," she said gently, "If Gary loves you, he won't make demands. Oh he'll want to make love to you; he wouldn't be a guy if he didn't, but he'd also respect your wishes too. Don't feel pressured."

"But I do feel pressured."

Jane squeezed her hand gently. "I know, sweetheart, but would you really be happy if all Gary wants you for is sex?"

Alison shook her head sadly.

"One more question and my last, I promise. Would you want to risk your future for a..." She paused and grinned. "...for a bit of rumpy-pumpy?"

Alison smiled sheepishly, her face still flushed with embarrassment. "I don't want anything to get in the way of my job and I'll talk to Gary when I see him." She looked longingly at Jane. "Will he still be allowed to visit me here?" She hugged the woman who had been nothing but a true friend and mentor since they had met. "Thanks for not being mad at me, Jane," she said sincerely.

"Of course he may come to visit," Jane assured her, "but I must insist you stay out of your bedroom, especially when I'm at home and more so when I'm not. House rules."

~ * ~

Ben listened for any sound that might tell him what was happening in Elizabeth's bedroom. It seemed he'd been waiting for hours, but in reality it was only minutes. He wondered if he should open the wardrobe door so he might at least see that his lover was all right. If she was sleeping, she would surely be fine; the heavy breathing he could hear was Walter, but he quickly realised it was he who was breathing hard and his heart was beating wildly in his chest. He would have to be very careful not to be detected. He felt helpless. He had to make a decision. He couldn't stay in the wardrobe all night...

~ * ~

Two days after their heart to heart, Alison came home in tears. "He finished with me," she told Jane. "He said if I wasn't prepared to satisfy his needs, he'll find it elsewhere."

Jane wasn't surprised. "I'm sorry, sweetheart, and I don't really know what to say to make you feel better."

"Don't say anything," Alison snapped. "This only happened because I took your advice..."

"Hey, hold on, missy," Jane retaliated. "That's all it was—advice. You chose to take it, obviously, so don't blame me. If Gary really wanted you, he'd respect your wishes. He's a lot older than you and so he should have the intelligence to know how to treat a lady."

Alison flopped down onto the settee. "He's only twenty, Jane. That's not old."

"Old enough to know better, Alison, but still not mature enough to accept his responsibilities. Did you tell him what you needed to do with your life before you made a serious commitment in a relationship?"

Alison sighed and the tears subsided. "I told him I didn't want to risk getting pregnant and he told me to go on the pill." She paused poignantly. "I don't want to do that, though," she continued quietly. "It was the pill that started all my mum's health problems, but Gary didn't understand that. How could he?"

Jane chose her words carefully. "Your mum isn't important to him, love. All he sees at the moment is sex for the sake of it. His whole attitude has proved that, to me at least. Most young men feel it's their duty to prove their manhood through sex. It's not making love, Alison, it's just pure, unadulterated sex. Girls make love; boys have sex!"

"You make it sound so cold and calculated," the girl stated.

"And so it is for them, that is until they really fall in love and then it becomes an act of passionate fulfilment," Jane explained. "Do you really think that's what you experienced with Gary?"

Alison blushed. "I didn't like it," she admitted. "I didn't feel anything except his..."

Jane noted the girl's embarrassment. "Too much information, love. You don't need to tell me the details, but I gather you are fast becoming clearer in your views."

Alison nodded. "I guess I don't love him like I thought I did," she said. "He didn't even say he loved me even when he'd satisfied himself." She paused and gasped audibly. "Oh heck, Jane. You don't think I could have got pregnant, do you?"

"Let's hope not, love, although it has been known that once is enough."

Alison's eyes filled with tears again. "What would I do?" she wailed.

Jane patted her knee. "We'll deal with it if and when," she reassured the girl. "We can't worry about anything like that until it happens."

~ * ~

Brad phoned that night and Jane explained what had happened. "I only hope I said all the right things," she told him. "When I left Australia, I didn't anticipate that I'd become a surrogate mother to a teenage girl. It wasn't on my agenda at all. In all my years of teaching, I never had to deal with anything like this, not even with Sally."

"I'm sure you did fine, Jane," Brad assured her. "From what I can gather, Alison is just a mixed up kid at the moment. Her hormones will be playing havoc and she won't know what she should do. First time sex is one big step to take and girls fall in love very easily at her age."

Jane laughed. "And how would you know that, Brad?" she asked good-humouredly.

"Mock ye not, Jane Peterson, my friend!" he protested vehemently. "Cheryl Deschamps declared her undying love for me when she was fourteen years old and demanded I kissed her behind the giant red cedar in the school grounds."

"And did you?" Jane asked, intrigued.

"Of course!" he stated confidently. "It was she who made me realise I wasn't interested in girls! I kissed her full on the lips as she pressed her developing bosoms into my chest and then I ran away and threw up!"

"Are you serious?"

"Of course not," he said, "but I did become aware of my sexuality at that time and it has got you out of your miserable mood, so Cheryl Deschamps has proved her worth twice now."

"I miss you, Brad," she said and she meant it.

"I miss you too, Jane, but I have some news for you," he told her. "I have met someone."

"Really?" she gasped.

"He was working in the office when I got back and we made a connection."

"Please don't talk about connections, Brad," she said sounding rather too emphatic. Her thoughts were agitated, confused. *Richard—the infuriating, wonderful Richard. Married, unavailable Richard. We had that undeniable connection.*

"Are you still there, Jane?" Brad asked.

"Yes, I'm here," she said almost wearily.

"What is wrong, my dear?" the ever astute Brad asked, concerned he had upset her just as soon as he had lifted her spirits.

Jane sighed. "I didn't tell you this when you were here, because I didn't want you to judge me."

"I would never judge you, my dear friend," he said gently.

"I know that really," she agreed, "but I haven't talked about this to anybody except my friend, Linda, who dismissed me out of hand when I told her. However, I do think about it a lot when I'm feeling vulnerable." She explained that when she was contemplating her future with Mick, she had made a strange, confusing, but wonderful connection with a stranger. "Nothing happened between us except a kiss, one kiss. It awakened all the sensual, sensuous, romantic emotions I hadn't felt for years and then he was gone."

Brad spoke quietly. "Dearest Jane," he said. "I sense you are experiencing regret that you didn't take it further."

"No point, Brad," she expounded. "He's married, happily married, so there was never a cat in hell's chance that it would go any further, but I still think of him and yes, I long for him at times. You would think that at my age, I'd know better. Women of fifty-one and a bit don't find love like that, do they?"

Brad sighed. "Jane, Jane, Jane!" he declared. "It is my belief there is always an abundance of love to give and receive when the situation is right. Age has nothing to do with it. I know you'll find love again. A woman with a relentless passion for life as you have will meet someone who appreciates you and all you have to offer. It is never too late to start again."

~ * ~

That night, Jane lay in bed staring through the darkness and seeing nothing. *When Brad told me he had met somebody to love, I felt so jealous. I am happy for him, truly I am. He's my friend and there will never be any romance between us, obviously.* She smiled in the dark. *How could I be jealous? You are stupid, Jane!* She turned over to make herself more comfortable. *I wonder if I will meet somebody to love again. I don't think I'm looking for true love at the moment, though. I need to complete my manuscript. My writing is my passion for now.* She chastised herself again. *Ben still has to resolve his problems, so forget your own, Jane. Is Ben like me?* she silently asked herself. *Or Brad, Alison, or Gary? Or is he all of us, or none of us? God forbid that he should turn out to be cynical like Richard..* Sleep evaded her, but she lay there just dozing until daylight crept in through the window.

Twenty-eight

Finding Ben finally came to a conclusion...

...Ben held his new wife's hand and introduced her to Old Joe, who smiled graciously, but Ben noticed there was something different about him, something weird about the atmosphere of the place. The long months he had been away had changed the old man and the house. They had unbelievably returned to the unkempt, dilapidated state they were in when Ben first arrived. At that time, he was trying to discover who he was, where he came from, searching for his past and, although he had learned much about life, had experienced things he would prefer to forget, he still didn't know anything about his parentage. He'd arrived at this house with a book in his hand, an empty book save for the address written on the back page.

Old Joe stirred in his chair. He heaved himself up, the ancient rockers creaking more and his old bones seeming to struggle to support him. He shuffled through the room towards the back door. Ben stood and reached out to open it, allowing the sun to shine glaringly through the open doorway. Dazzled by the brightness, Ben was unable to see as the old man slowly, yet with measured pace, descended several stone steps into a garden that had long been neglected, a grave wilderness, a place completely overgrown. Blinded by the brilliance of the setting sun, he followed in the old man's wake, signalling to Elizabeth to wait while he went outside. When he found himself at the bottom of the steps, the old man had gone. Inexplicably, Ben felt no urgency to call out after him. He experienced an unusual calm, a warm glow, an unfamiliar sense of belonging—his rite of passage to a new world. He turned back towards the house and looked up into the sky. The sun had gone and twilight shrouded the room where they had been sitting for... for how long? Ben didn't know.

His thoughts were interrupted by the slow creak, creak, creak of the rocking chair moving gently backwards and forwards, back and forth, slowly and deliberately back and forth, empty save for the flat, lifeless cushions ...and a book. He picked it up and walked slowly to the front of the house. The door was open, open to the world outside where the lights of life shone brightly in the friendly street. He halted in the doorway and smiled at Elizabeth. He couldn't remember when he last felt this way, perhaps when he fell in love with the woman who had become a part of his life and yet now, he felt a wonderful surge of happiness sweeping through his whole being, making him laugh out loud.

Still smiling, Ben remembered the book in his hand. "Outcast," it said, but when he opened it this time, he read out loud to Elizabeth, "A story of real life for my only love, Nan." by Benjamin Mbiti.

The young man was still smiling and tears were glistening in his eyes. "He was my father," he said softly, "He wasn't Old Joe at all. He was Benjamin like me. And Nan really was my mother. I don't understand why he ran away, perhaps I never will, but something tells me I shall find the answers in this book. From now on, I shall stand proud knowing I am their son."

~ * ~

Six months later, Jane found her life changing again. With her novel finally completed, and Ben eventually discovering his past and his love, she edited and perfected the manuscript several times before she requested an appraisal from a reputable literary editor. To her astonishment, he advised her to submit it to the publisher. She was not confident as she knew only too well that first attempts at writing a novel were always rejected. When just less than three months waiting was up, she received a letter which astounded her.

We have found your debut novel delightful and potentially of great commercial value. We would like to offer you a contract with us and look forward to working with you to make your writing a success. Please complete the attached acceptance form and we will begin what we hope will be a long association...

She shared her good fortune with Sally first. Her loyalty to her to daughter was her priority. She had missed her greatly in the past two years and she experienced all of Ben's emotions when she called to tell her the news. Speaking to Sally again was like rediscovering her past.

"Don't cry, Mum," Sally said as she heard Jane sob at the other end of the phone.

Jane took a deep breath to control herself. "I miss you," she said, still choking back the tears. "It has been too long and I have to consider returning to Australia; I just have to."

"When you're ready, Mum; in your own time," Sally told her. "We love you..." But her own tears were preventing her from speaking coherently. "Speak to you again later when we've both had time to digest the enormity of your success."

And what success! Book signings all over the UK, radio interviews, personal appearances and wonder upon wonder, an appearance on the Martin Dashwood *Saturday Night Chat Show*.

"You have certainly appealed to the reading public, Jane," the presenter said when he introduced her as the author of the new best seller, *Finding Ben*.

Jane smiled and tried to keep her nerves in check. "I'm astounded that my work has been so popular and in all honesty, I am still on cloud nine. It's a lot to take in. When I came to the UK, I intended to explore my options as a person as well as a writer. There must be something in the English air that has inspired me, in the Lake District particularly …does that sound cheesy?"

The presenter laughed. "Not at all, but I'm asking the questions, Jane! You write about Ben as though you are inside his head. Is he you, or is he somebody you know?"

"There are a lot of my attitudes in him, but he isn't me. I think he is a pastiche of several people who have crossed my path," she explained.

"Obviously some good, some not so good."

Jane nodded.

"I loved the ending. I never suspected the old guy was a ghost. Where did you get that idea?" Martin probed.

"I wanted the ending to be different, touching on the unbelievable and yet giving Ben the spiritual connection where he might find himself in exploring his past, discovering the present and looking forward to the future," she explained. "Often we don't understand that there may be some sort of inspirational force guiding us in what we choose to do. It is my belief that very little in life can be left to fate. Our destiny is in our own hands. I think Ben represented that."

"He did indeed," Martin said. "Thank you for giving us what is surely one of the best debut novels ever written. What comes next?"

Jane shrugged. "First I go home to Australia to catch up with my family and then perhaps I might be inspired by the Queensland sun to write my next novel. There are lots of ideas floating around in my head. There are characters just waiting to be explored..." She paused poignantly. "...and perhaps exploited." *Richard,* she incredibly thought on live television. *The unconventional, infuriating, intriguingly fascinating Richard.* She smiled appreciatively at her host. "Thank you for having me," she said.

"Our pleasure. Ladies and gentlemen, Jane Peterson." Loud applause faded out that section of the show making way for a group called Sweet Sensation singing the chart hit "If Wishes Came True." Jane couldn't help but smile.

Twenty nine

Jane returned to Coniston after the television appearance. With Alison away at university, she had time to assess her situation and plan her next move. Her ward was settled, so she might relinquish sole responsibility and allow Freddy and Victoria to take over her role. They were in London and much of Alison's training with English Heritage had been based in the capital. When she gained a place at Oxford, nobody was surprised. The girl deserved it.

"I'll never forget what you have done for me, Jane," Alison told her. "Please don't disappear in Australia and lose touch."

"As if I would, Alison!" Jane said affectionately. "I'm expecting you to come to visit me when you finish your degree course. You can bring Jonathan, if you like."

Alison laughed. "We're close, but I don't know where we'll be in three years' time. One day at a time, Jane. We are both intent on getting a first, so no risks are being taken, if you see what I mean."

"I see exactly what you mean, sweetheart. What I know of Jonathan, he's nothing like a certain person in Coniston." She paused briefly as both of the two women recalled the episode with Gary. "I'm serving out the lease on the cottage and then I'll make my plans to go home. Mind you, I'm homeless in Australia at the moment. I'll have to stay with Sally and Bill until I find somewhere to rent, or buy, as the case may be." She said it with a longing she hadn't felt in the past two years. "Your Uncle Freddy has made a studio flat for you in his house in London. I'm sure you'll love it."

"I know I will," Alison agreed. "If you'd asked me eighteen months ago if I'd be living with Uncle Freddy and Victoria, I'd have laughed in your face. Thanks for everything, Jane… oh, and great show on Saturday night. I was so proud of you."

"Out of my comfort zone really, but I didn't do too badly, did I?" Jane said modestly.

"You did a bonzer job," Alison told her in her best Australian accent.

"You just watch it, young lady," Jane said, laughing affectionately.

"What comes next, Jane?"

Jane was pensive. "I wish I had a crystal ball, but I have a few ideas for the next book."

"Anything to do with Ben?" Alison asked. "He was a great character, Jane. I don't know where you found him."

Jane knew exactly from where he came, but admitted to herself she'd had no idea he would have evolved as he did. "To begin with he was me —lost, floundering in the unknown, scared of being alone for the rest of his life, but then he found his strength in the people around him, even though some of them were evil bastards! Sorry, Ali, Australian vernacular."

"You know what, Jane?" Alison interjected. "We British aren't as stuffed shirt as you might believe. Vernaculate as much as you like!" They both laughed heartily. "I just made up a word!" Alison exclaimed excitedly. "Inform the Oxford University Press!"

"Must go, darl," Jane told her. "I'll call next weekend. Be good ...and if you can't be good..."

"Be careful, I know. Bye, pretend mum. Love you."

Jane was taken aback. "Love you too, baby," she said through her tears.

~ * ~

Jane considered flying out to Vancouver to see Brad on her way back to Australia.

"Oh Jane," Brad wailed when she called to inform him of her plans. "Jack and I will be in Russia."

"Russia?" Jane asked in dismay. "What the hell will you be doing in Russia?"

"My editor is sending me on the Solzhenitsyn trail," he explained. "After my article about you, he thinks I have the ability to draw out the best in a writer. I don't think I'll be able to interview the man himself, but who knows, I might get lucky."

"Brad, please don't take any risks. Make sure you're not trespassing, or doing anything illegal," she advised. "We hear such stories these days about journalists in foreign countries."

"Worry not, dear Jane," he reassured her. "I'll do everything right. Jack has a very sensible head on his shoulders; one of the many reasons why I love him."

"That's good," she said. "I'd like to meet him sometime."

"And so you will. We've already discussed a trip to Oz, maybe next year."

Jane was delighted and said so. "I'd better get a shimmy on then and find somewhere to live as soon as I get back," she said excitedly. "Mind you, even though I'm feeling very homesick at the moment, I'm quite nervous about going back. I have to face people whom I upset greatly before I left."

"Water under the bridge, Jane," Brad said with his usual wisdom. "Surely those people will show a modicum of discernment for your situation, especially now that you are a world renowned writer—congratulations on the TV appearance, by the way."

"How do you know about that?" she asked.

"CBC aired it here," he told her. "They have some connection with the BBC. You were…" He paused deliberately. "…AWESOME! That seems to be the in-word over here just now."

Jane laughed. "Thanks, darl, but like I told Alison yesterday, I was way out of my comfort zone."

"How is our ward?" he asked.

"She's great; settled in Oxford, in love again, looking forward to living with Freddy and Victoria during her holidays and…" She paused this time. "…well, I'll miss her terribly, but she'll keep in touch and the world's her oyster. I can't ask for more than that."

~ * ~

She travelled back to Australia via Rome, Athens and Hong Kong. As a completely unseasoned traveller, she decided she ought to see a bit of Europe before she returned to the Antipodes. Rome and Athens in particular provided her with a wealth of experiences she had never previously encountered. In Rome, she connected with a group of English amateur historians who were only too pleased to show her around and give her guided tours of all the famous historical sites. In the midday heat of Athens in August, she climbed the hill to visit the remains of the Acropolis— the Parthenon, sensed the spiritual inspiration from the sacred temple dedicated to the Goddess Athena and paid an extortionate number of drachmas for a glass of ice-cold orange juice when she returned to the foot of the hill. *These guys sure know where the money is to be made,* she thought, as she took a sip of the longed-for drink. *They have sussed out how desperately thirsty we tourists are after that long climb to the top of the hill and back. The wily old devils!*

After a frantic week in the Greek capital, having rejected several dinner invitations from white-shirted, sockless, olive-skinned middle aged men and fighting off persistent shopkeepers who typically lay in wait for tourists such as she, offering jewellery and souvenirs at grossly inflated prices, she flew out to Hong Kong to sample the shopping amongst the bustle of the busy city-state where east meets west. Three days were enough for her and she settled back on the plane that was winging her to the land of her birth. She was grateful that she had nobody sitting next to her and she didn't have to make polite conversation. Butterflies in her stomach were making it impossible to relax, but with the thought of seeing Sally and the children going round and round in her head, she somehow managed to doze on and off until the seat-belt lights went on and the pilot was telling them that they were making their descent into Brisbane airport.

Her luggage seemed to take forever to appear on the carousel, but when she retrieved it, she set off towards the arrivals hall full of excited anticipation at seeing Sally and Bill again. Pushing the trolley laden with two very heavy suitcases, together with precariously balanced plastic bags containing presents for her grandchildren, she eagerly searched the sea of expectant faces for Sally and her family. They weren't there. *Where are they?* she thought with some concern. *I e-mailed the time of the flight before I left Hong Kong.* She looked longingly at the automatic doors, thinking Sally might have miscalculated the time it would take to drive to Brisbane. *Surely they would have driven up from Coffs Harbour the day before and stayed with Mick—I cannot refer to him as Michael by which name he is apparently now known. Sally is usually so organised.* She smiled. *Like me. Why on earth hasn't she planned this better?* She sighed deeply and found a seat so that she might wait in comfort, even though she had been sitting on the plane for eight and a half hours. After half an hour, she decided to call. "Where are you?" she asked when Sally answered.

"At home. Why?"

Jane gasped. "I'm in Brisbane..."

Now it was Sally's turn to gasp. "You're two days early. Why didn't you let me know you were flying in earlier than planned?" she asked, not hiding the irritation in her tone.

"Welcome home, Mum," Jane said, showing that she was the one who should be irritated. "I know I gave you the right date, Sal," she continued. She sighed audibly. "Here I am at Brisbane Airport with nowhere to stay. Don't forget I'm homeless in Australia at the moment."

"I'm sorry, Mum," Sally apologised. "We've clearly messed up here. Could you possibly take the train to the Gold Coast and stay at the Sheraton, or somewhere? How about Hyatt Regency at Sanctuary Cove? Your status should now warrant such luxurious accommodation."

Jane laughed. "I don't think so," she said. "One book doth not a world renowned writer make!" She looked at her watch. "It's only ten-thirty. I'll have morning tea and then book into the Airport Hotel. I don't think I can face a train journey after the trip from Hong Kong." Her mind was busy plotting her next move. "I'll tell you what," she suggested. "I'll stay in Brisbane for a couple of days. I'll enjoy re-familiarising myself with the old place. If I do that, it will give you time to organise yourself. I'll take the train to the Gold Coast on Saturday. Gosh, Sal, it's so good to be back in Australia. I didn't realise just how much I have missed it."

Thirty

By Saturday, Jane had gone through the whole plethora of emotions. At first she was excited to be on home soil, but then being let down by Sally had both disappointed and irritated her. She lay on her bed in the hotel room and quietly seethed over the fact that her only child had not been eager to see her after her long absence. In more sane moments, her thoughts were calm and sensible. *Don't be selfish, Jane,* she chastised herself. *That was the old you; the new you sees other people's points of view. People make mistakes. You should understand that more than most. Maybe Sally simply wrote down the wrong date on her calendar. You've done that yourself on several occasions.*

Having rested and enjoyed the sights and atmosphere of Brisbane for a few days, she sat on the train and watched the Queensland countryside flash by as she travelled back to see her family again. She counted down the stations until she arrived at Nerang, knowing that her family would be waiting on the platform.

Two very enthusiastic children ran along the platform to greet her. "Nanna! Nanna!" they called excitedly.

"My goodness, how you've grown," Jane told them as she hugged and kissed them affectionately.

"I'm eleven, Nan," Jacob said sounding a little too pedantic for an eleven year old, but Jane smiled at the O'Connell trait he had obviously inherited.

"I know, sweetheart, and I'll remember in future that I must treat you as my little man and not my little boy," she said to placate him.

"And will you treat me like a little lady?" Holly asked innocently. "After all, I'm going to be eight next week."

Jane gave Holly an extra hug. "Indeed I shall, Miss Holly." She looked up to see that Sally and Bill had joined them. "Hello, darling," she said to her daughter and as tears coursed down both their faces, they hugged away the time they'd been apart, the regrets of having misjudged each other and silently understood that the bond between mother and child could never be broken in spite of iniquitous influences sometimes clouding their view.

Bill stood by and allowed mother and daughter their moment of reuniting. "Good to have you home," he said to Jane and took over the cases as they walked to the car.

They set off in the direction of Broadbeach amidst the excited chatter of the children who wanted to know what London was like. "Did you see the changing of the guards?" Jacob asked.

"Did you see the Queen?" Holly enquired sweetly. Both she and her brother had researched London online and Jane was delighted. "Did you go to the Tower of London where Anne Boleyn had her head chopped off?" "Could you see the blood?" "Were there wax figures of Prince William and Prince Harry in Madame Tussaud's?" Holly's eyes shone as she mentioned the young princes.

"Holly just loves the Royal Family," Bill explained. "Prince Harry in particular."

"I don't love him," she objected.

"Yes, you do," her brother teased.

"Don't."

"Do."

"Don't,' the little girl insisted and she swung a well-aimed slap across his bare leg.

"Ouch! Just you wait, Holly Mansell," Jacob retaliated. "I'll give you such a…"

"Stop it you two," Sally interrupted. "And keep quiet while I talk to Nanna."

~ * ~

Jane couldn't quite take in what Sally had told her. "Let me get this straight," she said cautiously. "Your father and his new wife have invited me to lunch?" She frowned questioningly. "How weird is that?"

Sally looked directly at Jane. "I think it's very civilised," she said forcefully. "He's moved on and you're happy with your life…"

"Your opinion, Sal," Jane interrupted. "How do you know I'm happy? I can tell you categorically that I'm not happy about having lunch with my ex-husband and the woman he shacked up with almost as soon as I was out of the picture."

Sally glared at her plain-speaking mother. "Please watch what you say," she demanded, albeit in whispered tones. She turned to Bill. "Will you please pull over for a minute, darl? I need to talk to Mum in private."

Bill shrugged, but obeyed anyway.

Once out of the car, Sally continued. "The children don't need to listen to this."

"Sorry, but you gave me no alternative. You put me on the spot in front of the children. Was that a deliberate ploy to prevent me from objecting too strongly?" Jane was becoming stressed. "What were you thinking, Sal? Surely you could see the problems in my accepting an invitation like that."

Sally sighed deeply. "I saw nothing wrong with it since Dad was big enough to extend the invitation to you. I think it was very noble of him..."

"Noble?" Jane questioned. "My guess is he just wants to gloat. How do think that makes me feel?"

Sally was becoming exasperated. "Don't do this, Mum," she pleaded. "Too many broken marriages result in unnecessary alienation from each other. Whether you like it or not, you have been an important part of each other's lives. You are my parents and my children's grandparents. What is wrong with us all being together on family occasions?"

Jane wanted to tell her daughter she was wrong to assume she would be comfortable with the situation, but ... "Put like that, it does seem acceptable, Sal," she conceded, "but in reality it isn't so simple."

Sally pressed her lips firmly together into a very fine line and took hold of her mother's hands. "Please, Mum. Try to understand it from my point of view. I don't want my parents to be at war. There will be many occasions when we need to be together as a family. I can't leave you or Sam out on birthdays for instance..."

"Pardon me for breathing, Sally, but Sam isn't family... if you insist on pushing the family issue..."

"She's Dad's wife!" Sally exclaimed. "She's become an integral part of our family as such. She's very nice and the kids connected with her straight away..."

Jane's spirit seemed to drain from her. *Don't mention connections, Sally,* she thought irrationally. *I know all about connections. You make them and then...*

"They call her Sam, not nanna or gran, just Sam," Sally continued. "What's your problem?"

Jane sighed deeply. "Look, Sal," she said as calmly as she could muster. "I can't say I'm happy about it, but I'll go along with it for now." She couldn't explain further, but silently thought: *This is not like me at all. I feel lost, alienated because I absented myself from the family circle, the family that continued a normal life while I was gone. I can't bear that this Sam person has taken over my role.* Her mind was full of turmoil again. She struggled not to weep. *Don't cry, Jane,* she silently willed herself. *You have to come to terms with the fact that you are a divorcee and you'll have to get used to these situations. You will be alone when others are with their partners, so get over it.* She took a deep breath in order to control her feelings. *Please give me strength to get through this ordeal.*

"Thanks, Mum," Sally said and squeezed Jane's hand. "I know you'll be fine. You're Jane Peterson, author extraordinaire!"

Jane smiled, but her heart was pounding in her chest at hearing her maiden name easily spoken by her daughter. *Alienation confirmed,* she thought sadly. *I am not an O'Connell anymore, so I guess that excludes me from family, by name at least.* Considering that Sally wasn't an O'Connell anymore either didn't enter her head. Try as she might not to be overwhelmed, she inwardly felt lost and was momentarily filled with sadness and regret.

~ * ~

It was a pleasant surprise to see how relaxed Mick was. "How are you, Jane?" he asked when he opened the door of his new house to them.

Jane felt her face flush and hated herself for it. "Good, thanks," she said quietly. "I don't have to call you Michael, do I?"

Mick grinned, the old boyish grin she had fallen in love with all those years ago, but she wasn't affected by it. "No," he said. "That's just Sam's name for me."

"Thank you for inviting me," she offered. "It's a bit weird, though." She detected that Mick looked a trifle uncomfortable, too.

He shrugged. "Sally really wanted us all together," he divulged. "It took me a while to come to terms with it, I must admit. I knew you would feel the same, but she can be very persuasive with her old dad!"

"The little schemer," Jane stated, suddenly aware of Sally's underhandedness. "She didn't tell me that. She allowed me to think I was the one who wasn't far-seeing enough to understand that exes can be together under one roof on occasions. If we are feeling awkward about it, what must your wife think?"

As if on cue, Sam appeared from the kitchen. Mick introduced her to Jane.

"I'm pleased to meet you, Jane—truly," Sam said. "I loved your book…"

Jane was taken aback. "Well, thank you," she said, her voice not hiding the surprise. "I hadn't realised it was in the book stores here. My agent has done well. I haven't been in touch with him while I've been travelling. I'll have to get in touch when I'm settled."

"I borrowed Sally's copy, the one you sent her," Samantha disclosed.

"Oh, I see," Jane said feeling a little slighted that the personally inscribed copy she had sent to Sally had been lent to Samantha, but she endeavoured to smile as they were directed onto Mick's new deck where Jane noted the similarities to the deck she and Mick had designed together. *Things don't change much after all,* she thought smugly.

~ * ~

Lunch was by far easier than she'd imagined. Conversation was light and, wonder upon wonder, Jane felt no animosity towards Mick; indeed, she felt Sam was good for him. He looked younger, fitter and very healthy. *I wore him down,* she thought. *We had drifted apart and I feel no antagonism for him anymore. I don't want to be with him and I don't blame him for moving on. He needs a woman in his life; he's a man, after all!* She dared to smile.

"Penny for your thoughts, Mum," Sally said across the table.

Jane laughed. "They're worth much more than a penny, babe. I was just thinking how happy your dad and Sam look and I'm delighted for them." She looked directly at Mick. "Good luck, Mick. I really am happy for you."

Mick smiled appreciatively. "Thanks," he said and then he looked very coy.

Bill noticed and, in a man to man way, he commented, "That's the look of a bloke who has something important to say, but doesn't quite know how to say it."

Michael looked appealingly at Sam who smiled and nodded slowly. He coughed deliberately. "We have something to tell you," he announced. "We are going to have a baby!"

Thirty-one

"Talk about a conversation stopper," she commented to Sally and Bill when they arrived back in Coffs Harbour. "I'm not so sure how I feel about it."

Bill was openly philosophical. "You really don't have to feel anything about it, Jane. You opted out of Mick's life, so what he does now really is nothing to do with you."

Jane was surprised at Bill's bluntness. "That's true," she admitted, "but it doesn't mean I can't have an opinion. Aren't you concerned that your children will have an auntie or uncle much younger than they are and your wife will have a sibling younger than her own children? It's not..." She was going to say 'not normal,' but thought better of it. *This is a delicate situation and perhaps better left alone for the time being.*

Sally was unusually quiet. "I'm with Mum on this one," she said. "Dad's too old to be having another child. More to the point, Sam is forty-two and having her first baby. It might be very dangerous, not to mention the embarrassment for me and the kids. What is Dad thinking about?"

"Shouldn't you have asked him when he made the announcement if you feel so strongly about it? But I'll go and make sure the children are getting ready for bed," Bill said diplomatically. "They've had a long day."

Jane went to sit by her daughter and took her hand. "How do you really feel, Sal?" she asked.

Sally's response shocked her. "Do you really care how I feel, Mum?" she asked in a way that could only be construed as tactless.

Jane did not hide her shock. "What on earth do you mean?" she asked, equally as forthright as her daughter had been. "How dare you question my feelings for you?"

Sally removed her hand from Jane's. "I dare, because you deserted me without so much as a by your leave…"

"I never deserted you, young lady," Jane replied rather more vehemently than was necessary. "True, we had a difference of opinion, but I never deserted you, darling. And if you want to go back over all that old ground, you misjudged me and refused to accept the truth. Would you still have been bearing the grudge if I hadn't made contact with you when I was in Coniston? I would really prefer you not to uproot all this again!"

Sally began to cry. "I felt abandoned," she admitted through her tears. "You had always been there for me and then suddenly you weren't. I'd put you and Dad on a pedestal as the perfect couple and when he told me you were splitting up, it shattered my world. All that on top of what I saw with you and your tutor forced me to cut myself off from both of you for a while. I felt let down…"

Jane sat motionless and allowed her daughter to unload, to unburden herself of the pent up emotions she had obviously been carrying around for the past three years.

"...I didn't want to believe what I saw, but it was so real, Mum. I'm sorry, so very, very sorry. I should never have misjudged you, but I convinced myself that you had feelings for the man in whose arms I saw you."

Jane's heart sank. *Oh my goodness,* she thought. *How astute is my daughter? I can't tell her she was right. I mustn't admit I think of him even now. He's married, happily married. Didn't he tell me that? Poor kid needs something, someone to reassure her that she was never abandoned.* She took a deep breath. "Sweetheart, there could never be anything between Richard and me so I'm not sure why you felt that way. I know that on the surface it looked like I didn't care about you when I high-tailed it to the UK. It was my way of dealing with the divorce and everything. I had tried discussing it with your father and with Linda, but I got short shrift from them both. I decided that talking to you about it wouldn't help, especially since you weren't feeling too kindly disposed towards me at that time. I'm not trying to exonerate myself. I didn't know how else to cope other than cutting myself off from everybody." She stopped as the lump in her throat was threatening to choke her and tears trickled involuntarily down her cheeks.

Sally wiped away her own tears and said gently, "I understand, Mum. Please don't torture yourself."

"But I need you to know I didn't abandon you. I was pig-headed and selfishly determined to prove to the world that I could make it on my own."

"And you did."

"But I was alone and very lonely on occasions and I didn't like myself for a while," Jane admitted.

Sally breathed deeply. "I felt alone too, especially when Dad told me he was seeing Sam."

"When did that start?" Jane asked, curious to know if her assessment of that situation was well-founded.

Sally's eyes glazed over again. "They never told me when they started seeing each other, but Dad was never around almost as soon as you left. He said he was on the boat a lot and stayed away every weekend. I got the impression he wasn't alone because he let slip a few things like '*we did this and we did that*' so I put two and two together. They must have been together. Oh don't get me wrong, Mum," Sally said firmly. "I was angry with him too and we didn't speak for months after I found out he was seeing Sam. I knew I was wrong about you, but I felt Dad had deceived us all in seeing Sam behind our backs."

"Before I left," Jane concluded.

"I didn't say that," Sally informed her forcefully. "Dad's reasoning was that he only started seeing Sam when your marriage was over. I can't put a date on it."

"You didn't need to, Sal. I know your father and he was away every weekend on the boat even when we were still together. I didn't suspect anything because I just thought he needed to be away from me," Jane explained. "Still, water under the bridge, as my friend Brad would say. I can let it go. What good would it do to rock the boat now? If you'll pardon the pun."

"I'm over it too, but I assure you, he didn't get away lightly. He did a lot of grovelling and soft-soaping before I was prepared to forgive and forget."

Sally smiled, albeit a half smile, but she still looked sad. "The thought of Dad having another child makes me feel lost and abandoned all over again. I know it's silly and a grown woman shouldn't be jealous, but I've never had a sibling, and this whole situation..." She paused to collect her thoughts. "... well, it makes me feel sick. Dad's a grandfather and he's fathered another child..." She stopped again and grimaced.

Jane shrugged. "It'll be good for his ego at least," she said with a grin. "It's not very usual for a woman to have her first child at forty-two and Sam will have to deal with all the ramifications of that, but your dad is not the first middle-aged man to father a child and he won't be the last. Charlie Chaplin was having children until well into his seventies! He fathered twelve children all together, so we can't condemn your dad for having two even if there are thirty years between them."

The two women laughed and the atmosphere lightened. "Thanks so much, Mum," Sally said and hugged her mother closely. "I guess we'll cope so long as I know you'll be around."

Jane looked pensive. *I won't be here forever, babe,* she thought. "Well, we'll think about that later. I won't be cluttering up your spare room for long. I need to find somewhere to live and have my stuff sent over from the Coniston cottage. Freddy and Victoria have allowed me to store it in their garage and will send it when I instruct them to do so. They are such kind people and I only met them by chance."

Sally gave her a hug. "I'm glad you made friends and from what you say about Alison, I'd love to meet her sometime."

"I'm hoping she'll come to visit when she's finished uni. You'll like her and I know Brad is coming next year. He promised."

Sally raised her eyebrows and fixed her mother with a knowing stare.

"What?" Jane asked.

"What about Brad? Did you have a fling with him?" Sally asked as she playfully nudged Jane's arm.

Jane laughed out loud. "Not at all," she said. "Brad and I could never be a couple."

"But you seem to be very close. All your e-mails were full of him," Sally reminded her.

Jane thought for a moment. Brad's sexual preference had never been mentioned and she really hadn't thought it would be significant when she arrived back in Australia. Apart from that, she had no idea what Sally's views were; they had never discussed the topic. "He's gay."

Sally was speechless for a moment. Her jaw dropped and she stood up from the sofa, her arms flailing as if she were about to take flight. Jane just watched in amusement.

When Sally regained her composure, she ventured to ask, "And when did you become so broad-minded, Mum? I can't believe you shared a house with a gay man."

"And why on earth not?" Jane interrupted. "He is one of the kindest and most caring men I know. He was my soul mate and I love him very much..."

"You *love* him?" Sally exclaimed incredulously.

"Yes, there are many different kinds of love, Sally and I love him, like a brother, like a best friend," Jane told her. "I'd trust him with my life."

Sally turned her back on Jane, an act of blatant objection and she continued with her condemnation of a man she did not know, had never met. "You shock me, Mother," she stated with undisguised disdain. "I don't know what has become of you," and she left the room without giving Jane the chance to respond, to explain how Brad had helped her in finding her inner self. She sighed, not out of resignation, but more as a sign of regret that she saw much of her younger self in her daughter.

How can a situation change so quickly? Jane mused. *We were getting along fine and then, bang! One bit of information and Sally went off like a rocket. She is so wilful, so opinionated...* She smiled. *She's me at her age! My goodness, how maturity changes one's views. But I will not let her abuse Brad nor any others I choose as my friends. She will just have to come to terms with the fact that Brad is my dearest friend and I cannot agree with her homophobic views.* Her mind strayed from Brad to Linda as she thought of best friends. *What do I do about Linda?* she silently asked herself. *I'm back in Australia and I haven't spoken to her for three years. That's very sad, so very sad.*

She retired early. It had been a long day and as dinner had been a strained affair, with Bill trying to keep the conversation flowing, she then decided she must find somewhere to live as soon as possible.

Thirty-two

Jane and Sally limped through the next few days and Jane decided it would be best not to mention Brad Courtney again for the time being. Two weeks into her enforced stay with her daughter, she decided she ought to contact Linda and hadn't the slightest idea what her reception would be. Tentatively she dialled the number.

"Linda Johnson," Linda answered cheerily.

Jane took a deep breath. "Linda, it's me, Jane."

Silence.

"Are you there, Lin?" she ventured as she heard a gasp from her friend.

"Yes, I'm here," Linda said, sounding awkward and clearly not overjoyed to hear Jane's voice. "To what do I owe this pleasure?" she asked with a definite hint of sarcasm in her tone.

Jane was determined not to sound upset. "I thought three years was long enough for us both to cool off," she said light-heartedly. "I decided to break the silence. It has to be a record for

"

us, Lin. We never stopped talking for long, even after the biggest of our disagreements."

"Oh, I see," Linda said haughtily. "You thought, did you?"

Jane was taken aback, shocked even by Linda's attitude. "I'm not sure what you are intimating, Linda. We have been friends for a long time and I thought..." She paused to correct her terminology before Linda began to misinterpret her intentions. "...I *understood* that our friendship would last forever. Now I'm confused and not so sure."

Linda was determined to make her point. "When you walked off saying, correction, *shouting* to the world that our friendship meant nothing, forgive me for assuming you wanted nothing more to do with me. You were very cruel, Jane, and being treated like that did absolutely nothing for friendship and yes, three years is a long time. You could have called to apologise, but you didn't." She made it very clear that she had harboured bad feeling since the day they had parted on the beach.

The new Jane was feeling vulnerable, but she felt the need to respond to what Linda had just said. "I know I ought to have done this sooner, Lin, and I'm sorry I left it so long. The longer I left it, the harder it became for me to contact you, but I'm here now. I don't want to upset you anymore. Please forgive me."

"You were very offensive, Jane," Linda continued. "I have thought long and hard during the past three years about what you said and I decided that I had put up with your judgmental ways for far too long. This worm has turned, Jane O'Connell."

Jane felt tears stinging her eyes. "I'm sorry," she said again. "I'm trying to apologise, Lin. I did say some nasty things in the heat of the moment and at the time I think I meant them, but I can only emphasise how sorry I am." She took a deep breath to steady herself. Quietly she asked, "Did you really mean it when you told me you wanted nothing more to do with me unless I sorted out my differences with Mick? I needed a friend's support at that time and rightly, or wrongly, I didn't think you were there for me. Please try to understand, Lin."

"You had an affair behind Mick's back, Jane! I could never support that."

"You are wrong, Linda, very wrong," she said gently. "I told you it wasn't an affair, but you got the wrong end of the stick. I met somebody in Noosa who actually helped me sort out my feelings for Mick, nothing more, nothing less. My life was a mess and, although I hate to say it now, you added to the chaos. I needed you to listen to me even if you didn't like what you were hearing. I reacted as the old Jane always reacted, speaking without thinking. Truly, that is not an excuse; it is fact. I realise now that I shouldn't have spoken as I did."

Linda sighed loudly. "You were always the same, Jane; you were right, everybody else was wrong. Well, I'm over it. A feeble apology for thinking you might have offended me really doesn't cut it. You called and I appreciate that, truly, but I haven't heard a real apology from you for your long silence. Anyway, it's four o'clock and I need to start dinner in time for when Bob gets home..."

Jane shook her head slowly as she smiled to herself. "Oh dear, Lin, I do so want to put all this behind us if we are able," she said. "I really hoped you might see the new me; the Jane Peterson who has been your friend forever."

"I can see what you are doing, Jane, but old wounds don't heal, especially when they fester for months on end," Linda said rather more forcefully than Jane liked.

"I'm trying, Linda," Jane said.

Linda was quick to interrupt. "Yes, you are, Jane, very trying."

"I called to mend fences, but are you telling me they are beyond repair? Hanging on to grudges for so long is not good for the soul," Jane said. Her tone was gentle, calm and appealing.

"And how would you know, Jane?"

"I do know, Lin, because I have spent the last three years in England re-inventing myself and believe me, my dear friend, it wasn't easy" Jane explained calmly and with a composure that belied the nervousness she was feeling inside. "I didn't like myself for a while, but for the record, Mick and I divorced; he's re-married. I haven't, because much as you thought I cheated on him, I had nobody into whose arms I might fall when I was unceremoniously dumped. Please try to understand that. If you feel you can't do it for me, then please think about it for old time's sake, will you?"

She heard Linda sigh. "I've changed too, Jane. I'm not ready to forgive and forget yet. I'm blaming you for this rift that has developed between us. Maybe one day, I might be able to forgive you, but not yet. Your call out of the blue has thrown me and that festering wound is still very raw, but I'll say one thing. If and when we are able to be friends again, I won't tolerate your judgmental views as I used to. You have no idea how hurtful you have been. You have to understand that."

 Jane felt sad. "I understand, Lin, truly I do. I'll look forward to hearing from you when you feel you are able to talk to me."

"I'll think about it, truly I shall, but for now, goodbye, Jane," Linda said with a strength Jane recognised as Linda's confident stand.

"Please don't say goodbye, Lin. Au revoir, please," Jane said and did not hide the pleading in her voice.

Linda had the last word. "Bye, Jane, for now," and then she was gone.

~ * ~

The following Saturday, Jane invited Sally out for lunch. "Please say you'll come for a girls' lunch, Sal. I would like to make amends for the past few weeks' angst."

They found a little fish restaurant by the jetty in Coffs Harbour and sat outside in the shade of the canopy that shielded them from the midday sun. "I missed seafood like this when I was in

England," Jane said as she tucked into her Moreton Bay bugs, prawns and smoked salmon. "In that respect, it's so good to be back."

Her comment wasn't lost on Sally. "Only in that respect?" she asked.

Jane smiled affectionately at her daughter. "Of course not just in that respect," she said gently. "Whatever you have been thinking, I love you with all my heart, but we don't have to share the same views on everything, Sal. It doesn't make you right and me wrong or vice versa. Surely we can respect each other's opinions."

Sally nodded sheepishly.

"Do you mind if I talk for a little while?" Jane asked.

"Not at all," Sally replied. "I think I need to learn how to listen." She grinned at her mum.

"That's my girl," she said, winking cheekily and then in contradictory mood, she continued, "I had the most terrible run-in with Linda the other day."

"So that's why you have been unusually quiet for the past few days," Sally commented. "Bill and I thought we'd done something to upset you ...again."

Jane looked sad. "I think my friendship with Linda is over, finished, done with, kaput," she said. "We fell out before I left for England. Let's face it, I fell out with everybody before I left for England and I never found the courage to speak to her while I was away. When I called a few days ago to break the ice, she made it pretty clear she had harboured grudges for three years and she really doesn't want to accept my apology for upsetting her."

"That doesn't sound like Linda," Sally interrupted.

"I know, but I found it very difficult to get her to listen to what I had to say," Jane continued. "I accept that I upset her and for such I apologised, but she upset me too. Maybe I'm being too sensitive, but it seems my feelings don't count. All I wanted was for her to say we both said things we shouldn't have in the heat of the moment, but she laid all the blame at my door and refuses to forgive and forget. I feel so sad, but the only consolation is that she said she would think about it."

Sally reached across the table and squeezed her mother's hand. "There's no accounting for how people change, Mum. You above all know that."

"Yes I do," Jane agreed, "and sometimes to my detriment, but it looks like Linda and I are going to find it difficult to be friends again."

Sally smiled. "I don't want to sound trite, but there's plenty more fish in the sea. You have other friends who won't be so judgemental, I'm sure."

Jane had to laugh. "Please don't use clichés, Sal. They were a real bone of contention between your dad and me when we could do nothing but find fault with each other. Your dad hated me for throwing hackneyed phrases at him to make my point. I got to the stage where I thought my life would be one big cliché unless I took..." She paused and giggled girlishly before she continued, "...unless I took the bull by the horns and let's face it, nothing ventured, nothing gained!"

Both women relaxed and laughed; friendly, loving, cheerful expressions of their closeness again.

As they walked along the jetty to see the day's catch being hauled in by the fishermen, they chatted happily about anything and everything. Telling Sally about the cottage in Coniston and hilariously and graphically describing the night the burly policeman knocked on the door, she suddenly announced, "I'm going house hunting tomorrow."

Sally wasn't surprised. "I knew you would tell me that sometime, but there's no rush, you know."

"I know that, but I won't outstay my welcome and I have to acknowledge the fact that Bill has been very patient having his mother-in-law under his feet for the past few weeks," Jane told her. "You need your space and so do I. I need to get on with my new book. I have so many ideas running riot inside my head."

Sally was delighted about that news. "Wow! My mum a famous author!" she exclaimed. "I'm so proud of you and I never did tell you how much I loved *Finding Ben*. That was very remiss of me and you never asked. The ending really made me think and I like a conundrum at the end of a good book."

"Thanks, Sal. That means more to me than any critique I have received so far."

"I recognised a lot of you in Ben and Elizabeth, but they aren't you at all in many other respects. That's bloody good writing, if I may say so." Sally linked her arm through Jane's as they walked along.

Jane thrilled at Sally's action. She chose her words carefully. "I'm going to live in Noosa," she stated quite categorically.

"Noosa?"

Jane nodded. "I found my haven up there on the Sunshine Coast. I can relax more there than in any other place..." She paused significantly. "...Well, perhaps not more than in Bracken Cottage, because that place was heaven on earth, but Noosa played a very important part in helping me to understand where I was going and what I wanted in life." She paused again as she thought of Richard. *He certainly helped, but he's gone now. He must be somewhere in London annoying his wife and driving her to distraction.* She smiled and sighed.

"A penny for them, Mum," Sally said. "You were miles away."

"Not many miles, Sal, but on my travels I met so many people who have been significant in helping me re-invent myself. I'll never meet some of them again, but I shall be eternally grateful to them." Her thoughts wandered again as they drove back to Sally's house. *How can I ever forget those people? Freddy who was really George; Bruce the country singer; even Barbara who helped me find a place to rent and also Freddy (the real one) and*

Victoria. I shall be forever in their debt, all of them in varying degrees. In his own typical unconventional way, Richard played his intrusive, infuriating part too in making me see where my future lay, but my undying love and affection will always be for Brad and Alison. They found me and I truly found myself.

Thirty-three

Her return to Noosa was a soul-searching affair. She drove her new car for the first time and once more felt her independence kick in. Being beholden to others for transport was alien to her, so when she invested her first pay cheque from the sales of *Finding Ben* in a brand new Mazda Miata, she knew she was making a statement. The drive to Noosa brought back memories of when she ran away in search of new beginnings. She had tasted the first signs of freedom then, but didn't find what she was looking for at the time.

Her heart to heart with Sally re-established the closeness of mother and daughter. *I needed that,* she reassured herself as she drove along the Bruce Highway, the top of the Miata down and the summer breeze blowing through her hair. *I love Sally and Bill and the children, but I couldn't live with them forever. I felt like I was an intruder. I know it was an intrusion of their privacy although they were too polite to say so. There's absolutely no way I would have wanted my mother living with me. I'm sure that's true of anybody, even though there is a lot of love between mother and child.* She giggled cheekily. *How on earth can they make love with a mother* cum *mother-in-law in the next room? Yes indeedy, my presence was an intrusion.*

When she thought of Mick and Samantha and the baby, she knew she had to find a place away from the Gold Coast. *I bear them no hard feelings and I wish them good luck; they'll sure need it with a new baby at their age, but I don't particularly want to be a part of their life, in spite of Sally's bold efforts to encourage her father and me to tolerate each other on family occasions. That's what it would be; toleration of each other. We don't belong together; we ran our course and it's best we live our lives completely separately. I don't want to be cooing over a baby in a pram if I should bump into them on Broadbeach Mall.* She smiled again. *Maybe when Jacob and Holly get married, we'll cope with being in the same place at the same time, but...* She sighed. *...not on a regular basis.*

Her quarrel with Linda still haunted her. *We have been friends for almost fifty years. How on earth can she throw away all that because of a difference of opinion? I miss her; I'm going to miss her for as long as I live, but she has to think about her own feelings. I can't tell her what to do. I thought maturity made us more tolerant of others, but with so much hatred in her heart for what happened between us, she'll find it difficult to think kindly of me. Opinionated though it might appear, it seems Linda hasn't yet reached that stage of maturity where she can forgive and forget. Hatred is such a powerful word and in spite of what she feels about me at the moment, I don't hate her. I just feel very sad that she is unable to view the situation with more understanding.*

Suddenly she felt very lonely. *I need to settle down in one place and make new friends, but first I need to find myself somewhere to live.*

~ * ~

To her delight, she discovered that a developer had bought Eden Sands with a view to extending some of the chalets at the far end of the resort and selling them as residential units. The resort would still accommodate tourists, but residents would have the security and privacy awarded by a gated community.

Her unit was right at the edge of Eden Sands, a stone's throw from the coastal path and the inlet she had adopted as her refuge before the sand castle builders had shattered her peace when she first came to Noosa. All that seemed a million years ago. Settling in with her belongings shipped from the UK and the buying of new contemporary furniture befitting the modern design of the unit, she began her new life with enthusiasm. With her new, sophisticated computer given pride of place in her office with views across the bay, she renewed her online friendships with her ex-colleagues and she wrote regularly to Brad and Alison. She joined social groups with the Eden Sands community: a book club, trivia nights and taking her turn to entertain her new circle of friends, which was both stimulating and great fun. Then she began her new novel, *Dare to Dream*. She knew the beginning and the end even though she wasn't quite sure what would happen in between. She was heartened by the fact that Ben had evolved in a similar way and she set about her task with great enthusiasm...

"What we need is a bit of magic in our lives," Aileen *announced dreamily.*

"I don't believe in magic," Belle stated caustically. "Fate perhaps ,but not magic. For goodness sake, Aileen, grow up. You can't honestly think that by waving a magic wand, all your troubles will disappear."

Aileen looked round the austere dormitory, remembering her friend's withering look as she delivered those scathing comments. "I just wish something good would happen," she thought. She stared through the darkness at the damp patches on the ceiling, the worn carpet on the floor and the rickety bed upon which she tried to sleep each night. "Does it always have to be like this?" she asked herself and she shivered as she pulled the paper thin doona up to her chin.

Aileen had grown up in that building and it was a place she refused to call home. Giving it that name would be admitting she was happy there and nothing was farther from the truth. She had never experienced happiness, as far as she knew. She supposed she should be happy to be alive, but that was too much to ask. The miserable, dank surroundings did nothing to lift her spirits and her housemates merely existed without hope, or ambition. Few, if any, of those around her had ever smiled, let alone giggled merrily like the girls she'd seen in the park when they were on their regimented weekly walk. She often wondered what it would be like to feel her belly jiggle with laughter, or have her sides ache through laughing too much. During all those years, the nearest Aileen had come to a smile was a snigger when the dormitory sergeant had tripped over somebody's shoes as she inspected the dorm one morning. She hadn't dared to laugh, because the consequences would have been unbearable, though the situation had given her a hint inside her stomach of what it might be like to laugh. Belle had been her only friend there and together they had survived their years in the State-run orphanage until they were sixteen and deemed capable of living on their own...

~ * ~

It was after one of her dinner parties when she had said goodnight to her guests and closed the door on the outside world that she returned to her lounge room and found James still sitting on her sofa and, she observed, looking very much at ease.

"Oh," she said not hiding her surprise. "I thought you'd left with the others."

"You know what thought did," James stated with an arrogance Jane hadn't noticed previously.

"Only thought he did," she quipped to maintain the upper hand.

James grinned. "You have all the answers, don't you, Jane?"

"Not all of them," she admitted, "but I'm always willing to learn. What are you doing here when everybody else has left?"

James shrugged. "I thought we might get to know each other a little better, on a more personal level."

Jane was quick to respond. "You *thought,* did you?" she asked pointedly. "Well, as you reminded me, you know what thought did."

"Touché, Jane," he replied. "I like a woman who thinks on her feet."

Jane didn't like his attitude at all. "I have to ask you to leave, James. Dinner did not include afters in addition to the dessert I served. I am tired and need to go to bed." As soon as the words were out of her mouth, she regretted them. *You idiot, Jane,* she silently admonished herself.

James jumped in with both feet. "I could join you," he suggested. "We are both consenting adults."

"I'm not consenting to anything, James. Now please go home before this turns nasty."

James stood up and forced Jane to take a step back to avoid his closeness, but he grabbed her arm and said, "Don't play the innocent with me. You are a divorced woman and obviously going short in the bedroom. I could fill that need for you and you know you want it." His face was so close to hers that she could smell the whisky on his breath.

She wrenched her arm free and moved quickly to open the door. Holding it wide, she said as loudly as she might without shouting, "Leave!"

James smiled sickeningly. "All right, Ms Peterson, I'll leave and allow you to go one step farther towards being a frustrated, lonely, old maid. Perhaps you will realise eventually that I was the best offer you'll ever get."

"Over my dead body, James," she said confidently. "And please don't expect another invitation from me and I shall make sure our friends know about this."

"They won't listen to you," James offered. "All the men think you're a stuck up cow anyway."

"Goodnight, James," she said forcefully as she helped him on his way with a gentle push and she closed the door with a flourish.

Phew! she thought as she returned to the lounge room and flopped into her favourite chair. *Is that really what the men think of me, I wonder?* She shrugged. *Their problem, not mine. James had had too much to drink, but I won't be asking him to dinner again in a hurry. Maybe he does need a woman— typical man being ruled by what's in his pants.* She sighed deeply. *Time for bed, Jane.* She smiled to herself. *Alone and happy with it.*

Thirty-four

Nobody threw a dinner party for a while after Jane's contretemps with James. There had been several barbecues in the resort, open to everybody, and Jane had gone to a couple. The first time she felt she was being watched all evening by the dishonourable James, but Connie told her not to worry and pointed out that he was eyeing up a group of younger, raucous women who appeared to be the worse for the drinks they had consumed.

"Maybe they won't be so fussy who they take up with," Connie said with a grin. "I can't believe we didn't see that side of him before."

Jane smiled weakly. "He was smart, I'll give him that," she conceded. "I actually felt sorry for him when he told us his wife had passed away."

Connie took hold of Jane's arm and whispered in her ear. "My Danny told me James was never married. He said it was a ploy James used to get women interested."

Jane gasped. "I met somebody like him in London. I should have been more astute." She sighed and looked around at all the couples in her circle of friends and realised poignantly that she was the only one without a partner. "I think I'll call it a night," she said. "See you at the trivia night on Tuesday."

"You don't have to go so soon, Jane. Stay a while longer and Danny and I will walk you home," Connie suggested.

"No thanks, Connie," she said quietly. "I've had enough for tonight."

Once home, she kicked off her shoes and switched on the television. "Movie time, I guess," she said out loud, but she felt sad, sadder than she had felt for a long time. *Seeing everybody with a partner tonight really got to me,* she thought miserably and stared round her lounge room as if searching for something that would ease her pain. *I'm alone and I'm lonely. I'm not going to put myself in a situation again where I'm the only woman without a partner. I feel like a spare part; I don't belong to anybody and it hurts.* Tears trickled down her cheeks as she watched Deborah Kerr and Cary Grant in *An Affair to Remember.* Her thoughts were confused. *That must surely be one of the most beautiful romance stories ever told. I thought I might survive on my own; I know I can survive on my own, but oh how I miss...* She stopped abruptly and said out loud, "Don't go down that road, Jane. Just go to bed and you'll feel better in the morning."

~ * ~

The next few months she spent working on *Dare To Dream* and found it cathartic in allowing Aileen to follow her heart against the wishes of her best friend and, in spite of the disapproval she was forced to suffer from less ambitious individuals, Aileen was pulling through. Jane made a conscious decision to refuse dinner invitations when the entertaining season began again.

"But James won't be there, Jane," Connie told her. "Please come. There will only be three couples..."

"That's just it, Connie. Three couples," she explained. "I feel awkward and it upsets me so I really can't see the point of putting myself through that."

"But it's us, Jane. We are your friends and we like your company."

"And I like your company too, but I hate being a woman alone amongst couples. A ladies' lunch is fine because there are no partners there, but sitting at a table when you all have a man by your side is just too much for me."

"You can borrow Danny; I don't mind," Connie said in an effort to persuade Jane to join them.

"Thanks, but no thanks, Connie. I'll be happier at home with my music and my TV and don't forget, I'm totally absorbed in my next novel, so I won't have time to be sad."

The winter nights were long and cold, but Jane immersed herself in doing the things with which she was most comfortable. During the day, she would walk along the headland avoiding the little sanctuary where she had met Richard. She deliberately did a u-turn before she reached the canopy of honeysuckle and jasmine she had so liked before. Now it looked dense and overgrown, untended, unloved. It seemed nobody had bothered to go there for the past few years.

On that particular morning, she decided she might just venture farther along the path to see what it was really like. *It can't do any harm,* she thought, and marvelled at how positive she was feeling. *Perhaps I can restore it to its former glory. It can be my project and it will certainly get me out of the house.* She was shocked to see the state it was in when she arrived. It was totally blocked off with overgrown weeds among what was left of the honeysuckle and jasmine that needed a strong pair of shears to tame them. The picnic table had gone and there was litter strewn everywhere: beer bottles, cola cans, chip packets, cigarette packets and plastic bags. *How sad,* she thought. *My memories of that place have been shattered in the space of a few seconds. Maybe that's what I needed. It finally lays the memory of Richard to rest.* The significance of the situation was not lost on her. *That's it then. Skeletons out of cupboard; ghosts exorcised.* She returned home and set about solving Aileen's dilemma in *Dare To Dream.*

~ * ~

For four years, they had been out in the big, wide world and living one day at a time.

"Belle?" she asked her friend as they sat huddled under the bridge trying to shelter from the torrential rain that had suddenly hit the country town where they hoped to find work. "Do you ever dream of a better life?"

Belle tutted. "No," she snapped. "How can people like us have a better life? We started off with nothing; we'll finish up with nothing."

"But even though we have nothing, we can dream," Aileen told her.

"Dreamers live in a fantasy world, Aileen, not the real world. We have to survive. We were put on this earth to scratch and scrape a living. We don't even know where we came from and who cares? I'll tell you who—nobody. We are twenty years old; at least we think we are. It's time you came down to earth, Aileen. Accept your lot with good grace," Belle urged. "Don't chase after the impossible."

When the telephone rang, it took her by surprise since she had unplugged the phone in order to cut herself off from everybody. "Hello. Jane Peterson here."

"Mum! Where on earth have you been? Your phone was just ringing out; you haven't picked up your e-mails; what's happening?"

"Hi Sal," Jane said. "Sorry, but I needed my space for a while."

"A while?" Sally asked in dismay. "A month is a lifetime when you are trying to contact somebody and you have no idea what's going on. Are you all right? We were all set to come up to Noosa and track you down if you hadn't answered your phone this time."

"You know you are always welcome, Sal, but don't just turn up. Give me warning so I can air the beds and do the washing up!" she joked.

"Ha ha, Mum. That's very funny, especially since the dishwasher does the washing up for you. We'll wait until the summer and then come and spend the holidays with you. We could always leave Jacob and Holly with you for the whole of the summer!"

"Whoa there, girl!' Jane interrupted.

"Just joking. I don't think they'd leave their friends for so long, and anyway, Jake's got a girlfriend. She's so cute!"

"I hope Bill has done the birds and the bees talk," Jane said seriously. "A thirteen-year-old's hormones can be pretty erratic."

"Stop worrying, Mum. It's all good," Sally told her. "Now that I know you are all right, I'll ring off. And check your e-mails. You must have hundreds in your inbox if you haven't opened them for four weeks."

"Okay, Sal, will do and thanks for calling."

She did Sally's bidding immediately and she did indeed have two hundred and fifty seven e-mails clogging up her inbox. Most were rubbish which she deleted without opening. Sally had e-mailed every day for a week and there was a strange one from Southport TAFE.

"I wonder what this is about," she mused and opened it to see why TAFE would contact her. She had given them her e-mail address when she did the fateful course so she wasn't confused on that score. She found a list of upcoming courses and the tutors who were involved. Her curiosity got the better of her. She scanned down the list for Information Technology and read: *Make a Home Business Work – Lucas Adams.*

Practical Home Projects – Helen Mary Hopwood

Computing for Beginners – Ric...

Her heart skipped a beat...

Computing for Beginners – Ricardo Giuliano

Disappointment overwhelmed her and for a moment she wanted to cry, but her telephone rang again and forced her out of her melancholy mood.

"Jane Peterson," she said.

"Jane, it's me, Connie."

"Hi Connie, good to hear from you. How are you?" she asked, as cheerily as possible.

Connie took a deep breath which Jane heard on the other end of the phone.

"Goodness, Connie," she said. "That was a deep one."

"I know," her friend replied. "It's just that I want to say this properly. We are having a dinner party on Saturday for an old friend of Danny's and wondered if you would come to make up the numbers. His name is Luke and he's on his own."

Jane sighed. "You're not trying to set me up, are you? If you have any ideas on those lines, forget it."

"Oh no, nothing like that. He is a nice guy, though, so please Jane, will you come? I do so want to make him feel welcome. Danny hasn't seen him since they left uni and he called out of the blue last weekend to say he'll be in Noosa for a few days. He's flying up from Melbourne on Saturday morning."

~ * ~

The day of the dinner party came too quickly for Jane, but she made sure she was busy during the day so as not to stress about what was in store. She spent the day writing. She liked her character, Aileen, and she wanted the girl's ambitions to be realised.

Aileen fell silent. She pulled her coat round her and looked sadly at Belle who had turned her back on the rain that was intermittently blowing under the bridge on the restless wind.

"Come on, Aileen," she said. "We're wet through already, so going out in the rain isn't going to make much difference, is it? The place can't be far from here."

Aileen remained silent, but followed her friend, both girls facing whatever the future held as the wind drove the icy spray into their faces. With heads down to combat the storm, they trudged along the dirt road to find the place named in the advertisement they'd seen in a shop window. 'Fruit pickers wanted for immediate start. Bunkhouse available.'

"My goodness," the portly woman exclaimed. "There doesn't seem to be much beef on the pair of you. Are you sure you're capable of lugging heavy fruit baskets? You're like a pair o' whippets and that's a fact."

"Wiry and fast," Belle told her, bristling at the woman's observations. "That's what whippets are. We're up for it, Missis. You just see if we aren't."

"And what about you, missy?" the woman asked Aileen. "You haven't so much to say as your friend here. Cat got your tongue, has it?"

"I'm as strong as she is," Aileen said defensively. "Please give us a try."

"Well, you've a few more manners than she has, I'll say that, but the pair of you look like drowned rats, so you do. Go over to the bunkhouse and dry yourselves out, then come to the house. We'll discuss the job then. I'll have a pot of tea ready and bite to eat."

"Does that mean we're hired then?" Belle asked without ceremony.

"It means I'm thinking about it," the woman told her pointedly.

"Thank you,' Aileen said quietly and Belle tugged her arm to lead her away before the older woman changed her mind.

"Why don't you stick up for yourself a bit more?" she asked Aileen as they changed and dried their wet clothes on the stove *in the bunkhouse. It was a wooden building, not much bigger than a garden shed, but it housed four bunks, a tiny kitchen and an even tinier bathroom. It was Spartan, but warm. There were no signs of any other people so they assumed they were the only hired help available.*

"I don't need to stick up for myself with you around," Aileen replied, "And anyway, it doesn't cost anything to be polite, does it?"

Belle's hackles were rising. "Polite doesn't get results, Aileen. People will think you're timid and weak. You need to show them you're strong. These folks expect us to be rough and ready. It's them and us. Them as have will always have. Them as haven't, never will have. It's the law of the jungle. Surely you have learned that by now.'

Aileen sighed. She loved Belle, but sometimes she didn't like her. She was the nearest thing she had to a sister, but it was obvious they were different, so very different. She chose not to reply.

By the time their clothes were dry, the rain had stopped and the sun was trying to break through the wispy clouds that had been left behind. They ambled across to the farmhouse where they discovered the woman laying the kitchen table for tea. "Come on in," she said. "I'm Mrs Fenton. Fenton's Fruit Farm. My husband's at the market today, but he'll be back later. The kettle's just boiled. Sit yourselves down and we'll discuss what's on offer."

Aileen whispered, "Thank you," but winced as Belle nudged her sharply in the ribs with her elbow.

"What did I tell you?" she hissed. "Don't be so polite and timid."

Aileen glared at Belle as she took her seat at the table. This is what she had always dreamed. To be in a warm kitchen, sitting round a table with a blue and white gingham cloth, fine white crockery set for a family and being fed little ham and cheese sandwiches whilst hot tea in large cups sent steam drifting up into the air. The nearest she had been to that was in the place where she grew up, but there the long trestle table had been bare and the benches alongside had been rickety and uncomfortable. They'd had a tin cup and plate and had to collect whatever food was provided from a serving hatch at the end of the room presided over by a menacing kitchen hand whose steely stare could have curdled milk. The farmhouse kitchen made her feel warm inside. Oh how she wished Belle would have these dreams too.

"And who are you?" Mrs Fenton asked.

"I'm Belle and that's Aileen."

Mrs Fenton smiled, thinking that the names should have been the other way round. "Well, hello Aileen and Belle," she greeted them, this time in a more friendly way. "Now then, let's see what we can do for you."

Three months later, the harvesting was complete and it was time for the girls to move on. They had managed to earn enough money to see them through the next few months should they not find work. They'd worked hard, eaten well in the farmhouse kitchen and they both felt much healthier than they had when they arrived on Mrs Fenton's doorstep, wet, bedraggled and penniless. "Mind how you go," the friendly woman said as they left. They hadn't a lot to say for themselves, but she'd warmed to them, to Aileen in particular.

What do you care? Belle thought, her expression less than friendly again.

"Thank you, Mrs Fenton," Aileen replied. "We will," and she waved to the lady who had shown them such kindness during the past few weeks, kindness to which they were so unaccustomed.

"God bless you, Aileen," Mrs Fenton said quietly and then under her breath, "Don't let that one lead you astray."

At five o'clock she decided to escape her fantasy world and face reality. *I need to shower, do my hair and make-up and decide what to wear.* She sighed. *Maybe I should just go in jeans and runners. I really don't feel like dressing up for a complete stranger.* She smiled. *I'm over dinner parties; I'm over socialising for the sake of it.* Then out loud, "I'm over men!" Later as she stood in the shower allowing the warm water to flow over her body, she began to relax. *You are becoming a right old grump, Jane. Just get over yourself and be more gracious in the fact that you have friends who care. Connie has been nothing but supportive of you. The least you can do is help her out and try to make her evening a success. It will do no harm to be sociable for a few hours.* She determined that she would enjoy herself. *Have a bit of Aileen's enthusiasm for life and dare to dream,* she thought with new resolve.

At six-thirty she was ready to go. Her chestnut hair, remarkably still her natural colour, shone in the glow of the evening sun. Her make-up was flawless and she had chosen a pale blue silk wrap-around dress that hugged her figure which she had managed to keep under control during her advancing maturity. She felt good and with that came renewed confidence. Connie lived just outside the resort on Noosa Parade and not too far to walk providing she was wearing the right shoes. Her antique silver sandals were perfect—low heels, sling backs and most importantly, very comfortable. Grabbing her evening purse and a light sweater in case the spring chill came in later, she set off for the leisurely stroll to Connie's house.

She arrived just before seven and noted there was only one car on the drive. Tentatively, she knocked on the door. "I hope I'm not the first to arrive," she told Danny as he welcomed her.

"No, we're all here," Danny said with a smile. "You look lovely, Jane."

"Thank you, Danny," she said returning his smile.

Connie came out of the kitchen and thrust a glass of red wine into her hand. "Gives the hands something to do," she said with a wink.

"Thanks," Jane whispered and walked confidently into the lounge room where the other guests were assembled.

The men were all looking out on to the garden and collectively admiring Danny's water feature forming the centrepiece of an immaculate lawn and didn't turn immediately. The ladies all welcomed her with smiles and greetings of, "Hi Jane, how are you?"

One gentleman, the guest of honour, Luke, turned round to see who had just arrived.

Jane stared incredulously at him. *This has to be a joke,* she silently acknowledged without openly disclosing her innermost thoughts.

Thirty-five

How she got through that dinner making polite conversation she would never understand. Luke sat to her left between herself and Connie. He chatted amiably to them both and often to the other dinner guests too. In fact, as dinner parties go, it couldn't have been better, but Jane's heart was beating wildly in her chest and often she thought he might have detected the shortness of breath, as she endeavoured to keep the conversation light and entertaining. If he did suspect anything, he didn't make it obvious.

After a delightful meal and wonderful after dinner drinks, guests began to leave and Luke had a quick word with his host. "Danny, I'll walk Jane home, if that's all right with you," he said.

Danny gave his long time mate a knowing look.

"Don't go getting ideas," Luke told him. "I'm just doing the chivalrous thing."

Jane prepared to leave alone. "Thank you so much, Connie and Danny. It has been a lovely evening. Goodnight and see you on Monday as usual."

"Just a moment, Jane," Luke called. "I'll walk you home."

Jane was surprised, since he hadn't made any special effort to speak to her alone all evening. "There really is no need," she told him.

"Not a need, but a desire," he said in typical manner.

Once outside the house and with the door closed behind them, she confronted him. "What the hell is going on?"

"Jane, Jane, Jane," he said. "I thought you had mellowed, especially since you went along with our little charade all evening."

"Don't start all that again, Richard..." She halted abruptly. "Or is it Paul? Or, holy cow, are you now Luke? Give me a break, will you? I'm beginning to think I'm going mad!"

"No, you're not going mad," he assured her. "I do tend to have that effect on people, as you well know."

He placed his arm across her shoulders and steered her gently towards the coastal path they had both frequently used years before. Jane didn't object. She needed the time and the fresh air to help calm her nerves. "What are you doing?" she asked again.

"Sh-sh," he instructed. "Let's just walk for a little while."

When they arrived at the picnic spot where they had first met, she noticed that the bench had returned. "I found the old bench at the far end of the path this afternoon. It's a bit more rickety than it used to be, but I think it will hold us," he told her. "The old place seemed unloved without it."

"That's what I thought," she said. "I tried to cut back some of the weeds yesterday."

"Let's sit down," he invited. "We need to talk."

"Wouldn't that be a little too conventional?" she asked.

"What do you mean?" he asked indignantly.

Jane laughed nervously. "You don't live by the rules of convention," she reminded him. "Talking is what ordinary people do and I would hardly consider you ordinary. You still make me feel very uncomfortable."

"You are getting defensive again, Jane."

"I am not," she objected. "And anyway, I think you owe me an explanation. Why the change of name again, and don't give me all that claptrap about being a different person to suit whatever you are doing. What a load of pretentious bull!" She was suddenly fired up and determined to get answers.

"My, my, Mrs O'Connell…"

Jane was growing more perturbed by the minute and knew she was in danger of allowing the old Jane to surface. "I have not been Mrs O'Connell for the past five years, not that you'd know anything about that," she informed him pointedly. "I am Jane Peterson."

"No!" he exclaimed. "The woman who had a bestseller at the first attempt? I don't believe it!"

"Well, there you go," she said, more calmly. "Have you read it?"

He looked sheepish. "Actually, no, but I shall now I know who wrote it. Am I in it?" he asked cheekily.

Jane sighed. "Well, if I'm honest, you may well be in there—not really you, but some of your bumptious attitude. I thought of you often when I was in London and in the Lake District."

"You were in London?" he asked incredulously.

Jane nodded. "For a little while, until I got fed up of life in the fast lane."

"I wish I'd known," he said wistfully, a trait Jane had never detected in him. "I needed a friend when I was there."

Suddenly she saw vulnerability in this man, a characteristic she would never previously have attributed to him. "Please tell me," she urged.

"I'm Lucas Adams," he admitted. "That's my real name; not Richard, not Paul Clemens."

"How did you get a job at TAFE under a pseudonym?" she asked.

"I obtained the position under my real name, Lucas Adams, but I asked that I might be known as Paul Clemens at that time. And before you say it, it was childish, immature and ridiculous. It was my way of hiding the real me. I was having an identity crisis, I guess. My wife had high-tailed it to London giving me an ultimatum. I could either follow her, or apply for a divorce."

"But you told me you were happily married," Jane said indignantly.

"I did and at that time I hoped I still had a loving wife. I knew you were unhappy..."

Jane nodded knowingly and Luke continued. "I didn't want to acknowledge the connection you and I had. It was so strong and in order to avoid having an affair, I treated you with undisguised arrogance and disrespect. I'm sorry, Jane."

Jane felt the tears filling her eyes. "You have no idea of the turmoil you created for me," she told him. "I wasn't ready to have an affair either, but I knew my marriage was over. I tried to hold on to it, but it didn't work out. I ran away to London; didn't like myself for a while, but then I met some wonderful people in the Lake District who unwittingly helped me re-establish myself as a human being again—well Brad and Alison together with my main character, Ben, who set out to find out where he came from and discover where he belonged." She sighed deeply. "All the time you kept creeping into my mind; messing with my head. You infuriated me, confused me and left me completely ill-at-ease. I continually told myself you were married and unavailable. To a point, that seemed to work."

He drew her close and kissed the top of her head. "Poor Jane," he whispered. "I'm sorry. I won't ever treat you so abominably again."

"What happened to your wife?"

"When I told you I was going to be with her in London, it was true," he said. "When I arrived there, I discovered she was living with a colleague from LSE—London School of Economics—a woman. She didn't want me at all. She more or less told me to go back to Australia as soon as I had got there. I had no idea a person could change her sexual preference on a whim. She had been so..." He paused to choose his words carefully. "She had been madly in love with me when we met, completely heterosexual, mad for it, if you'll pardon the expression."

Jane shook her head sadly. "I'm sorry," she told him. "I can't imagine how you must have felt." She felt her heart go out to him. "Can you and I start again, do you think, Luke?"

He cupped her face in his hands and kissed her lips gently. "Does that answer your question?" he asked.

She nodded and smiled. "Please don't walk away from me again," she pleaded.

"I won't. I promise." He kissed her again, this time with the tenderness and affection Jane had felt when he kissed her all those years ago. "Come on," he said. "Let me take you home."

Meet
Vera Berry-Burrows

Vera Berry-Burrows is a UK-born former teacher of English Language and Literature, living in Queensland, Australia with journalist husband, Alan. She has a son and two grandsons living in the UK. She has been writing for a number of years and has had numerous non-fiction articles published in the UK and in Australia. She was educated at Farnworth Grammar School in Lancashire, trained as a teacher at St Katharine's College, Liverpool and gained a Bachelor of Arts degree with the Open University.

Since she took early retirement in 1994 having been in the teaching profession for thirty one years, writing has become her compulsive hobby. CONNECTIONS is her third published novel.

Works by Vera Berry Burrows

Tomorrow Never Comes - Marriage, a new home and a new baby, Joel Thomas, all make up a perfect life for Nell Winston until suddenly her husband is no longer there and she turns into a woman possessed of compulsion to rule her son. Her strength is drawn from her unwavering sense to control until the young Joel decides to make a stand against her. Her domineering, self-absorption, along with egotistical stubbornness, takes her into a life that becomes her worst nightmare.

Joel's apparently selfish show of independence leads him along an extremely rocky road to eventual success in the Swinging 60's and with a complete reversal of roles, he takes charge of his mother's life. Will the new start in a different country bring the fulfillment they are both seeking?

Regarding Kimberley - Show business executive Kimberley Mason always felt something was missing from her life. She forms an association with a theatrical agency in Australia and uncovers a secret kept by her parents for thirty years. Revelations about her birth shatter her world. Discovering her real father is Australian television celebrity Joel Winston, she cuts herself off from the family she had always thought to be perfect

Leaving behind her past in England, she moves to Australia to be with the man she loves, her business partner, Simon Obertelli. Will running away ensure her future happiness or will the complications of accepting her famous father only lead to heartache?

Connections - Jane O'Connell did not envisage that her early retirement would completely disrupt her life. With too much time on her hands, she finds it difficult to adjust to her new existence. In her obstinate selfishness, she alienates herself from her family and friends. Running away from all things familiar appears to be her only option, but is it? Will the connections she makes really solve the problems she encounters in her life after work?

Family Matters - For three children left without a mother in the middle of World War Two, survival was all they could hope for. Their father struggled as a single parent, but instilled into his children, determination, ambition and self-respect so that they might succeed in post-war years and achieve everything which he was denied during his life.

This is their story.

My Name is Aphrodite - Rodi Bartlett sits on a plane taking her to the land of her conception. She can't call it the land of her birth because when her mother was sixteen years old, she had flown back to England from Corfu at the end of two weeks in the sun, unaware she was pregnant. When her mother, Adele dies young, details of the father, Cory Demetriou are exposed in her will and he has never been told of his daughter's existence.

Rodi's relentless search for the father she has never known, takes her to Corfu, mainland Greece and beyond. Filled with determination, setbacks, hope and love, this is the story of a young woman's quest to fulfil her mother's dying wish, but will Cory Demetriou accept her as his daughter twenty-six years on?

Dare To Dream - Left on the doorstep of St Anthony's Catholic Orphanage in Bolton, Northern England, Anne Marie O'Shea is placed in the guiding hands of another orphan named Bella Jones. As the years pass by, Bella accepts her lot for what it is; Annie dreams of a wonderful life, that special bit of magic that everybody deserves. When Bella is killed in a road accident at the age of twenty, Annie is left to fend for herself, to make decisions about her future and combat all the fears she has about forming lasting relationships. With numerous ups and downs, nurse training and emigration to Australia, a series of unbelievable co-incidences eventually puts the magic in her life that she could previously only dream about.

__Payback__ - Julietta's holiday becomes a nightmare when she is swept up in the frenzy of other people's abhorrent need for revenge.

www.ingramcontent.com/pod-product-compliance
Lightning Source LLC
Chambersburg PA
CBHW061031120726
47910CB00006B/2189